OPEN ALL NIGHT

a horror anthology
for the graveyard shift

edited by Eirik Gumeny

OPEN ALL NIGHT

Atomic Carnival Books
Albuquerque, N.M.

Second Edition

Paperback ISBN 979-8-9884520-2-7
eBook ISBN 979-8-9884520-3-4

Cover and book design by Eirik Gumeny

"The Clover Café" by Amanda Cecelia Lang originally appeared on the *Tales to Terrify* podcast

This book is a work of fiction. Names, characters, places, brands, and events are either the product of the author's imagination or used fictitiously. Any resemblance to actual persons, places, incidents, monsters, or pinball machines, living, dead, or otherwise, is entirely coincidental.

*When there's no more room in Hell,
the dead will walk the earth.*

Dawn of the Dead, George A. Romero

I'm not even supposed to be here today!

Clerks, Kevin Smith

Table of Contents

Editor's Note
Creatures of the Night

SLEEP AND I HAVE NEVER BEEN FRIENDS. One might even go so far as to call us nemeses.

As a child, resting fitfully, mind always, already, racing, chasing every stray thought, I found myself fascinated by the night. By the moonlight filtering in through half-closed blinds. By everything that was, or could be, happening beneath that big and empty and tomb-quiet sky.

Sleepovers during my pre- and mid-teenage years inevitably ended with my friends and I sneaking out and wandering through our stilled town. Not doing anything, looking for anything in particular, simply walking. Trespassing occasionally, certainly, but not maliciously. That was never the point. This was freedom for freedom's sake.

My twenties were an almost complete inversion, my sleepless nights filled with work, with *obligation*. Keeping open a Blockbuster until two a.m. or sitting at a chiming computer in a darkened office until midnight, until breakfast, running tech support for countries more suited to my nocturnal habits than my own. There were countless other jobs, too, temp work, overnight inventories, some ending later, some earlier. A local diner became a second home for myself and my nighthawk friends; we were on a first-name basis with the host and the waitresses, and served ourselves (and the occasional other customer) coffee and counter pastries. For a decade, I watched more sunrises than Must-See TV.

But then age and marriage and suburbia—not to mention a vested professional interest in keeping up with television in a timely manner, and, perhaps more importantly, medications specifically designed to quiet my restless mind—and suddenly all those big and empty and tomb-quiet streets started to feel a little *off*.

My home in Albuquerque is at the literal edge of the desert. If you were to look at a map, my neighborhood is a little protuberance bumping up into a seemingly endless expanse (depending on how zoomed in or out you are) of beige-brown. There is nothing to the west save scrub and sand for twenty miles at least, until you hit the Pueblo of Laguna. As a result, the nights are darker out here—so much darker than they ever were in New Jersey, in that part of the Garden State caught eternally in the creeping everlight of Manhattan.

Far from a city that doesn't sleep, Albuquerque—or, at least, my part of it—is practically comatose after eight p.m. Bats occasionally haunt the skies, while coyotes perched upon the mesa sing a somber serenade. Streetlights cast almost perfect cones of illumination, the sodium bulbs carving out *just enough* light to prove their existence, but no more. Taking out the trash is like walking into the poster for *The Exorcist*.

But that's what horror is, right? Everything's always the same, safe—until it isn't. What you're used to gets turned around and suddenly even minor concerns seem monumental, and monsters … well, they seem all the more monstrous.

Within these pages, you'll find various explorations of that idea. The normal turned strange and the strange made normal. Recurring motifs—diners and doppelgangers and dead sisters, old gods and creatures of the night coming to help and hurt in equal measure— abound and then aberrate. The same, until they aren't.

And through it all, facing down the demons of the dark, are the ones not being paid nearly enough to be there. The ones, like me, and maybe like you, called to by the night and coopted by commerce, scrambling for every dollar and every cent, no matter the real cost. The ones well-acquainted with all the misery, and all the mystery, that the graveyard shift can bring.

Eirik Gumeny,
September 30, 2023

Not Working
Russ Bickerstaff

I AM WORKING. BUT I'M NOT WORKING. Because I am malfunctioning and some cents. At least that's the way it feels. And yet I'm continuing to work. Otherwise I wouldn't be failing to work. Because I wouldn't know whether or not I was malfunctioning if I wasn't actually trying to work. So the only way I can truly know whether or not I'm working is to work. And in working I discovered that I am not working. Properly, anyway. There's something wrong. And I'm not sure what it is. But I have a sinking suspicion that it might have something to do with the time of day.

It's the middle of my shift. Which probably means it's the middle of the night. But it could also be the middle of the day. Depending on what day of the week it is. And then depending on what week of the month as well. And to a certain degree it also depends on the season. So there's that. And there really is all of that. And it really is difficult to tell exactly where I am in time. Because it's not like I'm getting a whole lot of feedback from outside. It's always the same kind of midday in the middle of the store like this. And I don't have a vision of any kind of window or anything like that.

I can look at my phone all I want. And I know that there are numbers there that would sort of correlate with some kind of time. But for whatever reason, numbers don't seem to mean a whole lot to me. Because the only numbers that are really important are monetary values. The amount of the merchandise and the amount of the money paid for the merchandise. And I'm not actually making change all that much. Which is to say that I'm not actually changing all that much. Because there's so much plastic. Just a plastic card and scanning and everything is finished. I'm not really doing that much. The numbers are sort of meeting last period and I'm sure if I really looked at the time I could probably work out exactly what time it was.

The way that the clocks work around here, I would only really know how long it was until the end of my shift. And even then I would only know that if I knew how long it was till the end of my shift. As it is, I picked up a few shifts from a few other people who are unable to make it in. And so, as a result, I'm not real certain or real clear as to when it is that I'm getting relieved. Other people who would've relieved me from my shift were unable to make it in. So I just kept working. And the people who would relieve them from their shifts also were unable to make it in. So I've worked their shifts as well. It seems as though there's a good chance that the person who is coming to relieve me of my shift is myself. Which doesn't make any sense. But that's pretty much the situation.

A dark-haired girl with the deepest blue eyes smiles at me. She just purchased something. And I just helped her purchase some thing. And I suppose I should feel pretty good about that. There was something about the way she was looking at me. Maybe it was sympathy or something like that. I don't know. All I know is that I feel pretty good. Like I'm still on top of everything. Not that I'm required to do a whole lot from where I'm standing. I just know that I am in a position where I need to maintain some small level of focus. And it feels as though I'm probably doing that right now. Though it is difficult to tell.

When I come in to relieve me, I am accompanied by a very familiar face. Cheery blue eyes. Long blonde hair. Does she seem surprisingly unfazed by the fact that I'm relieving myself? (Okay … that didn't come out the right way …) Which is to say coming in to relieve myself of work. Because I've worked long enough that I'm scheduled to come in now. And I am coming in now. But because I had to work all night, I'm the one that I'm relieving.

She seems perfectly OK with two of her boyfriends being the same. And being in the same place in two different places at the same time or whatever. I guess I should learn to accept that people are going to react to that sort of thing differently. They're going to take it in stride. Because, after all, things are a little weird in this shop. And things are a little weird around the shop as well.

Honestly, I can't remember when it was that I was supposed to arrive here. Originally. I mean, the more I think about it, the more I realize it's been a while since anyone else has worked here. I mean, now that I actually think about it, there's something very familiar about this whole situation. And it's the fact that when I came in here, I was relieving someone who bore the same image that I saw in the mirror every time. I guess I wasn't really thinking about it much. Kind of like the guy who is relieving me now.

I don't know. Maybe I'm too exhausted to really think about it that much. I just need to go home and get some rest. I know that I'll probably want to pick up some snacks somewhere to eat. But I know that I'm probably just going to fall asleep anyway. Better to get back to bed. I'll deal with it when I wake up tomorrow morning. Hopefully I don't wake up late like I did this morning. Or last night or whatever. Time will tell. I get the feeling it always does.

Factor Fifty
Tom Brennan

THE VAMPIRE WALKED INTO OUR DRUGSTORE at three a.m. to buy sunblock.

That first night, he didn't look too good. He wore these dark, dusty clothes, all creased, with bits of grass or hay sticking to them. You'd think he'd slept a few days in the back of a pick-up, you know the ones I mean? Wooden sides, you see them all over L.A., the Mexican gardeners like to use them.

Anyway, if we'd still had a security guard out front, there's no way the guy would've got in. But old Tony is still in traction after the robbery back in July and Pearson won't pay for another one: "The last one didn't do no good, right?"

So when the vampire walked up to the counter, I already had my finger above the panic button. A lot of good that would do.

"Uh, hi," I said. " Can I help you?"

The guy stared into the glass counters and cases where we keep the more expensive creams, lotions, gunk, and stuff. Pearson's is a small drugstore off Beverley Boulevard and Cahuenga, opposite a big mall and a couple of glitzy tourist hotels. It's mainly cosmetics, prescriptions filled, kids' toys. And there's a little coffee counter with three stools and an Italian espresso machine; Pearson bought the whole lot from a restaurant closing-down sale a block away.

"Sir? Can I help you?" I asked again, ready to press that button.

"I need something for the sun, Miss." He had a slight accent, nothing too heavy. He flattened his *a*s, made them sound like *e*s. Mrs. Stellway in my voice class, Tuesday and Thursday evenings, would have murdered him. I thought it was kind of cute.

"You need suntan cream? Lotion?"

He shook his head. "To stop the burning."

"Oh, right. No problem."

It made sense to me: he had business to take care of, he needed to be out in the sun instead of hiding from it. I could see it all: he'd stowed away on a boat from Europe, hiding in the hold until it docked at Los Angeles. Now he needed some protection because the sun hardly sets here. I watch TV, I know the routine.

I reached inside the counter and brought out tubes, bottles, and sprays.

"We've got this, a sun protection factor five … this one's a ten … there's a spray with factor twenty that goes on without feeling too greasy, or maybe a thirty?"

"I need more."

I reached to the bottom of the counter.

"Factor fifty. It's like wearing a lead suit."

He smiled and showed me perfect, narrow teeth.

"I'll take it."

While I bagged the cream, he pulled money from his pocket. I lost count of the different bills he had: U.S., English, Euros, Canadian, all kinds. When I helped him choose a crumpled twenty and a few ones, I saw how long and thin his fingers were, like a piano player's.

After he left, the rest of the night was pretty quiet. The cops came in for coffee around three, as usual, then the early birds, the janitors and cleaners, the diner waitresses on their way to work. I clocked off at eight and almost fell asleep on the bus home. I shared a two-bed sublet with a girl breaking into "adult" media; she's okay, very quiet, and she works during the day.

Because Lol, my agent, said to expect a casting call in the afternoon, I set my alarm for midday. But the call never came. So I worked out at the gym, made a quick sandwich, went to my evening class, *Acting Through Self-Exploration*, and then to work.

I didn't expect to see the vampire again. I had a dog-eared book, one of Stephen King's, open on my lap. I looked up and saw him—the vampire, not Stephen King—walk in.

"Hey," I said. "Not back for more sun cream already?"

"It is an excellent product."

He still had that accent, but he looked a lot better all scrubbed up. Clean slacks, an open shirt, leather brogues. He looked like a younger version of Conrad Veidt, the guy from *Casablanca*. His skin was still pale, of course, but his eyes burned dark blue.

I pulled out another tube of factor fifty and bagged it for him. I saw him looking at the coffee machine and offered to make an espresso. So we sat either side of the little counter, him on the customer stool, me on the employee one with the wobbly legs, and just talked. We swapped names, and I tried to pronounce his: Jaroslav, or -slev, something like that. He said I could call him Yaro.

I told him how I was only working nights in the drugstore to pay for my evening acting classes and my head shots. I had to explain that aspiring actresses needed lots of photos, good ones, for publicity. I mentioned my home back in Oregon but didn't say too much about my family, or about dropping out of high school.

Yaro told me how he'd been traveling for years; he hadn't seen his country in Europe for a long, long time. Home was someplace in Carpathia, but he couldn't go back there, not yet, maybe not ever. When he said this, he stared into his coffee as if he could see his home right there.

After that, Yaro turned up maybe every second or third night, usually around three. He must have had connections in L.A., because his clothes got smarter and he pulled up outside the drug-store in taxis. And he always left a good tip, ten dollars minimum; I never fished, and I never played on him. I guess he was just generous. And I think he liked the coffee and the company. Well, the coffee, anyway.

The way I saw it, Yaro had every right to be in L.A. It's like a big whirlpool that pulls in dreamers, the lost, the disconnected. And freaks. I mean, you wouldn't believe some of the people you see walking along the street in broad daylight. Weird isn't in it.

Whatever Yaro's business was, I never asked. I was curious, sure, but I didn't want to push it. He seemed nice, but I didn't want to end up as another one of the Undead. I've read enough King and Bloch. I've seen enough movies.

To be honest, I appreciated the company. I hadn't really made any friends in the four months since I'd arrived. And most normal people work days. Yaro was easy to talk to, telling me old stories about Europe, about remote, superstitious villages that hadn't even seen a TV or a car. And about people he'd known, friends and girlfriends, nothing too heavy.

Then Lol said I needed more shots, and recommended a really great photographer, a guy who'd started all the big female stars. But it was serious money. I took another job, in the mornings on the front desk in a beauty parlor, and then another one in a telemarketing place on the weekends. After two weeks of that, I almost fell asleep on the drugstore counter.

"You can't carry on like this," Yaro told me. "You look all drained and gray."

That's great coming from a vampire, I thought.

"I'll be fine. I just need to get these shots, then Lol says I've got a chance at a part in a big heist movie that's coming up."

Yaro shook his head. The fluorescent lights picked out the threads of silver in the black.

"After this, there will be more photographs, more shots."

I hid a yawn behind my hand. "What do you mean?"

"How long have you been with this agent of yours?"

"Lol? Four, almost five months. Why?"

"How many jobs has she found for you?"

"Look, I don't—"

He stared at me. "How many?"

"None," I admitted. "But she will. Once I get these shots."

"Trust me, my dear. She'll discard you when the money's gone."

Maybe it was a bad day. Maybe I was just overtired. Hell, I was wrecked. Anyway, I blew up.

"What would you know? You drift in from creepsville, some dump in Europe where they can't find their asses with both hands, and you tell me how I'm screwing up? Well, screw you."

Yaro folded up like a kid being told off, and I saw him for what he was. An old guy with a wrinkled, bone-white face. Not some vampire from the other side of the world. Not some prince with a secret, romantic past and superhuman powers. Just some old guy trying to muddle through, trying to make it as best he could.

And I saw how far I'd drifted from reality. I'd lost it. Taking a tired old guy for a vampire. Taking myself as an actress.

Yaro slid off his stool and placed too much money on the counter. He didn't look at me.

"I'm sorry, my dear."

I watched him walk to the glass doors and I wanted to yell out, wanted to tell him how sorry I was. But the glass doors were already opening.

Yaro never stepped through them. Two young guys pushed him back into the store with their hands on his chest. Both white, they had buzz-cut blonde hair and wide, druggy grins. I reached for the panic button.

"Yo, sister. Back off, there." The bigger guy raised the steel pipe in his hand. "You want don't gramps here to get blood all over his nice shirt."

I left the panic button and stepped away. The second guy, the one with the knife, made for the side of the counter. He gave the CCTV camera the finger and opened the till.

"Hey, Frank," he called out, "she only got fifty dollars in here."

"Shit!" Frank, the one with the pipe, pushed Yaro up to the glass counter. "Hey, where's the rest of the money, babe?"

I licked my lips. My heart wanted to leap out through my throat.

"In the safe," I said. "Pearson only keeps a cash float for the night."

"So, open the safe."

"I can't," I said. "I don't know the combination."

The one with the knife grinned at me and took a step forward. His pupils were wide and dark.

"We'll help you remember."

As I got ready to kick him between the legs, I looked over at Yaro. I've seen people scared before, people at gunpoint. Yaro didn't look like any of them. He looked sad.

"I think you should leave, gentlemen," Yaro said.

The one with the knife paused as if suddenly given a really difficult math problem.

"Say what?"

"He thinks we should leave," Frank said, grinning. Then his

grin vanished and he raised the pipe in both hands and brought it down.

I think I screamed. Then I saw Yaro holding the pipe in his right hand. Without any sign of strain, he crushed the pipe between his fingers. He never took his eyes off Frank's face. Then, before I could stop him, the other guy slammed the knife into Yaro's back. It sank up to the hilt.

Yaro trembled slightly. He turned and looked at the knife guy like he might stare at a gnat that had just bitten him. He grabbed the guy's jacket and threw him over to the other side of the drugstore. Twelve, fourteen feet, right through the air. The knife guy slid down the wall and into the racks of greetings cards.

The other robber let go the pipe and tried to punch and kick Yaro, but the blows just bounced off him. Yaro took hold of the guy's wrist, bent it backward until he screamed, and started dragging him to the exit. On the way out, he collected the other guy. He pulled the two struggling robbers through the doors like they were sacks of light laundry.

The automatic doors closed behind them. The background music carried on as if nothing had happened. I looked at the shattered glass counter, the upended racks and the cards strewn over the floor. Slow and calm, I took three steps and pressed the panic button. Then I passed out.

****

The medics checked me over and then the cops asked me what had happened. I told them it was a gang fight. They asked about the CCTV tape and I told them that Pearson had put in dummy cameras; he couldn't see the point of wasting money on real surveillance.

The cops wouldn't tell me what happened to the robbers. I had to worm it out of one of the medics.

"Jesus, it was bad," he said, checking the dressing over the cut on my neck, the one made when I passed out. "We found them by the dumpsters out back and I don't want to see anything like that again."

I couldn't tell any of them. They wouldn't have believed me even if I'd wanted to drop Yaro.

I gave Pearson a week's notice. He told me I could swap with Donna on the day shift, but I said I'd see out the week on nights. I guess I wanted to see if Yaro would show up. Four o'clock on my last night, there was no sign of him. Then the doors opened. I expected to see the cops, and I even moved toward the coffee machine.

"How are you?" Yaro asked.

"I'm okay."

We stared at each other.

"I'm glad you came in," I said. "I wanted to say thank you. And sorry."

He smiled. "For what?"

"For … for the things I said. I didn't mean them."

"I know." Yaro paused, then asked, "Do you think we could share one last coffee?"

As I made the coffee, I said, "How did you know I was leaving?"

"I didn't, but I'm glad to hear it. Are you going home?"

"I don't know." I set the coffee down in front of him. "I don't know about anything. Apart from one thing: you were right about Lol; she's been bleeding me dry for months."

He nodded. "I wish that I could be wrong. But I'm sure that not everybody is like her. Perhaps you just need to be more careful, next time. When you're ready."

We sat for a moment, on either side of the counter, as if the week before had never happened. Then I realized what he'd said.

"What's this about your last coffee?"

"I'm leaving," Yaro said. "Whenever things like … last week occur, I know it's time to move on. There are those who watch out for such events; they believe they see certain footprints."

"Where will you go?"

He smiled and shrugged. "Who knows? I have acquaintances in surprising places. And America is such a big country. Maybe I will stop off for a while in Oregon …"

I looked down.

Yaro said, "My dear, I would give anything to return to my own home. But I cannot. You have no idea how I envy those who have the opportunity to go back to their own families. I would give almost anything for that."

When he laid his hand over mine, I saw his long, thin fingers ended in beautiful nails. Sharp. Strong. Nails a manicurist would die for.

I smiled at him and said, "If you're ever passing though Portland—"

"I shall." He finished his coffee and stood up, leaving money on the counter.

"But how will you find me?" I asked.

He smiled and crossed to the front doors. Just before they opened, I could see my own reflection in the glass. Then the doors closed. Yaro walked into the night and I saw only the white and red lights of the streetlamps and the passing cars.

The Last Sunday
Patrick Tumblety

AN ELDERLY MAN LIFTS TWO SHAKY FINGERS at a bartender; the movement is answered by a shot of whiskey at exactly their height. The wattle of skin that hangs under his chin folds under his hand as he massages the fire down his throat. A drink that strong, not too long ago, would never have given him such irritation. Now it is almost too much.

His fingers form in the air again, like they used to when he was "playing guns" with his older brother as a child while they pretended to be soldiers. Back then, the barrel was steadier.

The bartender places his hands purposefully on top of the lacquered wood. The conversations around the tavern hush, and the old man can feel the weight of the patrons' eyes on the back of his head. He knows that the folks of Wheatfield are leery of strangers and especially cautious of liquoring them up.

Can't blame them, the old man thinks. *I used to be one of them.*

He lifts the frayed brim of his baseball cap to reveal his face, hoping to show the bartender some familiarity. If not in memory, then at least in the way that people from the same place tend to look like they're from that same place.

The bartender only sees him as a stranger.

Tears glaze over the old man's eyes. He pulls his brim down, then pulls on the collar of his patch-laden duster to reveal the silver tattoo of a razor-sharp tooth. An identification number is etched below the ink, still legible despite the drooping of the once-taut skin.

The bartender turns and returns the bottle of liquor to the bottom shelf. He reaches for one at the top. This action causes the bar's patrons to disengage their attention and return to their conversations.

"Had family that joined," he says as he opens the bottle and pours the shot, this time not paying attention to the level.

"They find him?"

The bartender shakes his head.

The whiskey helps the old man swallow this information.

What a waste of time, he wants to say, to perform such ceremonies when there are so many bodies and so many more coming. But he understands the need of trying to find closure when a family has already lost hope.

"They find some in the rubble," he offers. "Could have survived."

But the bartender is no longer listening. He's looking up toward the TV hanging from the ceiling in the corner of the room. Though silent, the images are a thousand unbelievable words. Spotlights from multiple helicopters sweep across last night's battleground, illuminating a clean-up crew as they insert hooks into a gargantuan mass of flesh and rip it into pieces. Stadium lights surrounded by military reveal men in hazmat suits as they fill bags with samples of the meat. Little stars burst from the black and disappear just as quickly as a horde of photographers and journalists use their cameras to capture the remains in their own way.

The news footage cuts to a ground shot of a demolitionist as he presses a button. The creature's left eyelid blows out of its head in gel-like chunks. When the dust settles, pools of unnatural colors sludge out of the empty socket where its eyes should be.

Their eyes melt the moment they die. No one knows why.

The old man looks away and gazes over the tavern crowd, the television's glow illuminating their faces. This little gathering is a perfect microcosm of humanity in the face of such unimaginable horror. Some are terrified. Some are enthralled. A few dare to form tentative smiles as they watch their enemy torn apart. Their differing reactions remind him of watching the newsreels that played before the Sunday cartoons at the local theater, back in the days when the Vietnam War consumed America's soul. Battle-ready soldiers charged through fields. Commanders regarded maps with admirable stoicism. Troops climbed onto tanks, pilots into cockpits.

The Last Sunday

None of the footage from the newsreels on those Sundays showed the reality of the war. The news always has to report some type of hope, even if it is a lie. How else will they convince a person to face something like that while still retaining the hope to live?

He had been too young to understand if the news was positive. Some of the images it showed were heroic, some were horrifying. He would look around the theater at the faces in the seats to gauge their reactions, but they were too varied to help his inexperienced mind form a conclusion.

He looked to his brother to know how he should feel.

His brother's stare would lower to the bottom of the movie screen when the bombs dropped and the tanks rolled. Only when the soldiers were on screen did his eyes lift and dart frantically across the screen from man to man.

He was looking for their father.

Even after the family heard Dad was not coming home, his eyes would continue to dart back and forth from soldier to soldier across the screen every Sunday.

"Were you there?" the bartender asks.

"Yeah," the old man laments.

"You survived. There must be some hope after all."

"I didn't survive," he says as he kills the shot and slams the glass on the counter to knock his mind back to the present.

"Either way, thank you for your service."

He pours another drink. The old man laughs and then knocks it back. He coughs as it scrapes the walls of his throat. He nods up toward the television.

"Don't thank me yet."

The helicopter's camera sweeps away from the carcass and zooms in on a full moon just above the ocean's horizon About half a mile from the shore. A school of green bioluminescent lights sparkles beneath the water and moves swiftly toward the beach.

The bartender looks away from the television. The color has drained from his face. He pulls a shot glass from below the bar, pours one for himself, and downs it. He tips the liquor bottle again but does not pour. After a moment of staring at the glass, he stands the bottle up.

"Then there's nothing left to do. I'm going to enlist tomor—"

"No!" The old man pounds the bar so hard that the wood snaps under his fist.

The bartender steps back. Conversations in the tavern die again.

"I'm sorry." He rests his face in his hands as he begins to cry. "I'm sorry."

"No problem." The bartender offers a towel to wipe the line of blood forming along the man's hand. The people of Wheatfield return to distracting themselves from their ultimate fate.

"I'm sorry," the old man repeats. "I've seen these things flatten twenty men with one foot. Hell, we put seventeen missiles into that one's chest and it didn't flinch. Get as far inland as you can and live the rest of your life before they come and swallow it away."

"Is that why you're here? Getting away from the battle?"

"I don't know …" The old man tries to find the words. "I needed to take a moment. Maybe get some perspective. Or advice."

"That's what a bartender does when he's not pouring drinks, right? But what can I say that will help?"

"Do you really think we stand a chance?"

The bartender contemplates his question for a few seconds. "I really do. You're proof of it. You survived last night's battle, and together we're watching them tear that thing apart."

The old man nods. "What if I were to tell you that yesterday I looked ten years younger than I do today?"

The bartender looks at him quizzically, but his expression changes as he realizes the subtext underneath the old man's words. "You're a Herald," he whispers, as though he's speaking at a funeral. His words the eulogy.

The old man stares beyond the wall of alcohol, toward the coast. A younger version of himself stands at the apex of a cliff that separates the sea from the shore. The company he commands stands behind him, strong and steady, until the ground beneath their feet begins to quake.

Each creature has a different appearance, but similar attributes. Some are amorphous creatures that the media calls "Sponges." The acid that covers their surface is deadly, but so soft that light artillery can quickly tear them apart. Others resemble large invertebrates such as jellyfish or octopi. These "Squids" have blubber that is soft enough to penetrate, but they are enormous, and their barbs and tentacles are swift and destructive. The deadliest of them are the bipedal horrors. Human-shaped and agile. Fish-like faces with enormous eyes. Wide maws with teeth the size of houses. Their leathery skin is thick and nearly impenetrable, and the ones with scales might as well be tanks the size of mountains. Their designation is "Leviathan."

Heralds—the men and women of high rank who are chosen to command the first wave—are responsible for pinpointing the category of the creature and any weak points before they make landfall.

Most Heralds do not survive their first glance at a Leviathan.

Some of the larger ones have porous flesh underneath their arms like fish gills. Some do not even have arms, but their mouths are larger and easier for the bombers to unload into. Heralds try their best to report what they see before the look into a Leviathan's eyes drains their life from their bodies.

The old man remembers seeing the creature's alabaster head rise above the sea, glistening under the moonlight, prominent against the black water. He does his best to concentrate on every part other than its amber-hued eyes as it reaches for the edge of the cliff and pulls itself onto land.

"Earholes!" he shouts into his transponder. He tries to look under or above the thing's joints where the helicopters and ship cameras can't see. "Gills at the base of its neck!"

A massive amount of seawater cascades from its skin, washes most of the calvary behind the Herald down the jagged ridge. The remaining soldiers chance a glance and then immediately fall back to the bottom of the hill.

Artillery lights up the night as bombs drop from the clouds like hail and tanks fire blindly, hitting leathery hide but doing little, other than making the monster annoyed. The massive head pivots away just in time for a missile to scrape across its skin and plunge into the ocean.

The soldiers that forget their training look up into the monster's eyes and stop firing. At that time of night, through such darkness, there is nothing to concentrate on except the massive, glowing eyes that hang in the air like sister moons. Their hair turns white and their bodies collapse. Some are strong enough to retreat a few paces before their skin becomes gaunt and their hearts burst out of their chests. Their bodies keel and tumble down the jagged rocks of the coastline like shredded rag dolls. One of the tanks stops firing and is squashed under the creature's gargantuan hand.

It is then that the monstrosity notices the sole human standing between its stadium-sized feet. It tilts its head down and stares directly at the soldier.

The soldier's hair and skin have already begun to lose their color. Somehow he is still standing, and because he is a soldier he remains standing, remembering the brave men and women he has trained with, as well as those that inspired him during the reels before "Cartoon Sundays." Those men only fought wars between humans, but regardless of the nature of the enemy, each soldier then and now faces the same fate. In honor of their memory, he wills himself to not look away from the glistening amber that is the creature's eyes.

Those skyscraper-sized orbs do not reflect his image, nor do they reflect the surrounding bluff. Within them, he sees another world. Shapes and structures and creatures that he does not fully comprehend, that he knows, even if he survives, he could never interpret. And if he could, he would still choose not to for the preservation of the listener's sanity.

Fear keeps his blood pumping enough to lift the transponder and push the call button.

"They're not eyes," he screams into it and then runs between the Leviathan's legs. With every step toward the dark horizon, he feels his life slipping away.

"Say again," the radio squawks.

The soldier clicks the call button as his body weakens. "They're doorways," he screams as his body collapses and falls from the cliff.

The man that washes onto the shore the next morning does not recognize his reflection in the water.

"Come back to me, sir," the bartender says, snapping his fingers.

The man, whose mind is much younger than his body, jumps like a child awakened from a nightmare.

"Sorry," he says as he pulls the brim of his hat down again.

"It's okay. I can't imagine what it's like."

"No, you can't, and no one should. No one should see what's beyond them."

"Beyond them?"

The old man shakes his head and points to the television.

"Tell me what you see when you look at that screen."

The bartender looks up at the TV. The news continues showing the scientists ripping the carcass apart, the journalists documenting their effort, and the soldiers lining up along the cliff, ready to battle the next threat making its way toward them through the black water.

"I see hope," he says.

The old man huffs.

"You don't think we have a chance?" the younger man asks, wiping away tears.

"I think you should take your family and friends to the center of the country and try to live until the end reaches you." The old man picks up the bottle of liquor and pours a shot into both glasses. He raises his glass in the air, and the bartender does the same.

"To the better days behind us," says the old man.

"To hope for tomorrow," answers the younger.

A bitter smile adds more wrinkles to the old man's face. He empties the glass and doesn't worry about the fire in his throat as he slides off the barstool.

"So what did you decide?" the bartender asks.

The old man pulls a generous tip from his pocket and places it under the glass. He nods toward the television. "Don't be surprised if you see me on the next reel." He walks across the bar toward the exit.

"Thank you for giving us a chance," the bartender calls after him.

The old man continues toward the door until he is stopped by the sounds of chair feet scraping against wood. Every patron in the tavern stands to watch him exit.

The soldier lowers the brim of his hat, but not just to hide his crying eyes. He realizes that those who might be able to recognize him have already mourned the passing of the man he used to be.

The old man exits into the night before the bartender discovers the yellowing ticket stub under the empty glass.

Whispers in the Dark
Bailee Smith-Garcia

LIKE MOST PEOPLE, I DESPISE MY JOB.

I don't know anyone who enjoys working in retail. You need incredibly thick skin to last there for more than a few months. I've lost count of the number of customers who've called me a bitch. I'd quit but I can't because it helps pay for my college tuition. Which is also the only reason I agreed to pick up my co-worker's night shift.

The cool spring air whips around me. Damn, I should've brought a jacket. It doesn't matter now, I'm already late.

I stand outside LARRY'S FAMOUS HARDWARE STORE. The blinking red and black OPEN sign hanging on the inside of the glass door flashes in my face. Right below the sign is a giant posterboard with the hours listed. Ugh, I don't want to be here. Regardless of what anyone tries to tell you, there's nothing glamorous about working in a hardware store.

I purse my lips into a thin line and yank open the door. The smell of floor cleaner and paint overwhelms my nose. I spot the bin on the floor with clearance tools spilling out of it. There's a giant spot of green paint drying on the white tile next to it. Seriously? No one wanted to clean that up?

There are rows of shelves behind the bin. They have everything from weed killer to nails and bug spray.

"You're late," Easton Calloway sings. He's a taller white guy with messy bleach-blond hair. Easton screams trust-fund baby, but his rich daddy cut him off, so now he has to work a minimum-wage job.

"By five minutes," I say. "It's not like you're ever on time."

He shrugs. "What are they going to do? Fire me?"

I scoff. As if this place would fire anyone. They're already short-staffed as it is.

I head to the break room to clock in. The break room is a closet. It has a microwave in it since we're required to take lunch, but I doubt anyone would ever want to stay here. I toss my hair into a messy bun. Only six hours and fifty-nine minutes until I get to go home.

When I get back up front, Easton is holding out a clipboard.

"You'll need to follow the spreadsheet and write how much inventory we have."

I scowl. "What century are we in when we have to use paper and pencil?"

"Don't be such a crybaby, Tara," he says.

"Fuck you," I say.

Easton laughs. "You better get started. They're doing the reset next week and Sam wants all this done by then."

I'm dreading the reset. Some company is going to come in and redesign the store for maximum profit. It's good for the owners but sucks for me. Customers will complain they can't find any-thing and then get mad at me when I haven't memorized where everything is yet.

Sighing, I head to the weed killer and start counting the containers on the shelf. I scribble down the numbers on the sheet of paper. It's going to be a long night.

For half an hour, I inventory all kinds of weed killers. Ugh, how can anyone work like this? I reach into my pocket for my phone and freeze. The sound of bare feet slapping against the tile breaks the stillness.

Why didn't Easton check for customers left in the store? I lay the clipboard on the shelf and step out to scold the customer, but there's no one there.

What the hell? No, that's not right. Someone's in here.

"Easton?" I ask.

He peeks his head out of an aisle. "Yeah?"

"Did you check for customers before locking the door?"

Easton rolls his eyes. "Yes, Tara. I'm a fuck-up, but you could give me a little credit."

I shake my head. "Are you sure you didn't miss someone? I heard someone running around."

"Aww," he says. "Don't tell me you're scared?"

"Shut up," I say.

He sighs. "Stay there and I'll go check."

Easton carelessly tosses his clipboard on the ground. He walks from aisle to aisle looking for people and then disappears to the back of the store. After a few minutes, he comes back up to the front.

"There's no one here."

"But someone was walking around in here," I say, frustrated. I wasn't crazy. I know what I heard.

"They're not here now," Easton says. "Tara, I think you're superstitious."

It wasn't a secret that I was cautious with the supernatural, but I couldn't help it. My parents told me stories like La Llorona since I was a little kid. But that wasn't the case right now.

"You don't believe me, do you?" I ask.

"It's not that," he says. "It's just … sometimes at night there are noises, but it's our imagination."

"What kind of noises?" I ask, but he doesn't answer. "Easton?"

"It's nothing. Sometimes the building creaks or some shit. It's not like it's haunted or anything."

"Haunted?" I ask.

Easton shakes his head. "No, it's *not* haunted. There's no such thing as ghosts. Come on, let's get back to work."

I roll my eyes.

"You're way too dedicated to this hellhole sometimes, Easton."

"Maybe they'll make me a manager," he says.

I snort. "As if, but keep kissing Sam's ass."

Easton flips me off and disappears into the aisle he'd been working in. I pick up my clipboard and try to go back to counting the weed killer and grass seed.

I count two kinds of grass seed, but I can't focus. God, I want to go home. A cool burst of air whips around me. Goosebumps appear on my arms. It's like the temperature dropped twenty degrees in a few seconds.

I glance towards the front door, expecting to find it open, but it isn't. What the hell? Maybe Easton's right and I'm just superstitious.

Taking a deep breath in, I turn back towards the grass seed. Get it together. I can survive for the next six hours. Plenty of people've worked here at night, right?

Maybe I should listen to some music. I scroll my playlist and find something I listened to in high school. I press play and set the phone on the shelf, but no music plays. My brows knit together in confusion. I turn the volume up but still nothing.

Of fucking course. Why would this night go smoothly? I close the music app and go to reopen it. The high-pitched screeching of a metal chain dragging across the tile stops me dead in my tracks.

"Very fucking funny, Easton," I say. God, what's his problem?

Easton peeks his head out of the aisle. "Tara, I didn't do that."

"Sure, you didn't," I say sarcastically.

He shakes his head. "I'm being serious. That wasn't me."

The metal chains rattle and clank together. My stomach churns. Who the hell is doing that? Why would someone want to do that?

"I told you someone was in here!"

"We should go check it out," he says.

My eyes grow wide. "We?"

Easton nods. "Unless you're scared."

"I'm not scared," I lie. "Fine, let's go."

We set down our clipboards and head back towards the buckets of chain and rope. It has to be some asshole who thinks they're funny and not a serial killer, right? My breath catches in my throat. I don't want to die in this piece-of-crap hardware store. My heart pounds in my ears.

Easton and I round the corner and freeze. There's no one here.

The chains are rattling and clanking against each other *on their own*. What the actual fuck?

The color drains from Easton's face. "Th-There's no one here."

"Wanna logically explain that one?" I ask.

"I …" He trails off. "We should call Sam."

"And tell him what, exactly?" I ask. "Hey, Sam, your hardware store is haunted. No, we haven't finished counting yet."

His eyes narrow. "Do you have any better ideas?"

"Nope."

Easton reaches into his pocket and pulls out his phone. With a few swipes, he brings the phone up to his ear. His brows knit together.

"What the fuck?" He ends the call and then tries Sam again. "There's no goddamn ringing."

I swallow hard. My music not playing earlier was weird, but it can't be a coincidence that Easton's phone won't work, either.

"I don't think our phones work here," I say, my voice shakier than I'm comfortable with.

"Fine, we'll go outside to make our call."

Before he can walk away, a piece of yellow rope flies out of its white bucket and wraps itself tightly around Easton's ankles. Easton curses, then smacks down on the ground, hard. The rope wraps itself tighter and tighter around him.

I scream and then clamp a hand over my mouth. This isn't happening. This can't be happening. I'm going to be sick.

The scissors next to the white bin soar through the air and crash down only inches from Easton. He scrambles away as far as the rope will let him.

Someone—or *something*—wants to kill him.

Wants to kill *us*.

Frantically, Easton grabs the scissors and cuts the rope. He jumps up to his feet. His hands are shaking.

"We need to get the fuck out of here."

I nod. I don't care if Sam fires us or not, I am not staying here. Easton and I dart down the aisle towards the front door. There's no logical explanation for what happened back there, and I'm not finding out.

Relief washes over me as I see the door. It's pitch black outside, but anything is better than here.

Easton reaches into his pocket and pulls out a keyring. He jams the key into the lock and turns it. Except it doesn't move. No! No!

No! Easton jiggles the lock and pushes on the door.

SNAP!

The key breaks in half, the majority of the key stuck in the lock.

"What the fuck, Easton?!" I scream.

"Do you think I meant to do that?!" Easton says. "We'll break the window."

"Break a window?" Was he out of his mind? Those glass doors were like a thousand dollars or something ridiculous. I know Sam's gonna take it out of my check, and I can't afford that. But what's the alternative? Die for a crappy, minimum-wage job?

"Grab something heavy," I say.

Easton looks around for something to break the window. He grabs a hammer from underneath the counter. We keep it there for threatening customers who get a little too grabby.

"Stand back," he says.

Turning toward the window, Easton raises the hammer above his head. Before he can swing it down, though, something seems to grab onto the tool. It yanks the hammer up, and Easton hovers about a foot off the ground. Then it hurls Easton back into the bin with all the clearance tools. He lands with a thump! All the clearance tools spill out of the container.

Easton whimpers.

"Easton!" I rush over to him.

Easton groans and tries to sit up. I put my hand on his chest to keep him from standing.

"Take your time, all right?"

He shakes his head. "We have to get out of here."

I open my mouth and then snap it shut. The gut-wrenching smell of rotten eggs and dead rat overwhelms my senses. I gag and try to keep down the iced coffee I drank earlier. I clamp a hand over my mouth.

An icy blast of air whips around us. A low whisper echoes through the building, but I can't make out what it's saying. It sounds like a guy, but I'm not sure. The whispers grow louder, but I still can't hear what it's trying to tell us.

"It's saying … lie?"

Easton shakes his head. "No, Tara, it's saying *die.*"

My heart pounds in my ears. Bile rises in my throat. Shit! Shit!

"No," I say. "No, we're not dying here." I *won't* die here.

God, I should've never taken this shift.

No amount of money could make up for *this.*

There's got to be some way out of here. I shove to my feet and stare at the tools on the ground: a hammer, a half-broken drill, a couple of drill bits, several packages of nails, and one little can of drywall texture mix. I reach down and pick up the can, squeezing it tight. It's decently heavy and might go through the glass.

"You will pay," a deep and grisly voice whispers. Whatever it is doesn't sound human.

"Paying for fucking what?" I demand. "We haven't done a god-damn thing to you!"

"You all have," the voice says.

Easton groans. "No, we haven't."

Taking a deep breath in, I lob the can at the door. The can smacks hard into the glass, and the glass shatters. Yes! We can leave. Relief washes over me; we're getting out of this hellhole.

"Tsk, tsk," the voice hisses, "you'll regret that."

The hammer rises and flies into Easton's head. Blood and chunks of brain matter splatter across my whole body. Easton opens his mouth, but no sound comes out. He falls flat on his face onto the hard tile floor, his head cracked open.

I scream.

"Easton! Easton, get the fuck up!" He doesn't move. Deep, dark red liquid pours out of his body. "Easton!" I sob, shaking his body. My hands are sticky and wet with his blood. Tears stream down my face.

"Help! Someone, please! He's going to die!!"

As soon as the words leave my lips, I involuntarily empty the contents of my stomach. Most of the puke ends up on Easton. The chunky, yellow-and-brown throw-up mixing with the blood. I gag again, but nothing comes up.

Easton lays still on the ground, no longer breathing. A low laugh echoes through the building. The hairs on the back of my neck stand straight up.

"You son of a bitch! You fucking asshole!" I sob. Why couldn't this be a nightmare? I wish I could wake up in my bed. Shoving to my feet, I take a deep breath. I only have one chance to get out of here.

I pump my legs as fast as I can. I kick at the rest of the glass in the door and the whole thing shatters, large, sharp pieces falling onto the sidewalk outside. As I step through, a sharp pain shoots down my leg. But I won't stop. I have to get the hell out of here.

It's pitch black outside and there's not a goddamn street light out. The wind blows strands of hair into my face, brushes them out. Spreads Easton's blood across my face. I'm going to be sick again, but there's nothing in my stomach.

I sprint down the parking lot and yell for help. My heart feels like it's going to pound out of my chest. Where the hell is anyone in this awful town?

But I can't stop running. What if it's following me?

My lungs start to burn. How long have I been running? It's hard to catch my breath. I stop and place my hands on my knees, struggling to catch my breath.

"Fuck," I mutter.

I glance back up to see bright white lights coming towards me. I bring my hand up to my face to shield my eyes. A car door creaks open and slams shut.

"Sheriff's department. What's going on?" My eyes adjust. The officer is several inches taller than me. He's a white man with short, buzz-cut black hair. His nametag says Deputy Lopez. Shining the flashlight at me, he gasps.

"Are you all right, miss? You're covered in blood."

"No … this is my friend's blood," I cry. "Something killed him."

"Something killed him. What killed him?" Deputy Lopez asks.

I shake my head. How am I supposed to explain this?

Deputy Lopez takes a step toward me.

"Miss, I need you to tell me what happened."

"A demon killed him."

The next half-hour is a blur. Deputy Lopez gets more cops here and an ambulance to evaluate me. I give them the address of the hardware store, and I can hear mentions of a body on someone's radio, Easton's body.

The EMTs look me over to see if I'm physically fine, and, according to them, I seem to be. But I don't feel right. I'm numb.

"Tara Rodriguez?" Deputy Lopez asks.

"Yeah?"

"I'm going to need you to answer some questions. I'm going to read your Miranda Rights now." The sheriff rattles off my rights, but I don't understand why he needs to. "Do you understand these rights?"

"Yes," I say.

"Did you and Easton Calloway have any problems? Any arguments between the two of you?"

"No." I freeze. Tears start to roll down my face. "You think I did this? I didn't do this. It was a demon. It was a goddamn demon!"

Deputy Lopez frowns.

"Do you have a history of mental illness?"

My mouth drops open. "Why the fuck would that matter? I'm not *sick*. There's something haunting that building. Can you do your goddamn job? I didn't kill him."

"You're going to have to come downtown to answer some more questions. You're not free to go."

"I want a lawyer," I snap. They're not going to blame me for this. I won't allow them to let more people die by not stopping this.

They'll hear the whispers in the dark, too.

Drained
Megan Kiekel Anderson

"Want me to wait up, Joel?"

Joel looked up from the barbeque sauce bottles he was topping off. R.J. was waiting by the front door, his coat slung over his arm and his keys balled in his fist.

"Nah, get out of here," he answered.

No sense paying the kid to half-ass. Not with the price of meat going up the way it was, the online-order apps skimming off his profits. Joel was already having to sell off the wall of arcade games he'd collected for the joint over the years. They were all lined up next to the old Bob's Bazaar Bizarre booth, a vestige of the building's past life as a flea market—one that had housed a serial killer rumored to have turned some of his unwitting customers into cannibals. It was fenced off now, but folks could see a collection of oddities through the chain-link.

Joel's patrons were mostly goths and true-crime soccer moms wanting to gawk at the Bazaar Bizarre. Kansas City didn't have many serial killers in its history. Robert Berdella's house had been knocked down—too many creepy lookie-loos for the neighbors' comfort—so this was the only good place for a pilgrimage.

Berdella had kept human skulls, shrunken heads, all kinds of fucked-up shit at his obscurity booth. Joel still couldn't believe nobody thought to check into the guy. Six men over four years he kidnapped, tortured for days or weeks until their bodies gave out. He raped most of them, invaded them with foreign objects, did sick experiments.

All the while, Berdella kept careful logs and over two hundred Polaroids of his sadism. If that seventh victim hadn't escaped, naked but for a dog collar and leash, Bob probably would have kept on killing indefinitely.

Some of the crime scene objects came up for sale a few years ago: a hacksaw, fireplace ashes, a camera, photos. It's not like Joel was doing anything like that. He wasn't hawking real murderabilia. He hadn't even sold anything original from the booth. No "Ethnological Curiosities from the World's Four Corners" for sale here. Barbequing was an honest living, and if he sold a t-shirt or a dog collar here and there, well that was just taking fair advantage of his luck of location.

In addition to the coins, the ancient art, and the shrunken heads, Robert Berdella had been found with an extensive collection of occult and witchcraft items, so it wasn't exactly surprising that there were rumors about a curse. About half of the Yelp reviews before COVID didn't mention the food; they were about the "creepy vibes" or the "feeling of something tingling down my spine!"

That was stupid, but, hey, stupid folks' money still spent.

Joel hadn't thought much about the symbiotic relationship he'd developed with those morbid psychos. But now that people weren't coming inside and the focus was suddenly on the food, the reviews were different: "dry burnt ends" and "Man these ribs aint got nothin on Slaps!"

Maybe the take-out crowd could imagine Joel was following in Berdella's (rumored) footsteps and serving up a little more than pork and beef, but that was it. And how many people got their kicks on cannibalism anyway? Not enough, clearly.

If no one was coming in to get the shivers, imagining Bob cotton-swabbing their eyeballs with bleach or pouring drain cleaner down their throats, there wasn't going to be enough to get by.

So, the arcade games had to go. He had skee-ball, a few classic arcade games, one of those dancing things the kids used to go crazy over. He had a pay-to-play pool table set up in the empty space near the wall, and, his favorite, four premium pinball machines. With a little luck, he could probably ride out the pandemic on the sale alone.

Joel wiped down the white-and-red-checkered vinyl tablecloths, hung up his grease-stained apron, and stretched. He should get some rest—he'd only have a few hours before he had to fire up the smoker—but he was wired.

What the hell. He could get in a few games before the guys from the laundromat down the street come to steal away the machines. Laundromat! Now that was a pandemic-proof business.

Joel unlocked his favorite pinball machine, Zombie King, and grabbed a pocketful of coins from inside the cabinet. He felt a thrill as he pulled the plunger and launched his first ball.

He got into a good flow quickly, landing his first skill shot and his locks for multiball. He racked up points with the zombie horde mushroom bumpers and loaded up balls into the graveyard pen guarded by the Zombie King toy. The toy was skeletal, sitting atop a throne with a knight's shield and sword. It rotated in its seat, brandishing its sword up and down when Joel landed a ball in the pen.

"I have a grave ready for you," the king called out.

Joel hit the combo he needed to get the middle field zombie toys to pop up, but nothing happened.

Goddamn it. This game was great, not least because it was easy to get multiball, but also to fall into the knockout hole, which kept the kids coming back, efficiently separating them from their quarters. But it had a serious design flaw on the pop-up mechs. The zombie toys were supposed to rise out of the field from trapdoor designs. The engineers must have been sleeping on the job when they designed the thing, because the thin wires powering the toys rubbed against the wood, wearing down as the mechs moved. He had to replace the wires on one of them at least every six months.

What are the chances all four would wear out at once?

He let the ball drain and opened the cabinet, raised the lock bar, and slid out the glass. He leaned the tempered glass carefully against another machine, jammed up the plunger from underneath so he could remove the balls, and lifted up the field. He checked the connections and, sure enough, every one of the wires was worn through.

Fuck. He'd have to go home and get his soldering kit.

He looked at his watch.

Waking up at dawn was going to be a bitch.

***

They heard the jingle of Joel's keys and the tumble of the lock. After a moment, his headlights washed a beam of illumination over the restaurant and then the darkness returned.

There was a soft clicking as the vivid flashing lights of Zombie King came to life. The only living thing in the restaurant was a mouse. When the machine came to life, it let out a terrified squeak and scurried back to its hole.

A chorus of moans erupted from the pinball machine's speakers as the LCD screen showed the zombie king launching from his throne, rushing to fill the screen, bringing down his sword on the viewer with his signature "I have a grave ready for you!" line.

A ball loaded in front of the plunger with a *thunk*.

"Player One," the machine growled. "Let's get ready to bash some zombies!"

The Zombie King toy reached down to the arms of his throne to push himself up, jeweled sword gripped in his fist. He slipped the sword into its scabbard, then stretched, yawning. He twisted from one side to the next, placing his hands on each hip in turn. His bones crackled.

The zombie horde on the mushroom bumpers peeled themselves from their two-dimensional prison, stepping into shape with a loud *pop!* one by one. They fell in line behind the Zombie King, stiffly staggering and moaning like extras in a cheap B-movie.

More of the undead peeled themselves from the art panels lining the field.

The Zombie King strode powerfully forward, stomping on each trapdoor in turn. They opened—*Ssst! Ssst! Ssst! Ssst!*—and zombies crawled from them as if they were tearing themselves from their graves.

While the zombies of the bumper horde were a repeated mass of a single image, the pop-up mechs had been rendered with loving care. The first had an eye dangling from its socket, its flesh the hardened char of a burn victim. The next had gobs of skin sloughing off its face, like wax melting from a taper candle. Another was missing its nose, the upside-down heart centered on its face surrounded by a halo of smeared blood. Guts spilled from the abdomen of the last mech toy.

They, too, fell in line behind the Zombie King, marching for the lockdown bar.

The Zombie King climbed the ledge, standing free beyond the glass for the first time since his creation. He raised his arms and gave a victory yell; the horde gave a joyous, moaning roar along with him.

The disemboweled mech tossed a rope of her intestines to the zombie with the dangling eye and repelled herself down the front of the machine, turning the keys in the coin door. Then Guts swung herself inside the machine, the impatient horde moaning above her. She reemerged with rings of metal stacked up her arms and her fists full of long wires, which she roped around her neck before climbing her intestines back to the top.

The horde got to work belaying down to the ground, using the supplies from the innards of the machine.

The Zombie King led the army, kneeling before Bob's Bazaar Bizarre and holding out his jewel encrusted sword as if to offer it in service. He stood again, motioning his subordinates ahead. They each kneeled quickly before stooping to step through the holes in the chain link.

Burn let out a moan of excitement when he climbed to the Tibetan exorcism knives. The mushroom bumper horde carried out a knock-off of a four-thousand-year-old Hittite figure of Astarte, goddess of fertility, like a line of ants carrying a slab of meat.

They assembled back at the pinball machines.

Eyeball tied the metal and wires into a grappling hook, catching the makeshift tool on the frame of Roller Derby, the neighboring machine. He climbed up and threw the hook again, this time looping it over a light fixture suspended from the ceiling. He tossed the hook back to the tiny zombies below. They heaved, pulling the rope to raise the goddess statue.

Tink tink

Tink tink tink tink

Beneath Eyeball's feet, roller derby girls were skating around their field, making wild jumps to tap on the glass above them.

Melted Face climbed to the top of the derby machine, too, and tapped back on the glass. The girls spun to a stop and looked up. Melted Face motioned their head up to the swinging Astarte statue above them. The derby girls rolled for cover as the zombies let the pulley go, the stone goddess raining down glass in tiny fragments.

Then out came the rollerblading girls, with their feathered hair and tight spandex unitards.

Two more machines to go.

Out came the rock stars with their electric guitars and wicked smiles.

Out came the green men from Mars with their huge, brain-exposed heads.

The strangest army of three-inch monstrosities ever gathered.

***

Joel unlocked the restaurant, sitting his toolbox on the floor so he could turn on the lights. The pinball machines were gone.

Joel stood in shock. What were the odds some pricks would steal the things the night he was selling them?

There'd been no sign of a break-in at the front door. It didn't make sense.

He heard a crash coming from the kitchen.

If those thieving fuckers were still hanging around, he'd catch them. They'd fucked with the wrong guy.

Joel stormed into the kitchen and saw … nothing. Someone had turned on the lights, but nothing was out of place. He ran over to the back door. He must have just missed them.

Clang!

Joel startled and spun around.

"Who the fuck is there? I promise you, you're going to regret this."

Where did the sound come from? The triple sink? There was nowhere to hide—

Before he had time to finish his thought, Joel's legs were swept from under him. He fell back. His head slammed on the grimy floor. Head ringing from the pain, he began flopping around, grasping, trying to figure out what was happening.

Joel was dizzy, disoriented. He forced himself to think past the throbbing pain in the back of his skull and the instant headache it brought along with it. Joel's blurred vision useless, he tried to kick his feet, but his legs were bound. As quickly as he made this realization, he was being pulled up by his ankles, hung like a pig ready for processing in a slaughterhouse.

Joel swung his head from side to side, but he saw no one.

He tried to pull himself up, to reach the wires that were digging painfully into his ankles through his houndstooth chef pants, but he was twenty years and fifty pounds too late for that feat.

"Aragh!"

Joel dropped back down, the force swinging him, and he hit his head again, this time on the shelf of a baker's rack full of plastic spice canisters. He heard the canisters tumbling to the floor.

He clutched his head, wincing in pain. He felt a gentle touch around his wrists, then before he could react, his hands were wrenched away from his face and pulled behind his back. The bindings tightened, wire cutting into his flesh.

His shoulder had already been sore. The strain of having his arms tied and pulled caused shooting pain. The overexertion made tiny tears in his muscles and ligaments. He imagined he could feel each microtear.

Joel whipped his head frantically now, but there was still no one. It was as if he was being attacked by a phantom.

"Where are you, you fucker? Face me!"

He heard a low, quiet moan. The rolling *woosh* and intermittent *thunk* he associated with roller skating.

Joel turned towards the sounds.

He'd hit his head, hard, twice. He was upside-down; blood was rushing to his brain. That had to be it. He had to be hallucinating.

The *Small Soldiers* nightmare he was witnessing was far too ridiculous to be real. He'd watched *The Evil Dead* and *Army of Darkness* one too many times. That was all.

Because, otherwise, minifigures were swarming from every possible hidden spot in the kitchen.

Tiny, busty lady in a silver miniskirt with a ray gun the size of his pointer finger: not real. Action figure-sized roller derby girls coming in fast: not real. Generic rockstar with hair made for headbanging and a guitar: definitely not real. Zombie horde limping toward him with his injector gun: not—

The zombies plunged the gun into the soft meat under his chin.

White hot pain erupted through his body.

Oh, God, it burned.

A sharp chemical smell filled his nostrils.

He screamed. The screaming made the pain so much worse. Tears streamed up his face. He could feel his throat swelling up; he gasped for breath, but couldn't get air in.

An unwelcome thought erupted through the fog of anguish: Bob Berdella tried to shut up his victims by injecting drain cleaner into their larynxes.

Joel squeezed his eyes shut, willing the pain and the hallucinations to go away. When he opened them again, his vision filled with the tiny figures still infesting the kitchen, busy movement all around him.

He flinched away from sudden burns on his arm. When he looked up he could see flesh already bubbling and blistering. Little green men were shooting him with hot oil from the fryer, pumped through their miniscule ray guns.

Joel tried to swing his body towards them to knock into them with his head, but it was useless. Attacks were coming from all sides now. He hadn't even registered the zombie horde with the toothpicks until they were jabbing them over and over again underneath his fingernails.

The rock stars carried a huge jar of cayenne pepper to the stainless steel prep table.

The Zombie King, surveying his domain from above Joel, nodded.

"Let us see what will happen."

Joel was confused; there was too much happening too fast. A pair of trapdoor zombies came at his teeth with pliers, but Joel bit down hard, bursting one of their heads with a satisfying *pop!* His mouth filled with the taste of burnt plastic.

Soon blood was rolling down his face. He didn't know where it was coming from, but he could feel movement from *inside* his stomach now. They were *in* him, sloshing around inside his organs and he was bleeding—

—bleeding—

—bleeding—

There was a loud rip, cold air on his now bare legs.

Oh, God, oh, God, one of the men Berdella killed died of an anal rupture. Bled out.

That was not going to happen to him.

The one who died fast, how did he go?

Joel felt himself blinking in and out of consciousness.

The pain was everywhere now, dull and sharp, shooting and throbbing, burning and—

—it was too much—

—too much—

—he was going to pass out but what would they do to him if—

Joel screamed out as loud as he could, the pain emanating from his ruined throat—

—excruciating—

And then they gagged him, the derby girls slapping high fives when the job was through.

Asphyxiation, Joel suddenly remembered.

That was how the first one had died.

***

The pinball toys hacked and stabbed, carrying pieces of bone and viscera in their little ant lines to the dumpster. Bits of Joel sprinkled the tops of the disassembled pinball machines, the prisons that would never again hold them.

Tossing body parts out with the garbage had worked before, when they were but one man. And there was so much less to dispose of this time.

R.J. would be coming in tomorrow.

Joel would be done smoking by then.

Stripped Down
Rik Hoskin

THE WOMAN IN THE SILVER BIKINI had Tom utterly besotted. Admittedly, he was drunk—drunk enough to walk into a strip club like this, still not drunk enough to forget Rachel. But the woman on stage—dark bangs that brushed the tops of her eyes; pale, slender body revealing itself sinuously, one layer at a time—was filling Tom's eyes and his mind in ways Rachel never had.

The clip joint was down a Soho back alley, one of those places where there was just a door and the illuminated promise of "Girls! Girls! Girls!" beside a bouncer in a too-tight suit. The lights on that sign were brighter than anything within, but what light there was caught the highlights of the dancer's metallic bikini, and her glistening skin and silver-painted nails.

Another gyration, another turn around the pole, and the bra came off, sailing from the stage to land square in Tom's lap. He grabbed it, feeling the body heat it trapped, and when he looked up the stripper winked at him. He was the last customer in the club, he realized.

Coyly, she turned her back to him, pulling down her panties in a staggered cha-cha-cha of her hips.

And then she was naked but for the heels, holding his gaze as he admired her body, touching her breasts as he watched. He couldn't remember the last time he had seen Rachel's body; they had argued so much in the last months and never made up, had discarded all pretense of intimacy.

The stripper's body was hot and slender, like the women Tom had dreamed about being with when he was a teenager, not like the ones he had dated. Her fingers held her nipples, caressing them stroke by tantalizing stroke. And then those silver nails dug in and she began to pull at her nipples, tearing them upwards, ripping them from her body, trailed by long strips of skin, up into her shoulder blades.

Tom vomited, tasting of beer and vodka, and stumbled out of his chair.

The bouncer was at his side instantly. "Show's not over," he said.

Tom found himself reseated—did he do that or the bouncer?—and watched as the beautiful stripper tore lines of skin from her body, each strip oozing with the red blossoms of blood that budded there to fill the space.

He watched, wanting to be sick again, tasting it in his mouth.

After the woman was done, stripped down to the frame beneath the skin, she came to him and she spoke, running her hand across his cheek.

"Your turn," she said.

Numb, he felt her nails dig in.

Always Hiring
Lydia Bugg

THE MOST HELPFUL THING I LEARNED in business school was how to eat shit while smiling. No theory, equation, policy, or quotation ever did more for me than learning to bite my tongue until it bled while my colleagues made their little comments. They said I was smart, "surprisingly." They pulled me aside and asked in a whisper if I had an OnlyFans, and when I told them no, they were shocked.

"You have an asset that's in demand, you should capitalize on that. Make that money, girl. I'm just saying. Everything is sex-positive now, so you should get yours. You know what I mean? You're not mad at me for saying that, right? Because I'm a feminist. I'm just trying to help you maximize your potential. Let me know if you want help getting set up or anything."

If I wore knee-high boots or bright colored heels, they were "hooker shoes." If I wore sneakers, I was "looking sloppy." If I didn't wear makeup, they would ask if I was sick. One of the few other women in my class would occasionally lock eyes with me over a comment like this, then we would smile and move on because we weren't like the other girls. We were actually going to graduate.

It was an impossibly long six years, but by the time I walked across that solid oak stage my smile was so wide and permanent I forgot how to make it go away. I was sitting at home alone in the dark, sipping wine, watching reality TV and smiling.

When I started working, the smile got even bigger. If they thought of you as a "mother" they would expect you to wait on them hand and foot, bring them coffee, do their paperwork — they turned into demanding, oversized toddlers. If they thought they had a shot with you, there would suddenly be a hand up your skirt under the table at the next meeting, no flirting, no dinner, just straight to insertion. My body was an asset in demand and these men were taught you had to be aggressive with the assets if you wanted to gain.

So, I got good at getting them to see me how I needed them to see me. I made them feel comfortable, but not indulged. I wasn't the mom or the girlfriend, I was the sweet little sister.

Then, one day, I was out, way out. So far out that I couldn't get a job anywhere. They said it was because of the cocaine, but come on. Who isn't on cocaine on Wall Street? That was bullshit. It was because my smile slipped.

I've been unemployed for six months, my savings dried up. I sold my West Elm furniture, moved out of the condo with the doorman. I was heading west because I figured it was better to be poor somewhere warm.

I stopped for gas—I don't know what town I was in, hell, I didn't even know what state. I'd been moving on instinct like an elephant headed to its graveyard.

But, now, the haze of my despair lifted and in front of me were two words on a bright red sign in careful white lettering: Always Hiring. I checked my hair in the rearview; I hadn't brushed it in days, frizz city. My eyes were bloodshot and rimmed with red. I pulled an old blazer out of my suitcase and smoothed out the wrinkles with my hands. You have to work with what you've got.

The woman behind the counter looked even more beat up than me, which I didn't know was possible for gainfully-employed people. If I looked like I hadn't slept in a month, then she hadn't slept in three. Her hair was half falling out of a banana clip, and her hand shook as she brought a paper coffee cup to her mouth.

"Excuse me …" I checked her nametag. Dale Carnegie says that people love to hear their own names. Hers read Caroline, Manager, so I knew I was talking to the right person. "Caroline, I saw the sign out front that said you're hiring."

She put down her coffee cup. In a measured tone, the slight twang of a southern accent peeking through, she said, "We are, but you have to really want the job."

I got her skepticism. My jacket was wrinkled but I'd bought it on Fifth Avenue. She must have been wondering how I ended up here.

"I do," I said. "I really do. I *need* a job."

The desperation was pouring off of me. It wasn't a good look, but I couldn't help it. Something I'd been working to keep tamped down for months was welling up inside me. The primeval fear of ending up one of those old, forgotten women haunting roadsides with bony, outstretched hands. I could see it so clearly.

My soul shivered.

I didn't know what Caroline would ask me next—my work history, my references—but it really didn't matter. None of my answers were the good ones. I'd found that out many, many times over the previous six months.

She didn't ask me about my greatest weakness, though. Instead, she looked me in the eye and said, "Beg me for it."

"What?"

"Beg me for the job if you want it so bad." Her expression was completely blank. It didn't seem like she was taking any perverse pleasure in this; she was just stating a requirement of the job, like *can you balance a register*? If I wanted it, I had to beg. It was simple.

The word rushed out in a whisper, "Please?"

She sighed and looked toward the security cameras that monitored the pumps.

"I don't know if that's good enough."

"What, do you want me to get down on my knees?" It came out more forcefully than I wanted it to.

Her icy expression didn't change as she said, "That would probably work."

So, I did it. I looked with disgust at the sticky, brown tile floor, covered in crushed Skittles and cherry slushie stains, then knelt before the counter, clasping my hands in a prayer position and raising them up toward Caroline like she was a god. But she was more important than God to me; *she* could actually answer my prayer.

"Please." My eyes welled with tears. "Please, I really need a job."

Now I had Caroline's attention. A small smile flickered across her lips. She *was* enjoying degrading me after all.

"This job," she clarified.

"This job, not just any job. I want to work here, *desperately*." In that moment it felt true. I wanted to work at this gas station. I could feel the need coursing through my circulatory system.

"All right, that should do it."

"You mean I'm hired?" I asked without rising.

"Yep, congratulations, you're hired. You can get up now."

It was difficult to pull myself up as all of the tension drained from my body. I did it. I was going to be able to take care of myself again.

"The shift is overnight, and you'll start tonight." She hopped off her stool and handed me a nametag with the word Employee above a blank space.

"Tonight? That's fast."

"Is it a problem?" Caroline reached out as if to take the nametag back, but I yanked my hand away before she could touch it. "There's a label maker in the office we can get set up for you, and you'll also need to sign some paperwork."

I followed her to the back of the store, past rows of snack cakes, chips, and candy. I noticed that the coolers were only about half-stocked with drinks. A thin layer of dust gathered on the glass. Wow, with a little bit of cleaning and restocking I could increase this place's profit in no time.

Caroline's office contained a tiny, paper-cluttered desk and an enormous filing cabinet. She motioned for me to sit in a chair that also doubled as a door stop. With the door closed, two people wouldn't fit in the room.

I filled in all of the typical information—name, Social Security number, and I made something up for my address since writing *wherever I park my car* wasn't an option. As I signed my name at the bottom I felt a small, sharp bite, on the tip of my thumb. How did that happen? I'd somehow managed to cut myself on the pen badly enough that I was bleeding. A few drops of blood already splattered across my signature.

"Oh, whoops, I'm sorry." I apologized for bleeding.

"Happens all the time," Caroline replied as she snatched the paper up and placed it in a manila folder. She opened up the filing cabinet carefully. It was so full that folders were popping out of the top when she shoved mine in. The drawer seemed to go on forever; the binders in the back were yellowing, and I thought I saw a few that looked like they'd been written on a typewriter. Wow, I'd have to convert them to digital as soon as possible. Another spot where I could find some profit. Caroline was going to have to watch her back. I'd have her job in a matter of months.

As I followed her back to the register I asked, "What about training?"

She pointed to a large black binder next to the security monitors, labeled *New Underground Gas Training Manual*. "That has all the information you'll need. There. You're trained." She held the glass door open for me and gestured to my car. "Come back when the sun sets."

"Right, a set schedule. I love that!" I chirped. Caroline remained stone-faced as she ushered me out the door. There was a pause. She clung to my upper arm for just a moment and looked deep into my eyes, as if trying to decide if she should say something. Her mouth quivered and she quickly whispered, "Don't eat or drink anything in the store. It doesn't like that."

"O…kay?"

Her face hardened once again, a decision made.

"See you at sunset."

I went to Walmart and splurged on an energy drink and a pre-packaged sandwich that I ate in my car. I took a nap in the back seat, feeling safe for the first time in a long time. When I opened my eyes again, the sky was glowing pink and orange.

It was time to get to work.

The Walmart parking lot had been teeming with life—birds, frogs, and cicadas calling out to each other in the fading light—but when I pulled into the gas station I noticed how silent it was. The bell above the door announced me, but Caroline was nowhere to be found. I called "Hello?" a few times and poked around, but since most of the store was clearly visible from the register I could see that no one was there.

The employee nametag sat on the counter, my name now in the blank space. I shrugged, picked it up, and put it on. This was another example of the inefficiencies of this place I could correct. I couldn't believe Caroline hadn't even stuck around to pass the station off to me.

It was time to get to work. I noticed a bucket and mop near the bathrooms, but I wasn't sure how to fill it. I ended up taking one of the largest slushie cups and filling it with water from the bathroom sink. Cleaning wasn't exactly my specialty, but since there didn't seem to be any other cleaning supplies around, I figured the best I could do was start with wiping down the drink coolers.

As I did, I started to notice some of the drinks inside. There were things I thought were discontinued years ago: New Coke, Tab Clear, Jolt. Then there were a lot of drinks that I felt certain did not exist: one was labeled Red Color Sugar Water, another said Nilk. It looked like milk and guaranteed "strong bone" on the label but was clearly misspelled.

I thought back to what Caroline had said about not eating or drinking anything in the store. Could that be because it would make me sick? Was everything expired and off-brand? I wondered if there was any way I could convince her to let me be involved with the purchasing around here.

Once I finished cleaning the cases, I started to wander the shelves, checking out the other products. There was specialized candy for every holiday, chocolate Easter eggs, peppermint sticks, and boxes of candy hearts all in a row. Mold was visible on some of the snack cakes, so I went ahead and threw them out. I considered going around and checking the expiration dates on everything else, but worried I might end up throwing out half of the store.

The only thing that seemed to be in perfect working condition was the cherry slushie machine. I stood in front of it for a while, watching the hypnotic turn of the bone-white paddle through the red liquid. The rhythmic pumping seemed to match with the pulse of my heartbeat.

Why was this machine so perfect? It was shiny and new while

everything else in the store decayed on the shelves. I reached out and pressed the palm of my hand against the front of it. Suddenly I was so thirsty. I thought again about Caroline's ridiculous warning. Then I thought about how she made me get down on my knees and beg.

Yeah, fuck her.

I filled a cup all the way to the top with free slushie. It was darker red than any slushie I'd ever had, and the sugary smell of artificial cherry was oddly absent. In fact, it didn't smell like anything at all. As I lifted the cup to my lips, a light in the back of the store flickered and went out.

"Great," I muttered, "another thing to add to my list of problems."

I shook my head and took a long gulp of the slushie. It tasted like nothing. I don't mean that it was bland, I mean it wasn't cold, it wasn't sweet, and it didn't melt in my mouth. It was viscous, it had texture, but no feeling at all.

I slammed it down onto the counter.

"Yuck, syrup must be out." Of course there had to be something wrong with it.

Suddenly I realized that I hadn't had a single customer yet. It was almost midnight. I figured it would be much later until things were this dead. I stared out the glass door into the pitch-black night. It felt like there wasn't another living soul for miles, and yet, somehow, it also felt like I was being watched.

Something made me wander over to the wall of security cameras and check them. There were the gas pumps in black-and-white, as well as a birds-eye view of the aisles and one of the bathroom doors. Although, now that the light back there had gone out, it was practically too dark to see anything. As I stared at that monitor, the one showing the gas pumps flickered and the image briefly changed. I jumped.

"What was that?"

There was just a flash of something else, something huge, then it was gone. I leaned in and tapped the monitor as if that would do something, but the image remained the same. The monitor above it, though, the one showing the aisles, flickered this time and I found myself face to face with a single, giant eyeball.

I propelled myself backward as far away as I could, gasping.

"What the hell?" I checked the aisles and looked at the camera, but, of course, there was nothing really there. The eyeball watched me, half-lidded, looking almost bored. Was this some kind of prank? An initiation into the gas station business? Like when the guys at the firm made me think I lost four hundred grand on my first day and then laughed at me when I started to shake with fear?

If someone *was* watching me, I wasn't going to give them the satisfaction of freaking out. I reached up and turned off the monitor with the eyeball. It appeared on one of the two remaining monitors. I turned that one off, too. Then it appeared on the final monitor. I flipped it off and stared at the blank screens.

They all came back on at once, all with the eyeball looking back at me. All three eyeballs blinked in imperfect unison.

My nose started to bleed.

"Okay," I whispered as I backed away from the monitors, all the way out from behind the counter. The monitors swiveled, all three eyes following my movement. I backed into the middle of the store, watching them blink.

"If this is a prank show or something, I want you to know I haven't signed a release and I *won't* and I know a lot of *lawyers!*"

That's when I noticed the floor was moving A slow, pulsating, up-and-down motion, the sleeping breaths of a giant. The movement caused me to stumble to the side; it was like I was standing on the deck of a rocking ship. I fell into a display of snack cakes and knocked it over, landing hard on my side.

The swaying motion rocked the entire store, knocking the employee handbook off the counter and into my side. I picked it up and began to frantically flip through, as if there would be some kind of simple explanation listed and the proper steps to solve my problem. All I found was unreadable gibberish. The manual was written in a language I'd never seen before.

As I lay before the slushie machine, clinging to the manual, I heard a low, ominous rumble. I looked up as a geyser of cherry slushie exploded into the room like a gush of arterial blood, or projectile vomit, something eerily reminiscent of bodily fluid in its undulating motion. I was covered in red liquid. It flowed freely down the aisles, coating the entire floor, more liquid then could have possibly been in the machine by far, a full underground lake of cherry slushie.

I had to drag myself through it in order to pull myself to standing again using a shelf.

"What is happening?" I called. "Please stop."

As if in response to my plea, the center of the floor began to crack open, brown tile disappearing into a deep, black hole. When I saw that, somehow I knew. This place, the gas station, had been speaking to me the entire time. It smelled my desperation from miles away and dragged me here. I was a sacrifice to an old god — something enormous, and hungry, and very good at disguising itself. I walked into its mouth voluntarily. I begged it to devour me.

The floor stopped moving and the slushie machine finally emptied. A sudden stillness engulfed the store, which was somehow *worse* because it left me face to face with the gaping darkness in the middle of the floor. It whispered to me and I felt my feet begin to move toward it. After all, I'm a woman of my word, and I promised, didn't I? Didn't I beg for this?

My hands clung to a shelf even as my feet carried me forward. A rustling sound broke through the silence as the candy on the shelves began to move. It rushed at my body in a wave, skittering up my legs like a plague of rats. A thousand tiny fingers made of expired Twinkies, melting chocolate, and moldy string cheese tugged at my hair and skin, pulling me to my knees, dragging me toward the hole.

I dug my fingernails into the floor. "No, no!" I begged for my life for the second time that day. Something about this scenario reminded me of my old job. This creature thought it knew what it wanted from me, but I had to convince it that it really wanted something else. What could I offer it, though?

As I rushed toward the hole, an unfriendly face appeared in my mind's eye: Caroline.

"I can help you!" I called out. "Promote me! I'll bring you twice as many victims as Caroline."

The tugging stopped. I had its attention.

"I can help you make this place more inviting, lure more people in. I'll go out into the world and recruit people, job fairs, that kind of thing. I'll get you on LinkedIn."

There was a long pause during which the sound of my own ragged breathing filled the room. The candy released me, scuttling back to the shelves and settling as if nothing happened. I crawled to the counter, my knees aching from the resistance, and pulled myself up. I saw there was something sitting in the middle of the countertop, a new nametag that said Manager, with my name underneath it. My pleas had been heard, my salary negotiated. I snapped it up greedily and put it on.

****

I tried to leave when the sun rose but found that I couldn't. The door was unlocked but simply wouldn't budge for me. Somehow I knew I had to prove my loyalty before it would let me go. I had to hire someone.

The man wandered in around noon. For him, the door flew right open. His name was Bill. He was dirty and not even coherent enough to attempt to hide the track marks on his arms. Somehow I knew he'd been thinking of robbing me, before he noticed the sign in the window. It whispered to him the possibility of a better future. He felt the spark of hope for the first time in years.

This hope was the bait the gas-station god hid its hook in.

"Of course we're hiring," I told him. "Night shift. You could start tonight if you really want the job."

It felt good to stand over him as he begged. The dignity I lost yesterday afternoon regained twofold as I watched him prick his finger and bleed onto the paper. This ancient, monstrous thing owned me, but as long as I was owned, I could wield its power. I would never beg again.

I watched Bill leave with his head full of dreams and I smiled.

Tonight we would feed on those dreams, and tomorrow I would go out and find us two more Bills to feed on. I would scour soup kitchens, AA meetings, underneath overpasses, anywhere the vulnerable gathered. I'd do what I always did. I'd survive.

Before I could finish celebrating, though, the employee manual slid itself across the counter, landing open in front of me. I could read it now.

> Congratulations!
>
> If you're able to comprehend the holy text, it means you've completed the New Underground Gas employee training program. Once you prostrate yourself before the altar and are accepted as a sacrifice to the one below ground, you will begin the process we like to call the three Cs.
>
> **Capture**
> **Corrupt**
> **Consume**
>
> In step one, you were lured to the station and bound to the one below, pre-consumption. Your filthy soul was then fully corrupted through your own tragic devices. This makes the soul more desirable and nourishing for our great ravager of the desperate. The final stage is what you are about to experience.
>
> We refer to this as consumption, but only because there is no word in any human language that can accurately describe the total, utter decimation of the human soul for the sustenance of an infinitely greater and wiser being. You may experience an astonishing amount of pain, endless screaming, fear, dissociation, pain, shock, bleeding, ripping, and

pain during this process, but you will not die!
Ever! Please be comforted by the knowledge
that this pleases our endless lord greatly.

The ground beneath me disappeared. I fell down through the darkness for what felt like an eternity, landing with a splash in a massive, roiling ocean made of gasoline. The smell was over-whelming, the fumes stung my nose and made my stomach turn. It whipped me back and forth in a churning, acidic current.

So this was what it felt like to be digested.

Why did they always tell me monsters want a pure sacrifice, a virgin in a white dress? Corruption was this monster's sustenance. It wanted to corrupt me fully, and then consume me, and the process wasn't difficult. As it pulled my head under, I realized I was right about one thing, though.

I would never beg again.

Closing Shift
Elena Greer

THIS WAS THE ABSOLUTE WORST-CASE SCENARIO.

Sitsi Hadwell watched, drumming her fingers against the counter, as the last of her co-workers pulled out of Early Rise's parking lot. That was supposed to be her. It was three a.m. and she was supposed to be in her truck, driving back to her shitty apartment. She was *not* supposed to be working the closing shift.

Lewis Myers, her least favorite of Early Rise's two managers, stepped out of the lefthand office, an armful of paperwork in his hold, fishing his keys from his jeans pocket. He never looked like he fit in the shitty diner setting, and Sitsi always pinned that on the fact Lewis took being the stereotype of a white frat boy a little too seriously.

Lewis didn't even look at her as he left the building, giving her a backhanded wave on his way out into freedom.

"Night, CeCe!"

Sitsi just nodded, waving her manager out of the building, watching him lock the diner behind him, get into his ugly green Porsche, and leave, too.

"It's pronounced *Sit-See*," she muttered to herself, turning to walk to the back of the kitchen.

The Early Rise Diner was the only diner in Doveport still open. A small, crumbling mom-and-pop that had served millions of people in the decades since its opening in the late 1930s. That, aside from some housekeeping and tweaking to fit the current day, looked the same as it had when it opened. Wide windows intercut walls painted a muted gray, the seating lines of red-and-white-leather booths. The main counter lined nearly the length of the diner itself, cut just a bit short to leave room for the restrooms and manager's office. Not too far from the swinging red doors that led to the kitchen, there was a rack settled in a window-shaped hole in the wall where the food would come and go. The stools lining the counter matched the booths in color and texture.

It was, unabashedly, the strangest place Sitsi had ever had the displeasure of working at. Her fellow staff were all rigid, rude, self-serving assholes with no room for compassion. The patrons were either half-decent teens and young adults, or older folks who made her nervous to walk to her truck at night. And they tended to come from all over; no two were the same.

Sitsi hated making judgments about people, but she couldn't deny that some of their mannerisms were odd. Sometimes a patron's teeth were longer than average, sometimes they drank from flasks she *knew* were not filled with beer or bourbon, sometimes the smell of wet dog or the copper of blood followed them like a plague. And Sitsi would swear by the Creator that she'd seen some have eyes that changed colors, or gazes that flashed with something she could only explain as ravaging hunger.

Early Rise not only attracted peculiar people, it also worked in peculiar ways. Early morning shifts were not the opening shift, rather a three-hour shift *before* opening, where one cooked bakery foods, set up the dining room and the kitchen, and got the stoves heated before the actual opening-shift crew showed up. The afternoon shift was the shortest shift, between the opening and evening shifts, only lasting three hours. No matter what, evening shifts spanned until past midnight. And the closing shift always happened in the after-hours.

Sitsi unhooked the bucket of cleaning supplies from the back hook, taking the broom, mop, and dustpan, and tucking what she couldn't hold against her side. Erika had been kind enough to write down a list for her to follow in a notepad, the instructions no different than the ones she got when she'd first started working early morning shifts.

- Empty and clean the coffee and tea machines
- Clean the soda and ice cream machine

- Return the menus to the menu holder
- Clean the bathrooms
- Clean the kitchen
  - Counters
  - Sink
  - Stoves
  - Ovens
- Wipe down the counters, tables, and booths
- Sweep the floors
- Mop the floors
- Sanitize the register, radio, etc.

Easy. Simple. She could do this, no problem.

Sitsi took pleasure checking each of the tasks off the list, since it meant she was one task closer to being able to leave. Her thoughts were plagued with dreams of her warm bed, in her warm apartment, with a warm and fresh johnnycake being eaten as she watched the latest stupid reality television show.

She was grateful she'd already changed into non-work clothes by the time Lewis had dropped the bombshell on her. It was infinitely easier to move in jeans and an orange-and-beige flannel than the itchy, yellow waitress uniform worn when she worked.

Sitsi was in the middle of drying off a metal tray when she caught a glance of herself in its reflection. The dual braids of bleached blonde hair she'd carefully done that morning were almost completely undone, the light amount of makeup more or less worn off completely. The bags beneath her brown eyes looked worse, and the planes of her narrow face and taupe skin were hollowed and sharper, like they always were after a long shift in the soul-sucking diner.

She was tired. She was exhausted from working a twelve-hour shift before closing had even been dropped in her lap. She never worked closing, and now she was stuck here. Covering for Erika because Lewis hadn't done his job right.

Sitsi sighed and rubbed her eyes with shaking hands, then

picked up the rag again to continue cleaning the —

She jumped as a bell rang out in the silent diner. She knew the sound all too well: the welcome bell above the front door.

Confused, she dropped the rag back into the sink, making her way from the back of the kitchen to the front counter. She pushed the swinging doors open and was met with an empty room.

"Lewis?" she asked, scanning the dining room with narrowed eyes. "You forget something?"

Nothing. No commotion from the office, no sound of Lewis' grating, condescending voice, only the buzz of the lightbulbs in the hanging lights and her own scratchy, Texan-laced tone.

Sitsi unlocked the front door, popping her head outside to glance around the dark parking lot. Also empty, spare her little truck parked right in the lights of the diner. She shut the door behind her, shaking her head as she pushed back to the kitchen to finish the last of the dishes.

She hummed quietly as she busied herself with work. As she deep-cleaned the kitchen top-to-bottom, scrubbed the ovens and grill tops until her arms throbbed in pain, wiped down the fridges and freezers until they were spotless. Every scratch on the checklist meant she was closer to going home. Every line through a chore meant one less minute in the hell on earth that was the Early Rise Diner.

Then Sitsi heard whispers of conversation, loud enough to shift her attention away from the dishware cabinet she was organizing. A frown formed at her lips. Her eyes could see just between the racks in the window, and all she saw was the dining room. No intruder, no speaking voices, nothing.

She walked around the counter, crossing the room to the modified 1945 standing radio, fiddling with the dials and volume, all of which played radio stations filled with music. Not talking.

Sitsi rubbed her eyes as she crossed the room again, muttering about making herself a quick meal before leaving, because the auditory hallucinations were getting out of hand. She'd barely stepped back into the kitchen when the counter bell dinged. Annoyed, she cracked the door open again, and was met with a still-empty dining room.

Sitsi took a snack break instead of cleaning and mopping the bathrooms. The boring sandwich, made of a burger bun and several slices of cheese, didn't do much in making her feel better, and settled in her stomach like a stone. Still, she ate it whole. Then a second one. Then a third one. Then, once she felt she had fed herself sufficiently, she wiped her hands on her jeans and returned her attention to the few remaining tasks she had.

The counter bell dinged again. She ignored it. It chimed again. She paid it no mind. Again, it dinged, and again, she dismissed it, this time with an irritated scowl and a shake of her head. Sitsi ignored every ding and chime of the stupid counter bell—until she heard something metallic clatter to the floor.

She balanced the mop against the wall, then took slow, halting steps towards the dining room.

"Lewis?" she asked, pushing the doors open slowly.

Sitsi stopped cold in the middle of the doorway, eyes wide as she scanned the room. The tables, which had been disasters of crumbs and unclean dishes, were spotless, as if there was never a mess in the first place.

She stumbled back into the kitchen, pulling a chef's knife from one of the blocks before returning to the counter, blood rushing in her ears.

"Seriously, Lewis, this really isn't funny," she said, the hand holding the knife shaking like a leaf in a hurricane.

No one was there. The dining room was as empty as it had been after Lewis left, and every other time she had checked it through her shift. Utterly, completely empty.

Turning, Sitsi tripped over her own feet, catching herself on the counter as the knife clattered to the tiles. Maybe it was the precarious positioning of the anti-fatigue mat. Or maybe it was the exhaustion from an already-long work day that had finally caught up with her. She wasn't entirely sure. She let out a choked sob, dropping to the ground with watery eyes and burning cheeks.

The tile floor was cold to the touch. It seeped into the denim of her jeans like a spilled drink, and Sitsi could've cried from the way it soothed her. She turned to lay herself down on the dirty tile floor, arms spread as far as they could in the cramped space. Her teary eyes flickered shut, and she took a deep breath in, then out. She inhaled slowly again, and exhaled slower. Her heartbeat slowed, the rushing of blood in her ears lessened, and her breathing evened itself. By the time she reopened her eyes, her mind felt clearer. More collected.

Fuck this, she thought. Fuck Easy Rise and their stupidly bizarre scheduling. Fuck this stupid shift. And *especially* fuck Lewis Myers.

Sitsi grabbed the side of the counter, grunting as she pulled herself to stand fully—and freezing just as quickly.

A woman stood in front of her, black hair a clean slice of the midnight sky, cropped short in a pixie cut. Her skin matched Sitsi's own, her lips painted a sweet cherry red, dressed in a white crop top and low rise pants.

A thousand eyes littered every visible inch of her skin. The sharp planes of her face, her stocky neck, her broad shoulders and toned arms, all of it covered in blinking eyes whose irises came in every shade and tone of color in the rainbow.

A rock formed in the base of Sitsi's throat. She hated staring, it was such a rude thing to do, but she couldn't help it. She wasn't sure if she was dreaming, if she was hallucinating from lack of sleep, or, worse, that the woman was real.

The thousand-eyed woman gestured to her left, to the little glass tray of croissants next to the register. Her request was obvious, even without words. Sitsi didn't move at first, standing completely still, before forcing herself to take a hesitant step towards the display. When the woman didn't move—beyond turning to watch Sitsi's movements—Sitsi inched closer to the kitchen door, dipping inside just long enough to grab a small plate, then stepped towards the bakery tray. The glass lid clinked against the porcelain tray as she lifted it, taking a croissant in her spare hand and placing it in the center of the plate before returning the lid.

Sitsi walked back to the woman, holding the little dish out for her.

The woman took it gratefully, the eyes on the back of her hand blinking as their hands brushed. She lifted it to her nose, inhaling sharply, and smiling in what Sitsi assumed was satisfaction. Sitsi watched in a hazed sense of shock and horror as the eyes across her lips blinked and widened, sharp little teeth peeking out from the space between eyeball and eyelid. The teeth took tiny little bites of the pastry alongside the woman's own teeth.

When she was done, the woman smiled again, and Sitsi forced a smile onto her face as well, opening her mouth to speak to the strange woman—

The bell rang out, clear as day.

"CeCe, why the fuck wasn't the door locked?" Lewis' voice cut through the diner, and both Sitsi and the woman looked at him. Sitsi in surprise and anxiety, the woman in annoyance and … something else. Something familiar enough that dread shot through Sitsi's spine.

Lewis stopped, eyes fixed in horror on the thousand-eyed woman, blinking rapidly as if doing so would make her go away.

"What the fuck—"

Sitsi blinked, and the thousand-eyed woman was across the room, throwing Lewis to the floor, the impact a sickening, echoing *crack*. Lewis shouted, clawing at the tile and the woman in an unsuccessful attempt to get out from beneath her. They tussled, and when the woman emerged victorious, she took Lewis' arms, one in each of her hands, and snapped them like twigs.

Sitsi jumped as Lewis screamed, a hand flying to cover her mouth as the woman twisted the limbs—the flesh writhing and bending and breaking in her vice grip—brutally, *slowly*, ripping them from Lewis' torso.

The thousand-eyed woman dropped the now-severed arms to the blood-soaked tiles, blissfully ignoring the horrific screams of the boy beneath her. She took Lewis' face between her palms, her mouth opening alongside her eyes, and took a bite out of the side of Lewis' face.

Sitsi dropped back behind the counter, curling her knees to her chest and covering her ears with her palms as Lewis' shrieks somehow got louder and infinitely worse. She couldn't see what was happening, but she could take an educated guess if the sound of shattering bone, tearing flesh, and bloody screams were anything to go off. Even when Lewis' screaming had lessened to a choked whine, and then to nothing at all, she could hear the woman's jaw working, the chomping of a million sets of teeth as they devoured.

Sitsi stayed coiled tightly against herself for what felt like an infinity, breathing hard and shaky through the gaps of her fingers, listening to the sound of cannibalism occurring barely five feet from her.

Only when the dining room returned to silence, when the only sound was the humming of electricity, did she remove her sweat-slicked palm from her mouth. Hesitantly, she uncurled herself, turning to sit on her knees and look up—

The gore-soaked woman was looking down over the counter. *Right at her.*

Sitsi's heartbeat stopped. The woman tilted her head in a curious manner, all eyes narrowed. Sitsi held up her trembling hands in surrender, and the woman's brow furrowed as she frowned for the first time, before shaking her head one time.

The message was clear, and Sitsi took hold of the counter to slowly pull herself into a stand, legs shaking, heart beating like a hummingbird's wings in her ears. She glanced to where she'd last seen her least favorite manager.

There was nothing left of Lewis Myers. No flesh, no bone, no hair, no clothes or shoes or even teeth. She thought it would've looked messier, uglier, but it was as if a child had licked it up like ice cream in a glass dish. There was blood, but only the blood that had seeped into the ridges of the grout and the tiny bumps in the hand-painted walls.

Sitsi looked back at the woman, who was holding herself with pride. She shoved a hand into her back pants pocket, pulling out a leather wallet and flipping it open. She thumbed through a multitude of bills, before pulling several hundreds out and handing them to Sitsi.

Sitsi wanted to protest, but took the blood-streaked bills with a grateful smile, pocketing the money. She'd barely whispered *thank you* when the woman grabbed her hand, not giving Sitsi time to react before she kissed her knuckles.

It was the strangest sensation, like a cat and their sandpaper tongues. The woman's lips lingered for a moment longer before she patted the top of Sitsi's hand with her other hand and let go. Then the woman smiled, and turned to the door.

"Wait!" Sitsi called out before she could stop herself. The woman paused, spinning back to her. Sitsi nervously grabbed a handful of brown paper napkins, holding them out for the woman to take. "For the road," she said, hoping her voice wasn't actually as shaky as it sounded.

The woman grinned, bowing her head in thanks before taking the napkins from her, dabbing at her blood-sodden top as she moved towards the door.

Sitsi watched the thousand-eyed girl leave and vanish into the deep dark of the very early morning, before retrieving the mop and bucket from the kitchen.

Someone needed to clean the mess left behind.

King Corn
Nathan Crowder

IT ONLY TAKES TWENTY-FOUR HOURS TO DRIVE from Las Vegas to Milwaukee, Glen had insisted. Less if you ignore the speed limit in some of the flatter states. He assured me he would do it himself—the reverse of his initial exodus from a few years ago—if he didn't have to stay by his mom's side while she recovered from knee surgery. Of course, he couldn't live without his precious Beemer even for a few weeks.

"And you've always wanted to drive it, Julie," he said, "so if you drive it up for me, I'll pay for your flight back home, pay for gas and meals, plus a fat two hundred dollars on top of it. What do you say?"

And what I say, of course, is "Sure," even though I want things between me and Glen to be over and don't know how to tell him yet. But his BMW was pretty choice, I had a few days off, and I might as well make some money instead of spending it curled up in bed watching K-Dramas on my phone. I could always break up with him over the phone from the flight home.

Great, in theory. Everything could be great in theory. I had hope, grit, determination. I was the boss of me or whatever bullshit affirmation I used to drag myself out of bed that particular morning. But theory never survived in the face of the rest of the world for some reason. At least not for me. And it always started small.

Case in point, the charger cable for my phone wiggled free somewhere on the drive. Between GPS directions and a steady playlist of '80s power ballads and '90s grunge classics, I was flying blind before I hit Nebraska. No big deal. I picked up a road atlas, a new charger, and a fistful of energy beverages at a convenience store in Sedgwick. My phone got back to charging, but slowly. To conserve juice, I switched over to radio, which was sub-optimal in the middle of nowhere, especially when I was counting on it to keep me awake.

Then, deep in corn country in Iowa, running on reserves in the ass-end of a dark, cloudy night, I found myself on the old highway instead of the main route. Nothing but cornstalks on either side of a road that probably hadn't been resurfaced in my lifetime, with occasional silos or farm roofs poking up above the stalks. There wasn't even a shoulder to pull over on, which was great if I wanted to blast through there at ninety miles an hour. But I couldn't trust my reaction time. Last thing I needed to complicate the evening was a high-speed encounter with a deer, or a cow, or whatever the fuck staggered out into my path.

It was kind of a miracle to come across lights in the darkness shortly after three a.m., when I was just about to fade for good. Positioned at a quiet intersection with a blinking red light like a cyclops eye, the twenty-four-hour diner named Cobb's Corner was like an oasis. The idea of a grilled cheese, fries, and a pot of coffee sounded like the best idea I'd had since leaving Nevada. I slowed the BMW and pulled off the road, parking far enough from any of the other half-dozen cars and trucks to avoid careless dings. Standing next to the car in the crisp night air, I noticed the Cobb's Corner mascot for the first time.

I guess you could call it a mascot, though the word wasn't quite big enough for what greeted me. An anthropomorphic ear of corn with long arms and legs and huge, googly eyes stood in the corn field next to the parking lot. Goddamn thing must have been forty feet tall if it was an inch, towering over a grain silo on the other side of the road. Just above its head, a narrow sliver of moon poked out from the shroud of cloud cover, then just as quickly vanished again.

"Jesus. That's a hell of a thing," I muttered, checking my bowling-style bag absently for phone, wallet, and pepper spray. A lady couldn't be too careful.

The diner wasn't huge, but it was well-lit and nauseatingly

yellow. I peered through the big front windows to see a plump, elderly waitress behind the counter chatting to a guy my dad's age with suspenders over a red flannel shirt, sleeves rolled up to his elbows. He would have looked like a farmer if not for the tan suit jacket and briefcase on the stool next to him.

A bell over the door jingled cheerfully as I entered and the waitress looked up from her conversation.

"Sit anywhere you want, darlin'," she said. Then she hoisted a pot of coffee from its burner and made her way towards the booth where I hunkered down. I guess the chances of someone coming to a diner at three in the morning in the middle of nowhere and *not* getting coffee were pretty slim. She flipped over a mug and started filling it without asking. Her nametag had a smear of dried ketchup on it, but beneath the mess I could see her name was Beth.

I picked up a folding menu from the condiment corral on the table and gave it a once over. Cornmeal-crusted fish, corn chowder, vegetarian chili with corn, corn dogs. Cornbread accompanied most of the entrees, too.

"Wow," I muttered. "Anything here not made with corn?"

Beth, consummate service professional that she was, didn't rise to the bait. I bet she'd heard that line once or twice. But the guy at the counter chuckled and spun around on his stool.

"You may not know it," he said, "but corn is in everything. At least here they're honest about it."

There was no grilled cheese on the menu, so I made my peace with a cheeseburger and fries. After Beth took my order and went to hand it into the kitchen, I offered a satisfied but tired smile.

"Not everything," I said. "One corn-free meal on the way."

This made him laugh even harder. He picked up his cup of coffee and headed over to my table, unbidden.

"Did I hear right?" he asked. "Cheeseburger and fries?"

"Yep."

He motioned to the bench across from me. I shrugged and he sat.

"Let's start with the beef. That's easy. Ninety-five percent of animal feed in the country is corn. It's where most of it goes, actually. The milk in the cheese for the cheeseburger probably has vitamin

D in it, which it gets from corn additives. There's cornstarch in the bun and on the fries to help them crisp up. There's corn syrup in the ketchup. There's corn in the coffee creamer, and the sugar packets there—if they don't say 'cane' or 'beet,' then it's corn, too. Fructose, maltodextrin, dextrin, dextrose, malt, glucose, MSG, the binders in whatever pills you take. Corn."

I stared at him skeptically, wondering if this was some kind of gag locals played on tourists. Not that I imagined this place got a lot of tourists, King Corn overlooking the road notwithstanding.

"Um ... bullshit?"

With the confidence of someone who has been using this line his entire life, he pulled a wilted white business card from his shirt pocket and handed it to me.

Dexter Wysocki
Sales Representative, MCP Refining
"Corn is our business."

"I'm guessing this is your first time through corn country," he said with a triumphant smile, before settling in for the conversation with a long sip of coffee.

He seemed harmless enough. Twice my age, the kind of build of someone who spent their life behind the wheel of a car or behind a desk. Dex here was the first conversation I'd had since leaving Nevada, and I didn't mind a little company while I waited for my food.

"First time east of Denver, actually. I didn't mean to interrupt your ... what, dinner? Breakfast?"

"Breakfast," he said, waving away my concerns. "If you want, I can go back to the counter, but God's honest truth, the waitress here is the worst conversationalist I've ever met. I swear, another fifteen minutes and she would have put me back to sleep."

"You slept somewhere around here?" I hadn't seen any indication of something that could pass for a motel nearby. There wasn't even a streetlight glow from over the waves of corn. Nothing but the lights on the silos across the road, a giant corn man in the fields, and a half dozen vehicles in the lot.

"I caught a few hours in the back of my car," he said, pointing to a blue sedan in the lot with Nebraska plates. "I don't sleep that much these days. Get to a certain age and sleep is a little too close to death, I guess. And work's had me running ragged the last few months, so I sleep where I can."

"Harvest time," I said, nodding like I knew what I was talking about.

"Well, soon," Dex said, shrugging uncomfortably. "For some folks, at least. A lot of the farms around here have been having a problem with smut, though."

I almost choked on my coffee, imagining how this old-timer defined "smut" and how it was causing problems with farms. He was gentleman enough to help me wipe up the coffee I'd spit on the table with a stack of napkins from the shiny chrome dispenser next to the condiment corral.

"Sorry," he said. "First time in corn country. I forgot. Corn smut is a fungal infection. Huitlacoche."

"Hweetlwhat?"

Dexter chuckled at my mangled pronunciation. "Close, but no. It's an Aztec word, I think? Like Centeōtl, the Aztec corn god."

"Corn god?"

He smiled. "Well, it was hundreds and hundreds of years ago. Corn came from here, you know. It was cultivated from a kind of grass by pre-Columbian peoples, then Europeans took it across the Atlantic, played with it some more, brought it back. But corn originated on this continent and has a special connection to the earth here. The huitlacoche, the corn smut, it doesn't happen any-where else in the world. It's an edible fungus, kind of tastes a bit like mushroom, and in Mexico they cultivate for it. It's a delicacy. Gives it a different flavor and more protein. Simply amazing in an enchilada. But this isn't Mexico, and it has a bad shelf life, so shipping it is hard if you don't have systems in place. You get a big outbreak up here, it's bad news because this isn't the right market for huitlacoche."

"So, all the corn out there …" I motioned towards the window and the landscape of waving cornstalks beyond the glass.

"Oh, that's all fine," he said dismissively. "These farmers got off lucky for a change. I joked about it a few years ago, that Centeōtl must have been angry with them or something, not that any of them knew what I was talking about at the time."

"Oh?" I looked around the diner for someone to either confirm or deny the story. We were still alone. Sound drifted from the kitchen, someone cooking to the quiet drone of country music. Hank Williams I figured, in the sense that I identified all faintly-heard country music as Hank Williams. But I couldn't see the cook from here. I couldn't see Beth either, and I could have really used some more coffee. It was just me and Dex, which felt off. I wondered if the other cars in the lot had people sleeping in the back seats, as well, given the lack of lodgings in the area.

"Things have been a bit rough since the new highway opened up. The road out there, the old highway? It used to be the lifeblood for a little farming town named Perryville about a mile or two to the east. They kept things afloat for a while, went all-in on corn, which is a viable plan as long as the crops are good. But there are always factors. Too much rain too late in the spring and you can't get the planting done in a timely manner. Or drought. Or pests. Or tornados. Or lack of farm labor. It's all a house of cards, and the last, oh, I'd say five or six years, well, they couldn't catch a break around these parts. I'm telling you, it was a relief to pull into the lot at sunset tonight and see all that healthy corn stretching off far as the eye could see."

"That and King Corn," I mumbled, thinking of their giant roadside icon.

He narrowed his eyes a bit at me and I figured the anthropomorphic corn dude probably had a different, more respectful name. I excused myself before he could launch into another explanation.

"I'm going to freshen up," I said, sliding out of the booth. "If you see the waitress, could you trouble her for a refill?"

The washrooms were down a short and poorly-lit hallway next to the kitchen. Faded posters for the county fair from the past several years covered the yellow walls, alongside a scattering of handmade flyers advertising handyman services and animals for adoption. The washrooms were along the left, facing the shabby, paper gallery, while at the end of the hall, a fire door to the outside stood slightly ajar.

A buzzing yellow light offered a glimpse of the parking lot and the side of a battered red pickup truck. I figured that explained where Beth went, out to grab a smoke while the cook made my dinner. I couldn't fault her for that. I remembered long, lonely shifts like this from my own food-service jobs when I was younger.

The washroom itself was small, with only a single toilet and sink, but it was clean and well-lit. After relieving myself of the gas-station hot dog, potato chips, and soda, all of which I was now confident had corn in them, I washed my hands, then rinsed my face with a damp paper towel. Surely my coffee had been refilled by now. If not, I wasn't above topping my mug off myself if Beth was still on her smoke break.

When I got back to the dining area, I was surprised to find that not only was my coffee mug still empty, but Dexter was nowhere to be seen. Cupping my hands against the light, I peered out into the parking lot to look for his car. It was still there, as dark, silent, and empty as when he'd indicated it earlier.

I muttered a low "What the hell?" to myself, then looked around the empty diner again. Not a single soul in sight. I felt a chill as goosebumps prickled my arms. I raised my voice and called out a shaky "Hello?"

I hated the tremor I heard in my voice. Goddamn it. I was a smart, strong, capable woman. I was not afraid of being in a diner by myself.

But this wasn't just any diner. It was a brightly-lit yet bone-chillingly empty oasis in the middle of nowhere. I would rather anyone else was with me at that moment, whether it be Dexter and his weird corn knowledge, or Glen and his, well, whatever Glen brought to the table when I still thought I loved him. But no. Just me and miles of corn.

At least my bag was still there, the sparkly vinyl winking up at me from the far end of the booth bench. I leaned in to retrieve it, digging around the cavernous interior for my pepper spray, then set the bag on the table. The little canister felt solid in my hand. Comforting. Made me think that maybe I was overreacting.

Maybe Dexter had gone to the restroom as well. Maybe he had joined Beth for a cigarette. In the relative silence, I could hear the sound of something sizzling on the grill in the back, and a scuffing sound of someone walking around in the kitchen. I wasn't alone. It was all okay. Everything was fine.

This was Iowa. Weird, dangerous shit doesn't happen in Iowa. I took a breath, then another deeper, calmer breath. I was making a big deal out of nothing. All this emptiness was getting to me because I was tired. Dexter had the right idea. I could benefit from a few hours nap in the car. Glen's BMW was certainly comfortable enough.

But first, another cup of coffee. Surely Beth wouldn't mind if I freshened up my cup, right? I picked up my empty cup, keeping the pepper spray in the other hand just in case, and made my way to the counter.

"Hello? I'm just going to grab a little more coffee if that's okay?"

I heard more clunking around in the kitchen, snatches of what sounded like a hushed conversation and shoes on tile. Through the window into the kitchen, I caught a glimpse of Beth's back and was weirdly relieved. It was nice to not feel so alone. Setting the canister of pepper spray down on the counter, I picked up the coffee pot to refill my cup. The black plastic handle of the pot was sticky. Like whoever had touched it last had syrup on their hands. A wave of revulsion passed through me, and I looked around behind the counter for a service sink or something to wash the gunk off my hands.

There was a wide, red smear on the white tiles behind the counter, like something big and bloody had been dragged away. The coffee cup slipped from my fingers and shattered on the ground, splashing hot liquid on my shoes and the blood trail before me.

I reached for the pepper spray, but knocked it over with my trembling hands. It rolled off the counter, clattered a few times, then rolled beneath the ice bin. I crouched to retrieve it, but it was gone to the darkness. Fuck if I was going to reach my hand into the shadows in this place. They could keep the stuff. I'd get another can in Milwaukee.

By the time I straightened and turned, Beth had emerged from the kitchen. Her apron was askew, a bloody handprint on the hem. In her right hand, she held a knife. Not even a big, Michael Meyers butcher knife; just a regular, serrated steak knife. Nothing fancy. But it dripped with fresh blood, assuring me that it was plenty stabby enough to be a problem.

"I was just getting more coffee," I said, voice flat, hands out before me defensively. "Sorry. I'm sorry. I didn't see anything."

Beth, for all her unhinged menace, didn't appear angry or murderous or, well, *anything*, really. She stared at me blankly, like she was looking through me.

"Centeōtl must be fed," she said calmly, taking a step closer.

I don't fucking think so.

I screamed, a howl of terror. Reflexively, I snatched the sticky coffee pot off the burner and hurled it at the advancing waitress. It cracked against her head, spilling hot, brown liquid down her neck and chest. It should have hurt. A normal person would have screamed, would have reacted in some way. Any way. Her wrinkled neck wattle turned red from the heat, but her expression didn't change.

Not a single bit. Not a twitch.

I backpedaled, feet sliding as I gripped the counter for support. I was aware I was treading on bloody tiles but no longer cared quite so much. I'd much rather walk through that mess than become part of it.

Beth took another plodding step towards me. Undeterred. Then her stained, white tennis shoes slipped on the coffee and blood and she went down. Hard.

Her head clipped the counter with a wet crack and she lay still.

I paused, chest heaving with panic while I tried to catch my breath.

Something was leaking from Beth's cracked skull—and it sure as shit wasn't blood. A stream of wet, yellow kernels spilled onto the tiles, pooled in her hair, seeped into the shadow under the counter.

Corn.

It was *corn*.

"Corn really is in everything," I mumbled, tipping perilously close to madness.

The little bell over the front door jingled and I turned, ready to shout at whatever luckless bastard had stumbled into Cobb's Corner, tell them to run. I could tell at a glance the warning was unnecessary. The line cook stood in the doorway, black apron slick with what I assumed was blood. A dripping, red cleaver was clenched in his right hand and he wore a blank look on his face like a mask.

"Centeōtl must be fed," he said calmly.

"Nope," I answered. I clambered over the counter rather than try to go around. Errant feet kicked condiment corrals and mugs and silverware to the floor in my exodus. I didn't let the mess slow me down. The line cook was already on the move, a wild, animalistic scramble, and I was determined to put as much distance between us as possible.

I hit the back door near the washrooms like a cannonball. The heavy steel door boomed open, caroming off some obstacle on the other side, but still offering me ample room to bolt out onto the weed-cracked asphalt of the back parking lot before it slammed shut behind me. Thankfully, there was no one outside waiting to jump me—though admittedly that concern didn't occur to me until it would have been too late to do anything about it.

I grabbed the side of the battered pickup truck and used it to steady myself as I passed, gripping at the corner of the bed to help me make a right-hand turn at speed without my sneakers skidding out on the weedy asphalt. The diner's back door slammed behind me again, letting me know not to slow down.

Another problem occurred to me as I neared the corner of the diner: my purse was still on the table inside.

And, yeah, I loved the smooth, shiny bowling bag purse. It was one of the few luxuries I had allowed myself when I got the first paycheck at my last job. And while I could probably replace it, my phone, wallet, and, most importantly, the keys to the car were in it. I tried to remember what the parking lot had looked like when

I went in, where the car was in relation to the diner's door in relation to the table holding my purse.

I couldn't just bolt straight for the keys. I'd have to double back once I had the bag, and that would give the guy with the cleaver too much time to close the distance and no time to get in the car safely. No, I had to be smart and control the panic.

The side lot was dark, but the closest vehicle was a semi tractor with no trailer behind. It was twenty feet off in the lot, practically butted up against the rows of corn at the lot's edge. The front lot wasn't going to be much better, as I remembered a half-dozen scattered cars and trucks plus all the lights out front to draw people into the diner. It all felt too exposed.

Making a split-second decision, I sprinted as fast I could across the open lot, around the parked semi, and into the corn. The ground beneath my feet was slick and muddy, and I found myself slipping once I got ten feet into the cover. I ducked quickly off to one side, then crouched and turned back the way I had come, looking for signs of my pursuer.

Through the dense green of corn stalks, I watched the cleaver-wielding line cook round the corner of the parked rig, chest heaving for breath. He was kind of a big guy, the kind of build you'd expect from someone who had played football in high school but let himself go as he hit his forties. Judging by how he was struggling, I figured this was the most running he'd done in twenty years.

He approached the corn about ten feet off to my right, wheezing like a rapidly deflating air mattress. He peered through the stalks while I crouched, shaking, breathing as quietly as possible. Thankful for the clouds overhead hiding the stars and moon, I shivered as his gaze passed over me and kept moving.

Carefully, and with reluctance, the line cook began picking his way slowly through the corn. I waited, motionless, as he passed by, barely six feet away. My nose was choked with the sweet smell of corn, mixed with the pungent, wet soil and fertilizer. I figured it was probably manure-based but didn't want to think too hard about it, promising myself that if I survived the night I'd burn these shoes. Glen would just have to live with it if I tracked some of the smell back to his precious car.

I waited until the sounds of the line cook vanished into the night, then began to pick my way silently back out into the lot. Once my feet hit asphalt, I moved at a fast but low walk back to the diner, peering over my shoulder now and then to make sure I wasn't being followed. I could feel eyes on me, burning into my back, but nothing stirred the corn except the errant breeze.

The diner remained empty. The waitress lay where she fell, head still slowly leaking its improbable yellow cargo. I grabbed my purse. Keys in hand, I went back to the car, the feeling of being watched stronger than ever. But I saw no people.

"Nerves," I chuckled to myself, trying to shake off the terror I had just witnessed.

Then, out of the corner of my field of vision, there was a hint of motion above the corn. I turned to look but it was only the giant roadside mascot I'd dubbed King Corn. I could have sworn when I pulled in that he looked out over the fields across the road, but now he had turned and bent forward, gazing into the parking lot of Cobb's Corner. Had he always been standing in that exact location? His cheery smile hadn't faded, but it didn't inspire joy.

A swirling scream of abject insanity clawed its way up from the depths of my soul as King Corn took a step closer.

"Centeōtl must be fed," I whispered, frozen in terror. Not that this was Centeōtl. It couldn't be. Not Centeōtl, but some middle-American perversion of the idea of him, maybe. Something misunderstood and old, twisted to suit the needs of the now by some miracle of desperate faith.

The keys slipped from my hand, into the shadows beneath a parked sedan with out-of-state plates. There might have been time to find them, to start the car and drive far, far away from here. If only I could move.

"Centeōtl must be fed," I whispered again, helpless as tears rolled down my cheeks.

Corn is in everything. And soon, it was in me as well.

The Clown and the Chalupa
Steve Loiaconi

DEAR DIRK,

If I were to chisel the Ten Commandments of Monster Hunting onto some tablet on a mountain, this would undoubtedly be one: nothing good happens in a Taco Bell after midnight.

That doesn't just go for monster hunting, of course. It's an immutable law of nature, one that Marley Bainbridge was familiar with from working the weekend late shift at the Taco Bell off I-84 in Fishkill. Deadbeats, burnouts, college kids tripping on shrooms and toad juice—the cast of characters looking for a gordita in the middle of the night in upper Westchester was alarming, disturbing, and occasionally entertaining. At age seventeen, very little surprised Marley. But I'll tell you, brother of mine, a grizzled dude bursting through the door at two a.m. covered in blood and bits of cream pie, that fazed her.

Limping toward the counter, I didn't have time to explain myself.

"I gotta use your john," I said.

"It's for customers only," she said, pointing to a placard on the wall. "Big old sign, right there."

"Fine." I glanced up at the bright menu board hanging above Marley, as if I hadn't hit Taco Bell on the regular in my teens. I slapped a five dollar bill on the counter. "Let me get one of those five dollar combo boxes."

"They're five ninety-nine now."

"Goddamn inflation," I grumbled, scrounging through my pants pocket for change. While I counted coins in my palm, she examined a red streak across Abraham Lincoln's face.

"What do you want in the combo?" she asked.

I shrugged my shoulders and disappeared into the men's room.

The bathroom was refreshingly clean, and I made a mental note to commend the girl behind the counter for running a tight ship. First, though, I needed to scan my arms and shoulders for bites and get the shards of pie away from my mouth and eyes. After a thorough rinsing, my face was clean and my hair was damp, but my clothes remained filthy. There was a fresh outfit in my car, but I had left it behind at the circus, so I was going to have to make do.

Meanwhile, Marley went about packing up a chalupa, a burrito, nachos, and a Diet Mountain Dew. I returned as she placed the food on a tray.

"You still got some, uh, meringue there," she said, pointing at a spot of egg white on the breast of my leather jacket.

"Thanks, doll," I said, brushing it off.

"I have a name," she sniped.

"I'm sure you do …" My eyes drifted to the nametag on her shirt. "Marley." I removed the jacket, revealing a sweaty, mud-caked tank top underneath. I rested the jacket on the nearest table and reached for the combo box. "Call me Brock, and don't eat any of that," I said, nodding at the lingering bits of graham cracker crust and whipped cream on the jacket.

"Why would I eat pie off a stranger's clothes?"

"I'm just saying, if you were so inclined, don't." Responding to the flummoxed look on her face, I added, "It's poison."

"Why are you covered in poisonous pie?"

"See, now—" I pointed at her with a chip dripping with lukewarm cheese sauce. "—that right there is a good question."

I didn't answer, though, instead turning my attention to the entrance of the restaurant. I silently scolded myself for not moving faster to secure a perimeter. If you or dad were still alive, I'd be hearing about that one for weeks. Without my supplies—again, sitting in the trunk of my car up at the big top—I could only cast a rudimentary protection spell.

Out in the otherwise empty parking lot, a clown rode a squeaky unicycle in circles. His white pants were polka-dotted with blood and gore, held up by suspenders made from wiry braids of blond hair. He was shirtless, exposing a back covered with scars and tattoos of guns and demons. He wore a cap with a sharp blade jutting from the top.

"Is that … a clown?" Marley asked.

"In a manner of speaking." I took a moment to ponder how to explain something that would almost certainly sound insane to her. "The best term I can come up with is wereclown. It's half-human, half-clown."

"Aren't clowns human?"

"Oh, you naive child."

The clown yodeled at the full moon, a war cry inviting more of its kind.

"Does that look human?"

Marley had that look on her face that people usually get when confronted with the reality of the supernatural: eyes wide, mouth agape, cheeks pale and clammy. There's no good way to ease a normie into this stuff.

I gave her a moment to take it all in while I surveyed the scene outside and sipped my Diet Dew. The warding spell was the best I could do in a matter of minutes, but it wouldn't hold for long. The clown was wobbling closer and closer to the door.

"Are you the only person here, Marley?"

She nodded.

"You run this whole place by yourself?" I looked around the large but empty restaurant.

"How busy do you think a Fishkill Taco Bell is at two a.m.?" I detected a twinge of pride in her voice. "I can usually handle it."

I paced in front of the counter, munching on the chalupa. Maybe I was just starving from all the clown-fleeing, but it was tastier than I want to admit. I craned my neck, trying to get a look into the kitchen, beyond the heaters and frying vats.

"Does this place have a back door?" I asked.

Marley laughed. "Not one that works."

"That seems horrendously unsafe."

"Feel free to call OSHA in the morning." She added with a stab of disgust, "Narc."

We were both jolted by the clown bashing its fist against the window outside.

"We gotta survive the night first," I said.

The clown pressed its face against the glass, his wide grin revealing misshapen, ink-black teeth and a thick, rotting, yellow tongue.

"I thought that thing couldn't come in," Marley said.

"That doesn't mean he isn't going to try."

I banged on the window, sending the clown back a few feet.

As the clown hopped back on its unicycle outside, Marley took a seat in a booth.

"What is a, uh, wereclown doing here?" she asked.

"Somebody in this town summoned a night circus."

"I don't know what half of those words mean."

"A night circus. A carnival of the damned." I gave it a moment to see if she registered any recognition, then continued, "Traditionally, it's a southern thing, like sweet tea and segregation." I slid onto the bench across from her and unwrapped my burrito. "They'd show up on the outskirts of town, pitch their tent, put up some signs. Then folks stumble across them, wander into the big top—because, you know, lots of people can't resist some pratfalling and casual animal cruelty. I don't see the appeal myself, but I'm not one to judge."

As I spoke, I struggled to keep track of the clown without making direct eye contact. I have heard some are capable of hypnosis.

"Inevitably," I said, chomping into the tortilla, "there would be a few kids who'd go missing when the circus was in town. Usually the black sheep and ne'er-do-wells, the ones everyone else could live without, even if they didn't want to admit it. Parents would tell themselves, oh, little Josiah or Cyrus must have run off and joined the circus, but that's not what happened."

I finished the burrito in a few bites—an impulsive choice I knew I might regret later. (*What else is new, Brock?* I don't want to hear it.) I checked my watch, calculating how much time we had until my warding spell would begin to waver.

"People like to think clowns live for laughter, that the smiles of the crowd fuel them. That's bullshit. They're soul-eaters, and they're always hungry."

The clown tapped on the door with long, cracked, red nails.

"Obviously, roadside circuses aren't so much a thing anymore, and parents are a lot less blasé about kids vanishing than they were in the good old days, so these troupes have mostly died off. There are still some out there, though, and they're always listening for a summoning spell that promises a good meal."

Marley looked up at the clown, who pointed at her, then drew a finger slowly across its neck and cackled. She pulled a cellphone from her pocket and began pressing buttons.

I reached across the table to stop her. "What are you doing?"

"Calling 911."

I sighed.

"You're just going to get a bunch of police officers killed."

"How do you get rid of them then?"

"Easiest way?" I chuckled. "Kill the schlamootz who invited them."

I assure you, that is the correct spelling of "schlamootz."

Anyway, when she heard those words, she froze.

"But I'm not going to kill you," I added (and I swear, I never seriously considered it), "so let's brainstorm something else."

"How … how did you know?"

"You got the stink of dragonsbane and elephant dung on you," I said, sniffing loudly for effect. "Yeah, that shit is a bitch to wash away."

Even before I ventured up to the circus to scout the scene, I had known Marley was the source of the summoning. A quick read of the spectrometer had shown me that as soon as I pulled into town. Call it overconfidence or inexperience, but I had hoped I could wipe out the clowns first and then deal with her. Instead, one had chased me across half of Fishkill before I tracked her down at work.

"I didn't know," Marley said. "I mean, I knew I was messing with otherworldly forces or whatever, and I knew there was some risk, but it was supposed to just be a dumb prank."

"It was dumb, all right," I mumbled.

You know how dad was with that "I didn't know what I was doing" shit. *Then why you were doing goddamn magic in the first place, numb nuts?* he'd always say.

"A couple weeks back, my little cousin Nico was being a jackass," Marley continued. "He came in here one night while I was working, swiped my keys from my jacket and tossed them in the dumpster. I really cannot communicate to you in words how disgusting it is wading through a Taco Bell dumpster on trash day. So once I showered and scrubbed myself, like, forever, I wanted to get back at him, and he's scared of clowns. Like piss-your-pants terrified."

"As he should be," I interjected. "Go on."

"So anyway, I was going to hire, you know, one of those clowns who works at kids' birthdays to spook him, but they are pricey." I nodded along, as if I knew. "Then I stumbled across this spell online. I'd never used magic before, but the stupid jade talisman was easy enough to find online, so I recorded a video performing the ritual over a little Judy Collins singing 'Send in the Clowns' and texted it to him. I didn't think anything was going to happen."

In the parking lot, the clown jumped rope with a strand of what I'm fairly certain were human intestines.

"Yeah, well, something happened," I said, slurping the last of my Dew. "Look, I can relate. My little brother was a shithead, too."

"What did yours do?"

"Everything better than me."

Hey, you outshine me enough, bro—in literally every way imaginable—can you blame me for taking it personal?

"I'm going to need the talisman you used for the ritual, Marley. It was, like, a monkey with a big dong, right?" I made a gesture approximating a monkey penis that I promptly regretted.

(Yes, I know. It's not a monkey, it's a wuzhiqi, but this didn't seem like the time for a lesson on ninth-century Chinese mythology.)

"Is that what it was supposed to be?" Her nose scrunched up. "I don't have it."

"Is it at home? I can cover you if you want to run back and get it."

"I mean, I threw it away."

"Well … fuck."

Who throws away an enchanted jade talisman that can summon a troupe of bloodthirsty jesters? I'm shaking my head in disgust on your behalf as I type this.

So eliminating the tether was out, and so was reversing the ritual. While my mind raced through the limited options remaining, Marley hopped off the bench.

"Who are you, anyway?" she asked.

"You ever hear of Dirk Drago? Senior, I mean."

"I have not."

I shook my head. "I'm really starting to think my dad's whole 'I'm a world-famous monster hunter' schtick was utter bullshit."

"What the hell is a monster hunter?"

I stared back at her. "Kinda self-explanatory, no?"

Honestly, I wasn't surprised she drew a blank on dad. As the otherworld increasingly bleeds into ours, it has become more common to encounter randos on a job who have at least some experience with the weird, but outside the mage community, monsters and the hunting thereof is still rarely discussed in polite company.

"How do you get into that business?"

"Looking for a career change?" I flashed a smile as I dumped what was left of my combo in the trash. "My younger brother, Dirk, Jr., was always supposed to inherit the family mantle, but he died last year."

We didn't have time for the full story: that my already-cruddy life spiraled into a pit of failure and addiction after dad's stroke, that you begrudgingly came to my aid when my gambling debts became soul-crushingly and life-threateningly severe, and that you wound up dead trying to balance the scales.

"Wait," Marley said, "your younger brother is Dirk, Jr. Why not you?"

Yeah, that still stings, bro.

"My dad never thought I was good enough for this gig."

She studied my pained face for a beat. "Was he right?"

"I want to say no—" I watched the clown send up another war cry. "—but the jury's still out."

You always insisted honesty was the best policy with the normies and I listened more than you thought.

Scrounging for anything resembling a weapon, I marched back toward the kitchen. As the clown dry-humped the window and moaned theatrically, Marley followed.

"No talisman—" I ticked off the obstacles with three fingers. "—more clowns coming down the hill, and that warding is only going to hold for about twenty more minutes. What do we do?"

We both took stock of our surroundings. Lots of sharp objects and things you could bonk someone over the head with, but nothing that could pierce jester skin.

"What if we spray it with hot cheese?" she asked, pointing at a tank of processed orange cheese sauce next to the grill.

"You think they might be lactose intolerant?"

She threw up her arms in frustration, like you would back when you tried to tutor me. Look, I would not deny that I was at times deficient in my studies over the years, but ever since I first read *It*, I've had a firm handle on clowns. Most of the known methods of eliminating them wouldn't do us much good in a fast food kitchen, though.

"To kill a clown, we would need a knife forged in hellfire or bullets dipped in ectoplasm. Or … heh." I smiled thick and wide like a chimichanga. "Holy oil."

I turned up the heat on the frying vats and waved Marley over.

"I need you to go online and get yourself ordained by any church you can find," I said, stressing, "as long as it's not, you know, explicitly satanic. Then you need to bless this oil."

"Why can't you do it?" she asked.

"Long story, but suffice to say, I have been deemed unholy."

Marley began scrolling through her phone as I stepped out to the dining area and approached the doors. I closed my eyes and touched the glass, assessing the strength of the magic coursing through it. The warding was about to wear out, but we had a bigger problem: a small car, about the size of a Mini Cooper, had pulled up next to the clown.

The horn honked, playing a discordant version of "La Cucaracha." The rear passenger door popped open, and a half dozen more clowns rolled out onto the pavement.

"Yeah," I said, sighing, "that ain't good."

I rushed back to the kitchen and found Marley whispering a blessing over the oil.

"All right," I said after she finished the prayer, "andale, andale, kid. Time to make a run for the border."

"You said this was my fault. I'm staying."

"You understand there's no prize for bravery, right?"

Maybe I was talking to you as much as her there. I never asked anyone to put their life on the line for me. I never asked you to risk everything to save me. I'm a fuck-up, I've always been a fuck-up. I know that. But I could have cleaned up my own mess if you gave me the chance.

The clowns swarmed the entrance, anticipating the spell's expiration. They giggled among themselves and honked their noses, communicating something. In the back of the scrum, a couple of them headbutted each other repeatedly.

Moments before the magic faded, Marley and I marched toward the door, pushing buckets filled with consecrated oil. Each had the long handle of a mop sticking out of it.

One hunter and one teenager against seven pissed-off wereclowns.

I offered her a confident nod.

"Let's make some clowns cry," I said.

I'm not sure she got the reference.

I shoved the door open, hefted my mop, and went straight for the tallest one. His skin sizzled as the oil splashed his face and white paint turned red. He screeched at the sky and collapsed onto the pavement.

Marley took a swing at a short, rotund clown with a pointed head who I could best describe as egg-shaped. Some of the oil spattered into his mouth. She shuffled back as he burned from the inside out.

I dodged a hurled cream pie that was likely filled with spiders or acid. Then I lunged at the one on the unicycle, pushing him through the window of the restaurant. As shattered glass rained down around me, I wrung out the mop over his head, watching him melt away.

Marley soaked her mop again and slathered oil on another clown who had been distracted by the screams of his tent-mates. She looked momentarily horrified, so I gave her a whistle of encouragement. You'd have liked Marley, bro. She had what dad used to call moxie. I didn't expect much from her, but she was unflinching in the face of sinister buffoonery.

People can surprise you.

While I marveled at her, one of the remaining clowns delivered a swift blow to my chin and shoved me off my feet.

I stumbled back, bumping into my bucket and tilting it sideways before I could regain my balance, then watching in what felt like slow motion as it fell to the asphalt. With the rest of my oil slithering toward a sewer drain, I recognized my mop wouldn't last much longer. Removing a lighter from my pocket, I flicked on the flame and held it to the grease-soaked cotton bristles. The mop immediately ignited, nearly singeing my fingers.

I charged at the clown who had pushed me, setting him ablaze. Then I chased another across the parking lot, lighting him up when he stumbled on a pothole and discovering that charred clown smells distressingly like carne asada. I looked back to see Marley holding the final clown's head down in her bucket. He flailed wildly until his skull dissolved, leaving only a few curls of red hair in her hand.

"If I'm being honest," I said, "that went better than I expected."

A brisk breeze carried the clown hairs away into the night.

Marley studied her empty, oily hands.

"That was gross," she said.

"But the flaming mop was pretty tight, right?"

As the clown corpses rapidly decayed into sludge, we stepped through the broken window into the restaurant, careful not to get any jester goo on our shoes.

"What do you do about the circus now?" she asked.

"I'm going to burn it to the ground," I said, "and then I'm going to salt the earth. Speaking of which, I am going to need the biggest bag of salt you've got."

I put my stained coat back on, futilely attempting to wipe away some of the pie with a cheap paper napkin.

"Is this a normal night for you?" Marley asked.

"More or less," I shrugged. "You?"

She thought for a moment. "Honestly, I've had weirder."

Back in the parking lot, I briefly weighed hopping on the unicycle to ride back, but I thought better of it and prepared to walk to the circus, sack of salt and lighter in hand.

"Important question, Marley," I said, staring up the hill at the light shimmering from the haunted big top and feeling a sudden hankering for one of those crunchwraps with the hashbrowns inside. "When do you start serving breakfast?"

Brock Drago
Fishkill, New York
November 2022

Ed's Worm Hole
Laura Garrison

YVETTE HAD ALMOST REACHED THE CLIMAX of *The Admiral's Main-mast* when the new cook interrupted her with a clumsy whack on the shoulder.

You could always tell when Yvette was at a good part in one of her stories, because the tempo at which she drummed her nails on the countertop kicked into a frenzied paradiddle that rattled the cups in their saucers. The regulars knew to wait until she resumed a steady *tap-tap-tap-tap* before requesting an extra biscuit or a double-scoop of stink bait, and the cook's faux pas elicited a handful of raised eyebrows and dismayed gasps.

The nights at Ed's Worm Hole—a combination diner and fishing supply shop which served the modest population of Lakeside twenty-four hours a day—followed a ritual pattern of activity. From the start of Yvette's shift at ten o'clock in the evening until about half-past midnight, students from the local community college sat pecking at their laptops and testing the limits of Ed's generous "free warm-ups" policy on coffee. The next wave shambled in after last call at the unnamed bar across the street, generally sometime between one and two in the morning, pickled in Mudthumper's brown ale and warbling ballads about ill-fated dalliances with slippery naiads.

Often representatives from that group were still snoring in the cracked vinyl booths when the serious anglers came in for breakfast. Everyone knew the lake's finest specimens could only be caught within an hour after sunrise. This was also the only window of time in which Old Suckerbitch, the fabled lake monster, had ever been glimpsed, according to the most reliable reports.

It was a quarter after five when the cook's blow landed, with sunrise pegged for 5:37 a.m., and the three fishermen at the counter, all brothers, went as still as statues on their chrome pedestals, waiting to see how Yvette would react. Rusty, the youngest at sixty-two, had just tossed back several ounces of scalding coffee, and a puff of steam issued from his open mouth, drifting toward the ceiling like a smoke signal.

Rusty was the quiet one, an artist who often returned to the lake with his watercolors after he was done fishing for the day. One of his paintings hung on the pine-paneled wall behind the booths, between a driftwood wreath and an old life preserver. It showed a pair of mallards floating side by side. They faced into the wind that was blowing through the pickerelweed and looked ready to weather anything as long as they could do it together. Rusty had been secretly in love with Yvette for the twenty-seven years he had known her.

With calm deliberation, the waitress placed a gum wrapper between the pages of her book and set it down, allowing her fingers to slide slowly over the glistening abdominal muscles on the cover. Her beetle-green eyelids flashed in the glow of the hanging lamps as she turned to the cook.

"What." Her tone was dangerously flat.

The cook—Gil, according to his apron—gestured at the griddle, where a pile of golden home fries sizzled expectantly, then held up a shallow stoneware bowl.

For a moment, it looked as if Yvette might snatch the piece of crockery and smash it over his fool head. But when she reached out, it was only to point at a stack of clean plates.

"No," she told him. "Those go on these."

Gil bobbed his head in assent, then slid a plate from the stack and began shoveling fried potatoes onto it with a spatula.

Yvette blew a stray curl of silver hair off her forehead and turned to the grizzled siblings. "New kid's dumber than a bucket of duckweed. Came shuffling in from who-knows-where and went right up to the griddle. I told Ed not to hire him, said he'd probably burn this whole place to cinders inside of a week, but you know Ed." A note of affection crept into her voice. "That man will never pass up a chance to help a sad sack get on his feet."

The brothers nodded at this, darting glances at Gil, who was still within earshot. But if he was perturbed by Yvette's assessment of his intellect, he gave no sign as he fiddled with the arrangement of the home fries with his floppy fingers.

"All right, that's enough," Yvette said, grabbing the plate. "It's not haute cuisine." She pronounced "haute" so it rhymed with "coyote."

She set the home fries in front of Lars, the middle brother and a known daredevil, who dispensed a glorious amount of Frank's Red Hot over them. He speared a potato with his fork and chewed thoughtfully.

"There might be a couple of leaks in his rowboat," he said, "but the lad gets a good crisp on his home fries, I'll say that much for him."

Lars took another bite, but this time his eyes widened and he pitched forward, slamming his face into his breakfast hard enough to crack the sturdy plate. Before anyone had a chance to react, he was hauled up onto the counter, legs kicking stiffly in protest, muffled groans emerging from the hot-sauce-dripping mask that obscured his features.

Hubert, the eldest brother and a respected sage, made a grab for him as he shot past, but he was left holding one rubber boot and blinking in disbelief as Lars flew off the end of the counter and arced toward the nearest window in the east wall.

Ed's Worm Hole was not equipped with air-conditioning, so the window was wide open to take full advantage of the summer breezes that swept over the lake. There was a screen in place, but Lars was traveling at such a speed that it popped out and tumbled into Ed's cucumber patch as soon as he struck it. Lars soared through the window as neatly as a paper airplane gliding through a tire swing.

A grassy slope led down to a strip of gravelly beach. The shallows were densely cropped with water weeds, extending for a few yards before dropping off with a suddenness that plunged unwary waders into the steel-gray waters. Attempts to sound the lake's depth had produced wildly varied results, but the most conservative measurements pegged it at seventy-five fathoms.

Lars hit the ground with a bone-crunching belly flop and continued with no slackening of pace, propelled across the grass like a log strapped to a rocket-powered skateboard.

Hubert and Rusty went to the window. The sky had brightened just enough for them to observe their brother's final seconds on land. Yvette hustled around the counter to press up close behind them, resting a hand on each of their backs. The three of them watched in stunned silence as Lars scudded across the ribbon of stones with a brief susurrus before plunging into the lake.

Rusty bolted out the side exit, ignoring the creaks of protest from his recent knee replacement. Hubert and Yvette hurried after him. Seagulls were already converging on the home fries that speckled the ground.

When he reached the spot where Lars had disappeared, Rusty kicked off his boots, fought his way through the snarls of weeds, and dove into the lake. He surfaced thirty seconds later, shook his head, then went back under. This time, a slimy rope from some underwater plant twisted around his ankle, and he had to yank at it with both hands before it snapped and fell away.

That second attempt left him shaken, but he tried a few more times before making his way despondently back to the shore.

"It's darker than a black bear's asshole down there," he said with a sniffle.

"You did all you could." Yvette handed him her handkerchief.

He nodded his thanks and honked into it.

"I just don't understand what happened to him," Hubert said. "One minute he was fine, and the next he was off like a comet from hell."

"It sure was perculiar," Yvette agreed.

She looked as if she was about to say more, but there was a clatter behind them, and they turned to see another screen tumble to the ground as the head of Brom Bones was thrust like a battering ram through the window beside the one Lars had sailed through moments earlier.

Brom Bones was not the man's actual name, but a nickname

bestowed on him by Ed upon observing his striking resemblance to Ichabod Crane's romantic rival. As Brom Bones generally arrived in a state of intoxication too advanced for intelligible speech, no one at Ed's Worm Hole knew him as anything else.

But while Lars had passed easily through the window, Brom Bones' meaty shoulders were several inches too wide, and his journey ended abruptly when they met the sturdy wooden frame. From this awkward position, he unleashed a series of ghoulish shrieks that threatened to shatter the glass panes above him.

Yvette, who had developed the same attachment to the Mud-thumper's ale crowd that a dedicated animal shelter volunteer might feel for the least adoptable dogs, braced herself against the sound and marched back up the slope. Hubert followed her.

Rusty gazed at the lake that had swallowed his brother while he peeled off his wet socks. The edge of the rising sun peeped over the horizon, and the water reflected the rainbow-sherbet sky.

Only three days before, Lars had nearly capsized their boat reeling in a fifty-two-inch muskellunge under a sky just like this one. Hubert had been fishing for blue gill in the shallows, so it had just been the two of them out in the middle of the lake. Lars had admired the sheen of the fish as it thrashed in the morning light and declared that it sparkled just as pretty as a mermaid. Rusty knew better than to suggest mounting it—Lars was strictly a catch-and-release angler, only in it for the thrill of the chase. He worked the hook out, patted the fish on the head, and heaved it back into the water. As he watched it swim away, Lars suddenly jerked back with a sharp intake of breath.

"What is it?" Rusty asked.

Lars squinted into the water. "A piece of tire tread, maybe. Only ..."

Rusty looked but saw nothing unusual. "Only?"

Lars shook his head. "Nothing. Whatever it was, it's gone."

A cry from Yvette pulled Rusty back into the present, and he squelched up the hill, droplets flying from his clothes with every step.

Brom Bones' piercing shrieks had subsided, but the man was clearly in excruciating pain. From the way he was wedged into the window frame, he should have been gazing down at Ed's cucumbers, but his neck was craned back at an unnatural angle. His eyes watered with strain, and his mouth was clamped tightly shut. Bits of scrambled egg clung to his wild beard.

"See?" Yvette stabbed a finger in the air. "Right there." She cupped her other hand under Brom Bones' trembling chin.

Hubert adjusted his wire-framed glasses.

"I'll be damned," he said.

It wasn't until Hubert made a fist in front of Brom Bones' face that Rusty spotted the translucent line protruding from the unfortunate man's lips.

"Knife?" Hubert asked him.

Rusty fumbled his cleaning knife out of his vest pocket and opened it. He brought the blade up in a smooth stroke beside his brother's hand. The tension in the line was so great that it snapped with an eerie twang the instant the blade touched it.

Brom Bones went slack, and several tablespoons of blood and saliva dribbled out of his mouth. He eased his head and shoulders away from the window, overbalanced, and sat down hard on the floor.

Yvette and Hubert went back inside, but Rusty remained at the window, looking in, thinking of Lars as he regarded Brom Bones with mounting trepidation. The man didn't bother trying to get to his feet, but raised a grubby hand to feel around inside his mouth.

Yvette sat on the floor beside him and guided his hand away. "Let Hubert take a look, hon."

Hubert had been a practitioner of family medicine in Lakeside for forty years before retiring three years earlier at the age of sixty-seven. Now he retrieved a five-gallon bucket from the storeroom, turned it upside-down, and sat on it.

"Open up," he said briskly, pulling out a penlight.

Brom Bones let his mouth fall open.

Hubert clicked the penlight on to peer inside and whistled.

Rusty had a pretty good guess as to what he saw.

"What size?" he asked.

"Hard to say." Hubert wiped away the condensation that had

fogged the lenses of his glasses. "One-aught, maybe."

"Baitholder?"

"Octopus."

"Oof." Rusty winced. "Can you push it through?"

"We'll see."

Brom Bones looked alarmed, but Hubert's still-agile fingers were already past his teeth. He managed one startled yelp, and then it was done.

Hubert held up a fish hook. The barb glinted cruelly in the morning sun, and the foot or so of blood-beaded fishing line trailing from it added a touch of barbarism.

Brom took one look and passed out cold. His head bounced once against the worn floorboards, then settled. He looked quite peaceful, so no one attempted to wake him.

"You think Lars—" Rusty broke off, not wanting to finish.

"Yes." Hubert frowned. "But who—and *how*—"

They all looked over at Gil, who was adding a rasher of bacon to a plate of silver-dollar pancakes. Orson the mechanic, an early riser who often popped into Ed's for breakfast before work, sat two places down from the remnants of Brom Bones' eggs, lost in the second chapter of *The Admiral's Mainmast*.

Yvette and Hubert scrambled to their feet while Rusty raced to the side door. Despite his wet clothes and bare feet, he reached the cook ahead of the others.

Rusty clamped a hand on Gil's shoulder, meaning to turn him around. To his horror, his fingers didn't close on flesh-covered muscle and bone, but sank into something much squishier. As the cook spun toward him with an awful slosh, Rusty saw he had a bite-sized pancake in one hand and a hook like the one that had caught Brom Bones in the other.

Rusty was still gripping a handful of Gil's loose shoulder skin, and now he gave it a firm shake that rippled through the cook in audible waves.

"Drop it," Rusty said.

The cook's head swiveled from side to side. Rusty regarded Gil's cloudy eyes and rubbery lips with consternation, wondering how

Ed—or any of them—could have mistaken this thing for human.

Instead of dropping the hook, the cook swiped it at his own hairy forearm. The first attempt glanced off and a needle-thin jet of clear liquid sprang from a tiny leak where the point had pierced the skin. Behind Rusty, Yvette swore, and Orson the mechanic finally looked up from his reading with a startled yip.

The second attempt was more successful. The moment the hook caught, the attached line tightened. Before anyone knew what was happening, Gil's skin suit was torn away. The effect was much like a magician whisking off a tablecloth, except instead of cutlery and wine glasses, what remained behind was a pillar of lake water with several dozen yellow perch swimming in it.

For several seconds, this bizarre entity held the shape of a man. Rusty heard, as if from a great distance, Orson's scream trailing off as he fled from the building. Then earth's gravity reasserted itself and the sculpture collapsed with a terrific splash.

At that precise moment, Ed arrived for the day shift. He lived in a studio apartment on the second floor, and he entered, as was his habit, from the storeroom. There was a beat-up radio in there, and he had switched it on while he was filling pint cartons with red wigglers.

Strains of a Patsy Cline tune drifted over the scene as Ed surveyed the room with his hands on his hips. With remarkable composure, he crossed to the damp patch of floor behind the counter where the perch were still flopping, picked a pair of them up, and ended their struggles with two sharp whacks on the counter.

"Best to get these on the griddle while they're fresh," he said. He grabbed a fillet knife from the block and sliced them open. "I take it he just now collapsed?"

Yvette nodded grimly.

"And you didn't notice anything before it happened?"

"No," Yvette said. "And, Ed—"

"Me, neither," Ed said. "Figured we still had some time. Thought she would—"

"*Ed*," Yvette put her hand on his arm. "She got Lars."

Rusty glanced at Hubert and thought he looked as bewildered

by this exchange as Rusty felt himself.

"Oh, hell." Ed sighed. "How'd she do it?"

"Fishhook in his home fries," Yvette said.

"That's a damn shame." Ed dropped the perches' guts into the trash, drizzled some oil on them, and flung them on the griddle.

"I am truly sorry, fellas," he said, nodding to Hubert and Rusty. "Your brother was one of the good ones."

"What *happened* to him?" Rusty blurted.

Ed glanced at Yvette. "You didn't tell them?"

"It all went to shit real fast, Ed," Yvette said. "There wasn't a lot of time to explain."

Ed followed her gaze to the windows and groaned as he took in the popped-out screens. "Are my cukes all right?" Then, seeming to realize how that remark may have landed with his audience, he added, "Not that it matters, of course." But he still looked pained at the thought of the damage his vegetables might have sustained.

"You gonna ask about Brom Bones?" Yvette inquired dryly. "He nearly met the same end as Lars."

"Oh, nothing could put a dent in that snap-turtle's shell." Ed rolled his eyes. "Old Suckerbitch would take one sniff and toss him right back up on the shore."

As if summoned to consciousness by that incantation, Brom Bones rose into a sitting position with all the grace of a zombie in a low-budget horror film. Ed snapped his fingers and pointed to the bucket Hubert had used as a makeshift stool.

"Make yourself useful, for once," he said. "Got some perch here heaving their last gasps. Pick them up and toss them in the lake, would you?"

"I don't work here," Brom Bones mumbled.

"You don't pay for your food, either," Yvette reminded him.

That got him the rest of the way onto his feet.

As Brom Bones moved unsteadily toward them with the bucket, Ed plated the cooked fish, grabbed Orson's uneaten pancakes, and ushered everyone into an empty booth. Rusty was surprised when Yvette slid in beside him, scooting in close so her thigh pressed warmly against his still-damp khakis.

After flipping the sign on the front door to CLOSED, Ed took the seat next to Hubert.

"So here's the headline," he said. "Old Suckerbitch is real, and at some point in the uncomfortably-near future, she's going to wipe this town off the map." He speared a flaky bite of perch on his fork and popped it into his mouth.

Rusty and Hubert exchanged a glance.

"I know how it sounds," Yvette said, "but he's not joking."

"Didn't suppose he was," Hubert said. "We've seen enough to convince us something far from usual is unfolding. But how can you know something like that for sure?"

"Because we made her ourselves." Ed punctuated this shocking confession by crumpling a strip of bacon into his mouth.

"You did *what?*" Rusty sputtered. "Where? When? How? And for *why?*"

Yvette ticked each answer off on her fingers. "We created the lake monster, in a laboratory, right here, about seventy years from now. We spliced human, octopus, and lichen DNA together in an attempt to design a smarter, hardier species."

Hubert adjusted his glasses. "What went wrong?"

"Nothing, unfortunately. We were entirely successful." Ed folded a pancake around a chunk of perch to make a tiny fish taco. "The result of our genome tinkering was supremely intelligent and practically immortal. But there were some unforeseen complications."

"Such as?" Hubert said.

"It was hideous, for one," Yvette said. "Our lab assistant went clinically insane, which was how we learned not to look at it directly for too long. Also, some octopuses are cannibals, and that wiring got crossed in an undesirable way. Found that out with another lab assistant, poor thing. Collected her remains in a twelve-ounce specimen jar."

Rusty rubbed his eyebrows. He felt a headache coming on.

"Could we address the part where you're from the future?"

"That's more of a show than a tell." Ed stood up and wiped his hands on his pants. "Right this way."

Hubert and Rusty followed Ed into the storeroom, with Yvette tagging along behind them. As they passed the windows, Rusty saw the empty bucket floating in the weeds. There was no sign of Brom Bones.

Ed cleared off the lid of an old freezer, piling wicker creels on a camp chair and stacking tackle boxes on the floor. Rusty noted the freezer was unplugged and secured with a combination lock. Ed had some trouble with the dial on the lock, which was coated with dusty grime, but eventually he got it open.

"What you are about to see," he warned them, "is a mite unusual."

He lifted the lid with an odd formality, like an undertaker displaying a top-of-the-line casket to a prospective buyer. But instead of satin lining, the interior was filled with pulsing violet light. The glow was so intense it saturated the whole room, washing out even the neon hues of the silicone lures.

Rusty and Hubert leaned forward to peer into the belly of the disconnected appliance. The purple brightness emanated from a round hole in the bottom, roughly eighteen inches in diameter. It was just possible to see the hole formed the entrance to a tunnel, a flexible tube of colored light that drifted softly in space as if it were being swirled about by a mild cosmic current.

"Ed's Worm Hole." Hubert sounded both amazed and amused. "I'll be damned."

"When our initial efforts to destroy the experiment were unsuccessful, we naturally concluded that the most efficient way of neutralizing the threat would be to open an interdimensional portal and pop it in," Ed explained.

"Naturally," Rusty echoed.

"We thought we'd managed it," Yvette said. "Until we learned there was a famously tragical event we'd never heard of before Old Suckerbitch had hitched a ride on the Einstein-Rosen Express."

Ed nodded. "Our actions had altered the history of Lakeside, which meant we hadn't sent her to another dimension—"

"You sent her back in time." Hubert said.

"Real far back," Yvette confirmed.

"We went after her," Ed said, "but the passage turned out to be unstable. It's fixed in place, but it moves around in time. It deposited us in 1996."

"And Old Suckerbitch?" Hubert asked.

"Based on her growth rate," Ed said, "our best guess is that she's been living at the bottom of the lake for about three thousand years."

Rusty gestured at the undulating tunnel of light. "How come no one ever discovered this thing? Before you came along, I mean?"

"Good question." Yvette smiled, and Rusty's heart hopped like a frog on a trampoline. "We think the lake covered this area for a good chunk of that time. After the water receded, the blackberry brambles ran wild, so the prickers might've been a natural deterrent."

"They certainly made our arrival unpleasant enough." Ed grimaced at the memory.

"Let me get this straight," Hubert said slowly. "A monster you haven't created yet has been lurking in our lake since the bronze age and is about to annihilate our town?"

"That's about the size of it," Yvette said. "There are stories about a tempest of blood and fish, and most of the townsfolk disappear while the rest have their brains soft-boiled in their skulls. But that's all we know."

"Old Suckerbitch has been laying low, growing bigger and hungrier," Ed said. "She seems to have developed in other ways, too."

"That trick with Gil was certainly new," Yvette said. "It almost feels like—"

"*SHE'S TAUNTING YOU.*"

They all jumped, and Ed lost his grip on the freezer lid, which clapped shut. Someone had slipped unnoticed into the storeroom with them, someone with a voice like a foghorn clogged with mud. Everyone turned to see who it was.

The emissary resembled Brom Bones in the same way a banana peel wrapped around a hundred squirming millipedes would resemble a tropical fruit. It knocked the ventilated lid from the closest bucket and hooked its clumsy fingers around a night-crawler. The worm stretched to an incredible length before it pulled free. The intruder put the end in its mouth and slurped it up like a fat strand of pink spaghetti.

"*AHH.*" It smacked its pale lips, and a trickle of lake water spilled out.

"That'll be five cents," Ed said tightly.

The thing that wasn't Brom Bones patted its pockets and attempted a shrug. Then its not-a-face brightened and it held up one bulging finger as if it had an idea.

"*WOULD YOU ACCEPT AN INTERESTING TRADE?*" The words fizzed at the edges the way an amplified voice did when the speaker was moved too far from the source. The thing shook its arm until something dropped out of its sleeve. It held it up for the room's inspection.

It was a Carolina rig, but instead of a soft bait, a human ear had been fixed on the hook. Between the lead weight and the swivel was a hazel eyeball, slightly rheumy with age.

Lars' eyeball.

Rusty started moving, but Hubert was closer and got there first, ramming his shoulder into Brom Bones' wide chest. The man-shaped vessel burst like a water balloon upon impact, spraying the storeroom with lake water and live eels.

As Brom Bones' deflating arm collapsed, it flailed up toward Hubert's face. The ear-baited hook embedded itself in the loose fold of flesh under Hubert's chin, catching behind the jawbone. Lars' eye dangled below it like a creepy pendant.

With a sickening feeling of déjà vu, Rusty watched as his brother was wrenched from his sight, whizzing through the open storeroom door and screenless window at dizzying speed, before following Lars' trail of flattened grass down the slope and vanishing into the lake with a splash.

Needing something to do with his hands, which were opening and closing helplessly at his sides, Rusty helped Ed toss the wriggling eels into another bucket. Yvette bent to pick an object off the floor—Hubert's glasses. She wiped them clean with the hem of her skirt before handing them to Rusty.

"Thanks," he said. "I don't know what to—"

And then she wrapped him in a bear hug that smelled like maple syrup and bacon grease.

"I'm so sorry, Rusty," she murmured.

He let himself be held for a moment while Ed slipped out to dump the eels. He was sad for his brothers, of course, but knowing their deaths were harbingers of the town's imminent demise gave his despair an edge of desperate vitality. Hubert had once observed if they had been on the *Titanic*, Lars would have hurled himself at the iceberg and pummeled it with his fists, while Rusty would have apologized for bumping into it. Now Rusty thought he needed to channel some of Hubert's wisdom and Lars' scrappy courage.

Thinking about the infamous shipwreck gave Rusty a glimmer of an idea.

"What time does the museum open?" he asked Yvette.

Lakeside's only museum housed an extensive collection of antiquities that had been left to the town by a wealthy corset manufacturer with a keen interest in famous explorers.

She raised an eyebrow.

"The Hall of Adventures? Not until ten."

"And does Ed still lay in a supply of fireworks for the fourth?"

Ed returned in time to field this one himself. "Sure do. But I don't see that we've much to celebrate at present."

"Not celebrating," Rusty said, rubbing his hands together. "Exterminating."

****

It was almost noon when Rusty dragged himself back to the storeroom. The brass and copper diving suit he was wearing had helped him get close enough to Old Suckerbitch to deliver a diving-bell's worth of semi-legal explosives into a tooth-studded circular orifice he only glimpsed through the bleary window in his helmet.

Ed had been less fortunate, unable to help himself from

directing the beam of his lamp directly onto his own creation to see what it had become. Rusty had hauled him back to the surface, but his thinker was busted beyond repair. When Rusty bid him a sad farewell, Ed was laughing like a maniac under a sticky shower of blood and flesh chunks—human as well as fish. Their efforts had wounded the monster but did not kill her, which only added to the chaos and destruction. Rusty's brave plan had failed, and the town was doomed.

Yvette's end, at least, had been quick. A coiled tentacle, a single squeeze, and a pop that would echo through Rusty's nightmares, if he lived long enough to have any.

Rusty gathered the remains of his strength to remove his gloves and unscrew his helmet. He pulled a handful of inventory forms and a pencil from Ed's worktable and began to write, filling two pages with cramped cursive. Then he folded the note, tucked it into his scuba suit, and crawled to the freezer. He was relieved to see that Ed had neglected to refasten the lock. Using both hands, he pushed the lid open, bracing himself for the rush of swirling violet light.

Given what he was leaving behind, the glowing tunnel looked almost inviting. Which was good, because Rusty didn't know how many times he would have to go through it before he came out where he needed to be. Some disasters, he now understood, could not be prevented, no matter how bravely one fought against them. But that didn't mean there was nothing he could do. There was still a chance to make things different. Better.

He pulled himself up to the edge of the freezer, scrabbled over the rim, and dropped headfirst into the wormhole.

"Godspeed," he whispered, not sure if he was wishing himself luck or merely describing his current velocity.

✻✻✻

Rusty read over the lines a second time, scratching his head. This was all very confusing, and he wouldn't have believed a word of it under normal circumstances.

But.

He'd gone to the restroom after his second cup of coffee, as he always did, and when he returned, the note had been on his stool.

"What's this?" he'd asked his brothers.

"A man in a very strange getup left that for you," Hubert said.

"He raced in and out of the storeroom," Lars added. "Must be an old friend of Ed's."

"Emphasis on the old," Hubert muttered, although he was getting pretty gray around the temples himself.

Rusty recognized the handwriting—how could he not?—and skimmed the note, then read it again slowly, giving himself more time to absorb the words. He wondered if it could be true. He studied Ed, who was turning sausage links on the griddle with a pair of tongs.

Then he looked at Yvette.

She was standing across from him, reading *The Pirate-King's Peg Leg* and drumming her nails on the counter.

When he'd turned thirty-five a few months before, Rusty thought he would follow his brothers into cheerful bachelorhood. Then Ed's Worm Hole had opened its doors and Yvette had served him a side of rye toast, and he had wrestled with a brief but intense desire for another sort of life, the kind where people did the things they liked to do in those romance novels she was so fond of. It would never happen, though. He was far too shy. Unless …

He squeezed the note in his hand.

If I can do all that, he told himself, *surely I can do this.*

He sat up straighter and cleared his throat.

Yvette looked up from her book.

"Yes?" Her brown eyes were curious, but not annoyed.

This was it. He had her attention. So much depended upon what happened next. Every detail seemed to press upon him with extra significance—the smell of the sausages, the clink of Lars' fork against his plate, the breeze that swept through the window and cooled his flushed cheek. *Now,* it urged. *Now.* And he heard himself form the question like a man reciting a line from a dream.

"Sure." She smiled. "That sounds nice."

Hubert gave Rusty a nod, impressed, and Lars dug an elbow into his ribs.

Yvette went back to reading her book. It might have been his imagination, but Rusty thought maybe the patter of her nails was just a bit faster than usual.

Cherry Boy
Danger Slater

NOBODY WANTS TO BUY MY CUM ANYMORE and it's a goddamn shame.

I've spent the requisite ten thousand hours mastering my technique. I know how to maximize my output. Like a tube of toothpaste, from the bottom to the top. Please bring me a second cup, nurse. And, no, I don't need any visual aids. Do what you love and you'll never work a day in your life, right? I've probably sired hundreds (if not thousands) of children over the past two decades. I've hustled more gravy than the line cook at a Thanksgiving buffet. I'm a hero to the women in this town.

Except now when I go around to the sperm banks, they all tell me the same thing: "I'm sorry, Mr. Slater, but we have a strict age limit on donorship. The cut off is thirty-nine years old, and, as of last week, you no longer qualify." These rules are as draconian as they are arbitrary, and, frankly, I find the whole thing unacceptable.

The first time it happened, I thought the receptionist was just new.

"I'll excuse your ignorance, ma'am," I said, "because I can only assume you are uniformed. You see, I'm a bit of a legend around these parts, and, as such, I demand you purchase some of my jizz this very instant. Look in my file. Look at the gallons upon gallons I've given. Plus, I believe I was one punch away from getting my free ice cream sandwich. You can't deny me that."

She shook her head, half in pity, half in disgust.

"Look, we don't want your old-man sperm, you creep. Now get lost before I call the cops."

"Fine." I put up my hands. Backed slowly toward the door. "I guess I'll just take my business elsewhere."

But elsewhere didn't want me, either.

And so that was that.

***

I've tried selling blood and the even more lucrative plasma, but the rules on these types of donations are even more draconian than semen, and you can only come by the clinic so often before some nurse starts going on and on about your "safety" and cuts you off. *Of course* I don't want heart failure or whatever the hell else they're always blabbering on about, but, also, I have bills to pay. Rent. Electric. Sewer. Cellphone. Car insurance. Health insurance. Gas. Groceries. And don't even get me started on the student loans. Here I am, well past my prime sperm-donating years, and I've barely made a dent in my student loans.

I really thought things in my life would've fallen into place by now. It feels like I was handed a Lego set with a few pages missing from the instructions. I'm doing the best I can with what I've got, but this bullshit does not look anything like the Millennium Falcon pictured on the box.

***

I'm not lazy. And I'm not afraid of hard work. I'm always sniffing out new and exciting money-making opportunities. This is the only way I've managed to survive.

I subscribe to a lot of email lists that offer paid market-research gigs. I'm talking focus groups, mock juries, opinion panels, and so on. Companies are always looking for insight into the heads and habits of the common man. And I just so happen to be a common man. I get hired a lot.

What they do is send you a short survey to fill out. Real basic stuff. Name. Age. Location. Annual household income. And then a few seemingly random questions tacked on at the end that'll often hint at what the panel might be about.

Q: "What do you think of cherries?"

> A: "Funny you should ask, because cherries
> are actually my favorite food in the world. I
> eat them all the time. My nickname in college
> used to be Cherry Boy, if you can believe it. I
> always had a pocket full of cherries wherever
> I went."

Okay, okay, I was exaggerating a bit on that one. In fact, if I'm being honest, I actually don't like cherries at all. But it's important that you appear enthusiastic on these forms whenever possible. They like to hire enthusiastic people. That, and so long as you match whatever demographic group they're looking for, and you're in.

And it just so happened that my age and location and annual household income were *exactly* what those cherry people were looking for. A simple taste test for $150. All I had to do was eat whatever they put in front of me and answer whatever questions they asked. It didn't matter if I liked cherries or not. All that mattered was, at the end of the day, I was going to get paid.

***

Amid a sea of nondescript office buildings I found the one I was looking for, perhaps the most nondescript of them all. It was the kind of building you could drive by five times a day and not even notice. And at night? Forget it.

Under a single, flickering flood light at the edge of the parking lot, a single, flickering sign was lit: UNITED FLAVORS AND FRA-GRANCES. There were a few cars scattered about. My other taste-testers, I assumed.

I wondered if Bethany would be here, too. I met her at a mock jury about eight months back. A mock jury is when lawyers hire people like me to pretend to be a jury so they can present their arguments-in-process and get feedback before the real trial. Sort of like a practice run.

The one Bethany and I met on was some kind of medical malpractice suit. Apparently some doctor left his cell phone in a patient he was performing gallbladder surgery on. Every time a text came in, the phone would vibrate and the patient would shoot bile out of his dickhole. The infection got so bad he was in the ICU for a week.

Oh, wait. I forgot I signed an NDA for that one.

Forget I said anything.

Anyway, Bethany ends up at a lot of these things, too. The second time we ran into each other we shared a knowing nod. The third time, we verbally acknowledged the fact that we recognized each other. The fourth time, we finally exchanged names. If she were to make it here today, this would be our fifth panel together.

I'm not necessarily one to believe in fate, but in a lot of ways I feel like the universe is trying to bring her and I together. How else could you explain this constant running-into-each-other-ness? Five panels together would be no mere coincidence. Five panels together would *mean* something.

***

Up a staircase. Down a staircase. Two lefts. Three rights. Then I finally found the room I was looking for. A paper sign with the word TESTING was taped to the door. There were five panelists in total, a mishmash of ages, races, and genders, encompassing the widest demographic spectrum United Flavors and Fragrances could find.

When Bethany walked through the door, my heart began to flutter. And it fluttered even more when she smiled and greeted me.

"Hey, stranger."

"Hiya, Bethany."

"So waddaya think? Cherries?"

"That's what I figured, from the way the questionnaire was leading us. Luckily, they're my favorite food in the world."

"Oh, they're my favorite food in the world as well. They used to call me Cherry Girl in college."

"No shit? They called me Cherry Boy!"

We shared a knowing wink. This was not our first rodeo. And who knows who was listening?

A sweaty man in wrinkled trousers came out a side door and introduced himself as the administrator before explaining how this particular taste test was going to go.

"Well, as some of you may have surmised, the taste test today is going to be on cherries. Maraschino cherries, to be exact. Like the kind you put on top of your sundae. We're going to be putting you in booths where you'll be served a variety of different maraschino cherries. All you have to do is eat them and answer a few questions on the computers that'll be set up in the booths as well.

"Please be honest when answering these questions. This isn't a quiz; you're not being graded. You're here because we want your opinions: the good, the bad, and the ugly. The test will go on until we've gotten your feedback on all of the samples. When you're done, we'll already have your checks made out. You can just grab them on your way out the door.

"Any questions?"

There were none.

***

The booths were divided up by partitions so that we sat separated, almost like cubicles. Bethany was on the left side of me and an elderly Mexican-American woman was on the right. It was a small space. A bit claustrophobic. But I could handle a little claustrophobia. This wouldn't take long.

I sat at my desk. There was a little mail slot-style hole in the wall in front of me, through which the cherries were going to be distributed. Next to me was a big, boxy computer from what I assumed was the mid-'90s, with a five-buttoned keyboard attached to it, numbered one through five. The rating system, no doubt. One typically meant STRONGLY DISLIKE and five typically meant STRONGLY LIKE. Buttons two through four didn't matter at all. Those numbers were for cowards and those kinds of people didn't qualify to be here in the first place.

"Hey, Bethany, can you hear me?" I asked.

"Yeah, I can hear you," she replied.

"No talking," the administrator said to us and to everyone. "The test begins now."

***

Through the slot, a plate was passed with a single maraschino cherry on it. I was to eat the cherry and rate it on the scale attached to the keyboard.

Easy-peasy.

I popped the little red bulb into my mouth and was immediately assaulted by a maelstrom of flavor, both painfully sweet and toe-curlingly tart. I scrunched up my nose as the intensely fruity scent wafted up the backside of my nostrils. I almost vomited but managed to quell my stomach by thinking of cool and calm ocean breezes.

This was, quite possibly, the worst cherry I ever ate.

Of course, I'd already told them I loved cherries on my intake survey. I even went so far as to call myself Cherry Boy. I knew that administrator dude said to be honest, but I was already dishonest when I was filling out the paperwork, so I couldn't contradict myself now. If I did, they'd know I was lying and they wouldn't hire me again in the future. I really had no choice.

"How would you describe your experience with Cherry No. 1?"

I hit the five.

STRONGLY LIKE

***

This continued for another twenty cherries or so, each one inexplicably

115

redder and sweeter and tarter than the last. I found myself growing more and more nauseous by the bite.

"Hey, Bethany, how're you holding up?" I whispered.

"Not great," she replied. "I'm hoping this'll be over soon."

The administrator stomped over toward us. "Who's talking?"

I didn't want Bethany to get in trouble so I said, "I was."

"Is there a problem, Mr. Slater?"

"I just might need a break soon."

"There are no scheduled breaks. We need to keep this moving so the next group can use the facilities when we're done. They'll be eating mustard. All sorts of weird mustard. All you have to do is shut up and eat your cherries and press your little button. It's not fucking rocket science."

"I could use a break, too." The voice of the old lady on the other side of me was weak, undoubtedly suffering through these cherries as well, one after another. "I need to use the bathroom."

The administrator scoffed.

"So use the bathroom, Mrs. Vasquez. Nobody is stopping you."

I heard her chair slide back, but before she could stand up, the administrator pushed it back in and pinned her against the desk.

"Whoa, whoa, whoa there, grandma. Nobody said you could get up."

"But you said I could use the bathroom."

"I did. And you can."

"But where am I supposed to go?"

"I'm sure you could figure *something* out."

There was a tense moment of silence, interrupted by what I could only describe as the sound of a large quantity of wet spaghetti filling up a pair of pantyhose. Then the smell hit me.

"It's bright red!" I could hear the old woman scooping handfuls of slop out of her undergarments. "My shit is bright red! I'm bleeding internally! Call the ambulance!"

"That's just the dye they use on the cherries. Relax." I could hear the facilitator scribbling something down on a clipboard. "This is actually an interesting development and the exact kind of thing we're conducting this study to find out."

"It's not dye!" the old woman wailed as she writhed around in the ever-growing puddle of viscera cascading out of her. "There are chunks of intestine in it! There's my spleen! And my duodenum!"

The facilitator stopped writing and leaned in.

"Hmm. Yes," he said, "that is your spleen, isn't it? This is even more interesting than I thought. Head's up, everyone, some of these cherries may cause rectal hemorrhaging. If any of you feel like you're about to shit blood, please hit the HELP button on your keyboards."

"The keyboards don't have HELP buttons," a voice called out from the other side of Bethany.

"They don't?" The facilitator scribbled on his clipboard some more. "… *add help buttons …*" he mumbled. "Okay, thank you for that feedback. Hopefully no one else will die during this and we'll be able to finish on time."

"Oh my god, she's dead?!" Bethany cried out.

"Huh?" the facilitator replied. "Oh, yeah, I think so. I mean, I'm not a doctor, but she's lost a lot of blood and is no longer moving. I'll call a custodian once we finish up in here. Anyway, back to the test!"

****

The variation between each cherry was subtle as they grew sweeter and tarter still. It was clear they were building toward something, some unapologetic and unknown apogee of flavor of which the general cherry-eating public had never even conceived. I didn't know how many more we had to go, but I was surprised we already eaten as many as we had.

"How would you describe your experience with Cherry No. 108?" STRONGLY LIKE

"How would you describe your experience with Cherry No. 109?" STRONGLY LIKE

"How would you describe your experience with Cherry No. 110?" STRONGLY LIKE

"I can't take it anymore!" a masculine voice from the other end of the room screamed.

"I thought I said no talking!" the administrator chastised.

"I don't care about your stupid rules anymore. I don't care about anything! I have died and gone to hell and this whole operation is being run by demons!"

The administrator scribbled some more on his clipboard. "... *hallucinations and violent outbursts* ..." Then he said, "To address your concerns, Mr. Kulkarni, I would like to assure you that you are still alive and well, and that I am not a demon or any other kind of supernatural or malevolent entity. We here at United Flavors and Fragrances have only one goal in mind: to create the best-tasting and most emotionally- and spiritually-satisfying maraschino cherries the world has ever seen. If that makes us evil, then I guess George Washington was even more evil because all that guy ever did was cut down cherry trees and lie about it.

"We at United Flavors and Fragrances would *never* harm a cherry tree. We are bringing cherries to the people. I can think of no more noble and altruistic a pursuit, and you should consider yourself lucky to play even a small part in it. What you are doing here, you are doing for the good of all mankind."

A single gunshot rang out and a body hit the floor with a thud.

"Goddamn it," the administrator grumbled. "Listen up, if any-one else brought a weapon into the testing facility, please relinquish it now or you won't be paid at the end of the session."

***

Two panelists had died already. There were three of us left. The cherries kept unrelentingly coming. And it crossed my mind more than once that perhaps this wasn't a cherry taste test at all, but rather some kind of ruse for a psychological experiment. Maybe they wanted to see how long we would eat these horrid things before attempting to escape. Maybe they were making these cherries taste bad on purpose. Maybe the sweetness was *supposed* to be punishingly sweet. Maybe the tartness was supposed to be taste-bud-murderingly tart.

The flavor of these cherries was almost impossibly bad. I didn't doubt that they could have been developed in some kind of military lab to be used against enemies of the state and other defectors.

One time, I got hired to test out a VR headset, and while me and the other participants were waiting to be let in, a gorilla burst into the lobby and started maiming everybody around me. It was a bloodbath. I thought I was going to die.

Well, it turned out, the blood and guts were all special effects, the other participants were paid actors, and the gorilla was just a man in a suit. Apparently, the real test was put on by psychologists to see how long it would take a grown man to shit his pants under a situation of what they called *implausible duress*. The whole thing was a setup to gauge my genuine reaction.

At the end of the session I was given fifteen dollars and a bus voucher, so I guess the whole ordeal wasn't a total loss. But, still, I would've preferred to play with some cool VR gear.

I didn't get the impression this taste test was a setup at all, which, if I'm being honest, was an even more terrifying prospect. United Flavors and Fragrances simply wanted to develop a better maraschino cherry. If we died in the process, that was just the price of doing business.

The 187th cherry came through the slot. I picked it up and readied my mind and body to swallow the thing. But a thump from behind the wall distracted me.

I leaned over and looked through the opening. A set of wide, desperate eyes greeted me back, framed in the small rectangle like a pair of scuba goggles. I nearly fell back in my chair.

"Jesus Christ!"

"Shh! Keep your voice down! They don't know I'm back here."

"Who are you?" I asked him.

"I'm one of the other panelists," he said. "Perhaps you saw me when that administrator dude was giving his little speech at the beginning? Asian male, age 18-30?"

"Oh, sure. I remember. Green Shirt Guy. How did you get

behind the wall?"

"I forced myself through the slot."

"What?"

"Yeah. And it wasn't fuckin' easy, either, let me tell you. I had to break a few of my bones. Most of them, actually. It hurt like hell, but I managed to ooze my way through."

"What's back there?"

"Just a few automated robotic arms and shelves upon shelves of cherries."

I immediately broke out in a cold sweat.

"How many cherries are we talking about?" I asked.

"More than I can count."

"More than a thousand?"

"I can count to a thousand, man."

"Do you think they're gonna make us try them all?"

"I don't know, but I'm not about to stick around and find out. I'm gonna make a break for it."

"I don't think that's a good idea. They're pretty serious about us finishing the test. They didn't even stop for a medical emergency or a suicide. Plus, you'll be forfeiting your payment."

"Fuck my payment. These cherries are disgusting and they're making me sick."

I completely agreed with him, but I didn't say so out loud. I needed to keep up the charade in case this guy was a ringer and this I-broke-every-bone-in-my-body bit was some kind of subterfuge to make sure I answered my questionnaire truthfully.

"I'm sorry, sir, but I don't agree with you there. I am a Cherry Boy and I STRONGLY LIKE all the cherries I've eaten so far."

"Did you get hit in the fucking head?"

"No."

"Then you have the worst sense of taste in history. Best of luck to you, bud. I'm gettin' the hell outta here."

His eyes disappeared and I heard the scuff of his sneakers as he ran across the tile. A locked door handle rattled. Then another. And another. Then a few expletives. And then the sound of an alarm. More footsteps, a whole gang of them, this time approaching. One of the previously-locked doors opened and what I assumed was a team of security guards stepped through.

"Please return to your seat, Mr. Lu. Nobody has to die tonight."

"Fuck you, pig."

"All right, have it your way."

The roar of the flamethrower was louder than his screams. A few seconds later the stink of charred flesh came wafting through the slot as maraschino cherry number 188 came my way.

***

After that, time kind of lost all meaning. Maybe thirty minutes passed, maybe it was four years. I was lapsing in and out of a diabetic coma. The human body was not built to consume maraschino cherries in such excess.

Sticky red syrup was caked all over my face. Drool and vomit splattered in a bib-like pattern on the front of my shirt. I could hear Bethany quietly weeping.

"Stay strong," I said to her as I ate my 368th cherry. "We're gonna get through this."

She sniffled as she swallowed her 368th cherry down as well. "I don't know if I even want to know the kind of person I will become after being reshaped by this stupid taste test."

"You wanna know what the most ironic part of all of this is?" I said.

"What?" she replied.

"I don't even like maraschino cherries."

"I don't like them, either."

"I wish we were on that mustard test he was talking about. Now mustard I can get behind. I put that stuff on everything."

"Didn't you say everyone in college used to called you Cherry Boy?"

"I just made that Cherry Boy thing up so they would hire me. Everyone in college used to call me Freckle Dick on account of all the freckles I have on my dick. I graduated twenty years ago, anyway. Nobody calls me Freckle Dick anymore except for my family and a few close friends."

"My nickname in college wasn't Cherry Girl either. It was Sunscreen."

"Why was it Sunscreen?"

"Because I always had sunscreen on me. Like, in my bag. My friends weren't very clever."

"Did you realize we've done five of these opinion panels together?"

"Have we?"

"Yup. Five. And the only thing I know about you is your name."

"What else would you like to know?"

"I want to know everything. Like, what's your favorite movie?"

"Oh, that's a tough question. I'm freezing up here. I feel put on the spot."

"Well just name a movie you like then. It doesn't have to be your absolute favorite."

"I like *Legally Blonde*."

"I don't think I'm familiar with that one."

"It stars Reese Witherspoon as sorority girl-turned-law student Elle Woods?"

"Oh, wait, is that the one where she goes to Yale or something?"

"Harvard Law, yeah."

"Harvard. That's gotta cost an arm and a leg. I went to state school and it still cost me hundreds of thousands of dollars. I'll never be able to pay off the loans. I wonder if Elle Woods is still paying off her student loans like I am."

"Probably not. I think she was rich to begin with. Then she becomes a lawyer at the end and gets a job at a prestigious firm, so I can only assume she becomes even richer."

"Whoa. Spoiler alert."

The administrator appeared behind us.

"No talking! Holy fucking *shit*, how many times do I have to fucking say it? There are, like, three rules here. Do you two idiots want to get paid or not? If so, then *be fucking quiet* before I *drag you out of here by your ears* and put you both *out of your misery like the lowdown, dirty dogs you are!*"

"Sorry, sir," I said.

"Sorry, sir," Bethany said.

The administrator gave us both the stink eye and wandered wearily away.

***

I wish I could tell you something exciting or adventurous happened after that. I wish there was some kind of big, third-act twist where Bethany and I discover the *horrible truth* about this facility and the two of us were forced to make a daring escape. But that's not how real life works. This had been the most psychologically and physiologically torturous panel I'd ever been a part of, but at the end of the day a job was a job, and I considered myself lucky that opportunities like this presented themselves to me. A lot of people fill out those intake surveys and not everybody gets selected. I was just happy my intestines hadn't ruptured like they did with that old woman.

My belly *had* distended outward like a basketball, though, and I was covered in so much sticky red paste that I resembled a giant cherry myself. I had literally become the Cherry Boy of my own legend.

"How would you describe your experience with Cherry No. 1893?"
STRONGLY LIKE

"How would you describe your experience with Cherry No. 1894?"
STRONGLY LIKE

"How would you describe your experience with Cherry No. 1895?"
STRONGLY LIKE

And then a horn honked. The computer screen went blank for a second before the words THANK YOU appeared. The administrator approached, clipboard tucked up into his armpit, a big smile on his face, carrying two sealed envelopes.

"All right, unless you have any questions for me, that about wraps up this evening's test. I just wanted to say 'great job' to those of you who survived. I know eating 1,895 maraschino cherries in a row is no small task, but the opinions you provided here today are invaluable to us at United Flavors and Fragrances, and we appreciate both your time and your candor."

I could hear Bethany moan and groan in pain as she stood. She
was in rougher shape than I was. Somehow she'd lost a few teeth
over the course of the panel. Maybe her cherries had pits? Maybe
the sugar rotted them out of her head? I didn't know. I certainly
wasn't going to ask either. That'd be rude.

The administrator handed her her check.

Then he handed me mine.

"If you … got any other gigs … in the future … reach out…" I
said to him. I knew this wasn't a great experience, but most people
don't like their jobs. And I still had rent to pay.

****

Bethany and I made our way out to the parking lot just as the sun
began to rise. Orange and purple waves rippled across the sky.

"Hey, Bethany?" I said to her just before she got into her car.

She stopped and turned around to face me. "What's up?"

"I was just wondering if, um, maybe you wanna go out with
me sometime? Maybe get some coffee or a cocktail or something?"

"You mean like a date?" she asked.

"Yeah, like a date," I replied.

She smiled at me. I smiled back.

It was going to be a beautiful day.

Meaningless Flesh
J.A.W. McCarthy

IT WAS A REASONABLE ASK, EVEN FROM THE START. And I wanted that boy anyway, so it made sense. Like me, Anne longed for our separation. Freedom, even while we held each other close, leaned on each other, our spirits breathing and beating and pulsing as one.

I ate and she watched. I kissed and fucked and plunged my hands into whipped cream and silk pockets and the depths of animal fur, all while she hovered in a numb sort of longing. It was as opportune as it was accidental, giving in to the strange urges that weighed on me even heavier than my sister did.

Words were not enough. I could give her the language—silky, slimy, salty, sweet—and she could picture every action of her nonexistent limbs, her nonexistent tongue, but without the flesh to explore, it was meaningless.

To have a body is a delight and a terror all at once. I owed my sister that pleasure. That pain.

***

Jamie came in every Saturday night for the midnight screening. This week it was *Trainspotting*. He'd seen it five times already, which was why my stomach did a pothole dip when he walked up to my ticket window.

"Seriously?" I teased him. "Your Kelly Macdonald crush is out of control."

He blushed, his gaze drifting down to my hands on the keyboard. When his eyes met mine again, a lock of sandy hair flopped into his face. James Fucking Dean with his pinched smile and those starbursts bookending his eyes.

"What makes you think I'm not here for Ewan McGregor?"

"Kelly's cuter."

"You look just like her," he said.

It was my turn to blush as I printed a comp ticket. I would've anyway, even without the compliment.

You're right — he does kinda look like James Dean. East of Eden *Dean. Shy. Sad.*

I smiled at Anne's comment, the best I could do while making change and engaging in small talk with the customers in line. She hovered just behind me, a light pressure on my shoulders, a gentle pull of my neck. Without means to touch me, she'd gotten quite adept at distracting with words. And when she wanted my attention, she knew just what to say.

Remember how you used to stare up at that Rebel Without A Cause *poster on your ceiling and touch yourself?*

"He's dead," I muttered.

The two women at my window gave me matching quizzical looks.

"Enjoy the show." I forced a smile as I handed them their tickets.

I wanted to remind Anne that I'd been scratching my thigh — and so what if I had been touching myself; I'd run screaming from Catholicism same as I'd run screaming from our parents' house — but I couldn't let that slip with customers still in line. Like any other twin, she couldn't hear my thoughts. I was too easily baited; like most sibling relationships, we traded off being the antagonizer, the other falling into the push-pull role of gleeful victim and thrill-seeker.

Once I got through the line and midnight struck, I closed my window and gave the usher, Jonah, the all-clear to lock the lobby doors. I printed the nightly sales report while he helped Abby behind the concessions counter, but, really, I was watching Jamie. I liked how he lingered with his cup of shitty coffee — I'd told him a million times he could bring in something better from the cafe down the block, but he insisted the theater's stale sludge was preferable — pretending to examine the faded movie posters and peeling wallpaper that decorated the tiny theater's moldering lobby. He always waited to enter until Jonah shut the double doors, shooting me a shy smile as the thunderous trailer music swallowed him into the dark gullet inside.

I bet he fucks like James Dean.

I turned back towards the closed ticket window, the dingy backroom lights of the University District stuttering to life as the neon shut off.

"How would you know how James Dean fucked?"

How would you? You're gonna have to ask him out, you know. He's way too shy.

"You really think he's into me?"

You know that "You look just like Kelly Macdonald" comment nearly killed him. How long do you think it took him to work up the nerve? That's love.

"'Love' is a bit much."

"Huh? Caroline?"

I turned around to find Abby and Jonah staring at me from the adjoining concessions counter. What they must've thought of me, always talking to myself—I could accept that. It was the being twenty-two to their eighteen, the non-student working full-time at this failing movie theater for rent money instead of spending money, that gutted me.

"Nothing," I said, sliding out of my seat. "Once you finish with the soda machine, you can leave. I'll count out the drawers."

At least, in the ten months I'd been here, I'd worked my way up to manager. While the owner and projectionist, Randall, hermited away in his attic-booth, only coming downstairs for the bathroom and stale coffee refills, I had the honor of dismissing the rest of the skeletal staff and ushering the last patrons out into the night once the film ended.

Though there was only a set of double doors between me and the dozen people in the theater, I often felt like the last person on earth on these nights. They might as well have been sealed into another dimension, leaving me staring through the glass into the real world—sidewalks empty, windows going dark as people with money and better jobs and lives crawled into bed, spooning and dreaming, while I tried so hard to appreciate that extra seventy-five cents an hour that my managerial position brought, how it was enough to get me something better than stale popcorn for a dinner a couple nights a week.

Anne was all I had, sometimes the only voice I heard all day, asking me to describe the taste of the popcorn and butter for the millionth time, until I felt more sorry for her than myself. Though we longed for separate physical bodies, she was my other half, the only barrier between me and the emptiness.

The lobby fell into silence as soon as Abby and Jonah left, only the crisp whisper of ones and fives brushing against each other as I counted out the concessions and ticket drawers. There'd been a time or two when I'd peeked into the theater halfway through the film to find it empty, the patrons having slipped out the emergency exit into the alley. Still, Randall had insisted on letting the film finish.

Since Jamie started coming in, though, I didn't mind anymore. I was willing to stay for him, his shy smile, our debates over who had the best falafel in the neighborhood, the way he got excited about Mary Harron and David Cronenberg. The thought of how nerve-wracking it must've been for him to compliment me ... Now that Anne had planted that delicious possibility, I could see something other than this place, something new and solid I could start shaping my body around.

After delivering the cash up to Randall, I slipped into the theater, taking a seat in the back row. Jamie was several rows ahead in an aisle seat, the same seat I would've chosen—easy access to the bathroom, we'd both joked. I watched the light from the projector halo his head in gold, screen grime sliding over him then brightening, turning the back of his head into shadows and strobes I wanted to read like tea leaves. My hand rose, reaching through the empty space between us.

You have to do something.

"He's not that shy," I whispered. "Maybe he's just not interested in me, not like that."

He comes here every Saturday night.

"He's a night owl. He likes movies."

He lingers in the lobby and stares at you. He doesn't talk to Abby or Jonah, just you.

Anne smoothed herself down the sides of my neck, her humid weight enveloping me, pressing harder as she settled onto my shoulders. Sometimes I thought she might burst through my skin. I *wanted* that, even if it left me nothing more than an open wound.

You have a body, Caroline. You have hands and lips, and you get to touch—to feel. Don't waste that because you're insecure and shit. All I have is what you tell me. What I wouldn't give …

A sparkle of gray-green light washed over Jamie, golden embers sparking on the edge of his lip as he turned his head to glance back at the doors. Was he thinking of me, what he'd say on his way out tonight?

I stood up and made my way down the aisle to sit behind him. The rusty seat creaked in acknowledgement, a swinging groan and squeal that caught his attention so that he glanced back briefly. A smile bloomed on his face as his eyes focused on me.

You could find out if he kisses like James Dean. Tonight, when he's leaving. He wouldn't say no.

My hand lifted again, outside my conscious control, this time dangerously close to the back of Jamie's neck. It wasn't that Anne had any power over my motor functions. We had always wanted the same things; we were always in sync whether she was the echo or I was. Without her prodding, I would've still been in our parents' house, forbidden to speak her name, forced to pray for a soul that had never been dead.

Jamie shifted in his seat, his head bowing slightly to sip his coffee. The hairs on the back of his neck caught the light, flitting in and out of view like fireflies. My hand hovered, fingers stiff and trembling. Another inch and I would know the downy softness of those hairs, the topography of his scalp, the goosebumps that would surface at my touch, the meaty, mineral tang of his skin. I could bathe my tongue in its oils, heavy-bottomed and viscous, same as the loneliness that balled tight in the back of my throat on these late nights in the theater.

Anne slunk under my raised arm, a little nudge. But I didn't need her push this time. My breath grazed unknown flesh, an exhale enough to part a path through that sandy hair. He had to know how close I was—and he wasn't moving, wasn't resisting.

Anne was right. An invitation. A dare.

I envisioned the soft pad of my index finger gently kissing the back of Jamie's neck. The barest swipe. Then me, leaning back in my seat just as he turned around, my bemused smile, waiting for him to turn back to the screen before suckling flakes of skin and oil off my finger.

But, even without Anne still pressing on me, my hand wasn't mine anymore. Not when my finger jabbed into the back of Jamie's neck. Not when my fingernail cleaved his tender flesh, drawing blood.

Or I didn't want to admit it was mine.

"What the—?"

Hand clamped to the back of his neck, Jamie swung around and scanned the empty seats before settling his gaze on me. I had my hand in my lap, but I was still leaned forward, mouth open and eyes wide. He examined his fingers in the dull light of the screen, rubbing them together, recognizing the unmistakable slickness of blood.

His brow furrowed. I braced myself to dart out of there, call in sick for the next two weeks, figure out another way to make rent this month. But his eyes flicked up to mine and all he said was, "Mosquito?"

Holy shit, Caroline. Anne trilled low in my gut.

Once Jamie turned back to the screen, I examined the finger that had unintentionally gouged him, a tiny curl of dry, paper-white skin and fresh blood gathered in the cup of my nail. In the projector's light, his blood glowed cherry red, the tip of a cigarette, a fire that teased my tongue. Anne nestled against the back of my neck, the comforting weight of a warm water-bloated washcloth.

I slid my finger into my mouth and sucked. My tongue nuzzled under the nail, seeking the pressure of that ridge, leaching out copper and salt, an oily, meaty hint of scalp. Staring at the back of Jamie's head, I sucked greedily, no longer able to differentiate his flesh from my own. Anne's silence was a surprise, but she knew I was memorizing every flavor, every texture for later tonight, when I could describe them to her. She didn't need to know I was saving these details for my own enjoyment as well.

And then the screen flickered.

It was a flash of light, like the moment the projector overheats, when the picture distorts, right before the celluloid ignites. I turned around, but there was nothing strange about the projector window, the soft rattle of its forward motion evident in the silence. The few other people in the theater glanced around, too, then back at a screen that was now white. Jamie turned to me, his mouth forming a comical O.

"Randall must've fallen asleep again," I said. "I'll go check."

As I started up the aisle, Anne was a hot breath urgently prodding the back of my neck.

Caroline?

Even without corporeal form, my sister still had her needs.

"I don't know," I whispered. My tongue probed the divots of my molars. "It's blood. Dirty pennies, salt—"

No. Look.

As I turned around, *Trainspotting* came to life again, the reassuring roar of Begbie starting a bar brawl. The picture, though, hadn't returned, not fully. On the edge of the screen, like an image under vellum, the faint outline of a face surfaced from the blur of drab beiges and browns. Dark eyes, high round cheeks, one corner of a wide mouth flicked upward, same as I'd seen in childhood photos—as familiar as the one I saw in the mirror every day.

But that wasn't my face. It wasn't a hallucination born from a shared fantasy, either. It was what we'd dreamed of since birth.

My sister.

Her face.

Anne eased from the back of my neck. By the time I made it to the theater doors, I couldn't feel her anymore.

Meaningless Flesh

***

When I was little, our mother would tell me I had to drink all my milk and eat all my broccoli so my body would grow and be strong. Every meal, I choked down that calcium and Vitamin C, imagining a doll-sized arm sprouting from my own, a little leg emerging from my thigh, Anne's auburn head crowning from my scalp. With each bite, my sister blanketed my shoulders and back with warm encouragement. Every tingle, every itch was pure hope—Anne growing appendages of her own, pushing up under my skin, ready to burst from my body and into the world to *really* hold my hand, *really* pull my hair, really be more than a delusion or a phase in the eyes of our parents. Her own person, with her own body. She cheered me on as I chugged a gallon of whole milk, then whispered soothing words as I vomited a white and yellow swirl onto the kitchen floor.

The truth was, if I'd succeeded—if she'd gotten a body—they would've cut her out of me. Without full detachment, she'd be a fifth limb, an extra pair of thumbs, a vestigial tail. A deformity. The doctors would've tossed her in a bio waste bin and I'd never have the one person who was born to understand me, to know the true, most vulnerable me. The weight of what was once a sentient phantom limb.

Anne didn't die in our mother's womb, absorbed by my developing fetus. Same as me, she was born. In fact, she came out first, her cries—silent to the doctors, the nurses, even our parents—the rope that pulled me into the daylight behind her. While I was swaddled, she spooned me. In our crib, I kept my limbs close to make room. When our parents kissed me goodnight after a bedtime story, they were kissing Anne, too, whether they accepted it or not.

They gave me two names, so I gave her one of mine: Anne. I learned quickly that when I spoke of my sister, our parents saw an abomination possessing their only child. Holy water and daily confession couldn't smother her, not when my body continued to grow around her, an armor, a vehicle, a palm to hold my invisible twin. We grew together, strong and intertwined as redwood roots.

Before the theater, before what happened with Jamie, Anne's life was secondhand. That was what pained me the most, that she could never be more than an observer. My hands and lips and tongue were wholly mine. I was the padding on her bones, the echo in her ears, the film over her eyes. How could I resent sharing what I had when nothing would ever be her own?

Even though there was a chance I might lose her—with her own body she could move to a different city, run away with someone else—I yearned for her freedom. There might come a point where I was left alone with my failures, but I knew, even if she gained autonomy, Anne would always come back to me.

The things she whispered in my ear were never foreign, never shocking. The urges were all mine, whether she encouraged them or begged me to rethink them.

What she wanted—what I wanted—was worth every gallon of milk I vomited, every broccoli floret propagating between my teeth like moss, all the times I cut myself open to see if anything had sprouted from my bones.

I would've done much worse just to see her face.

***

I spent the following week buoyed by the sight of my sister's face, supping from the image I'd seen on the movie screen. Doubt chewed at my every thought, of course; what I'd seen could've been the ghost of Kelly Macdonald from an earlier frame. As much as I wanted to believe I'd caught a glimpse of Anne—a body that could've been hers—Randall assured me that he'd seen nothing more than a blip on the screen, a splice between two frames that hadn't been as smooth as he'd intended.

Still, Anne crystallized in my mind, her image clear and material, her higher cheeks and wider mouth—those subtle differences—proof that what I saw was not a hallucination of my own image. She assured me that had to be her face because we saw the same thing and we couldn't both be hallucinating.

I sat in on every show during my shifts and came in on my days off—something I'd never done—in the hope of seeing her again. We discussed it when we were alone, the circumstances that conjured her, and both kept circling back to Jamie. Maybe blood and lust were all it took to make a body.

I wasn't sure if Jamie would show for the Saturday midnight screening of *Scream*—he'd mentioned slasher comedies weren't really his thing—but when he did, Anne reminded me that this was crush behavior, as far as a shy creative writing major was able to go. When he greeted me, he said my name, and I savored the harsh thinness of the long *I* on his tongue, the bob of his chin, the little ridge of dry skin poking out from the center of his bottom lip giving me something tangible and irresistible to focus on as my sister contemplated how the other parts of his body might taste.

As usual, once I waved him in, he bought a coffee and lingered in the lobby, perusing the various Open Mic Night flyers from the neighborhood cafes until Jonah shut the double doors. I wasn't planning to make a move, but in the quiet of the lobby Abby and Jonah were a pair of exclamation points as they cleaned up concessions. Their whispers were bright and clipped, an occasional giggle lifting love-drunk voices, the rags in their hands making overlapping circles against the doors of the popcorn machine. They suppressed sheepish grins when I caught their gazes. After clocking out, they slipped into the supply closet where we kept our coats and bags, and emerged holding hands.

"Don't," I said to Anne once they were gone.

She slunk around my shoulders, light as a warm breeze, then landed heavy against the back of my neck.

Go in there and sit next to him this time. I bet he—

"I said, don't."

The thrill of touching him. And getting away with it. The way he tasted … Don't lie. You loved it.

Near the end of the movie, I slipped into the theater. Only a handful of people remained, scattered about. Jamie was in the back row this time, right on the aisle; he offered me a smile when he saw me come in. I waited for Anne to press against my upper back, but instead she lightened as I squeezed into the row and took the seat beside him.

"How is it?" I asked.

He shrugged. "Not bad."

I tried to focus on the screen. As I searched the white walls and appliances of Stu's kitchen for that face—Anne's face—I could taste the mineral tang of Jamie's blood patinating my molars, that curl of dry skin reviving on my tongue. Flesh and blood for another body. Anne never needed to say the words. She'd coaxed me out of the womb and I still never knew who was following whom.

So I did it. I leaned close to Jamie, and when he turned to me, I kissed him.

It was easy, but it wasn't a good kiss. We were clumsy, both trying to lead, our mouths bumping hard enough to clink teeth. After a stifled laugh, we readjusted, fat, throbbing lips finally latching, jaws unhinging as if we both hadn't realized how famished we were, too much want and saliva filling the soft pockets beneath our tongues. Anne cradled the back of my head, gently pushing, and I raced against Jamie, inhaling coffee and spearmint gum, pulling whatever I could into myself, my teeth catching that dry little flag of skin sticking up from his bottom lip—

"What the—"

Jamie pulled away from me, the tip of his tongue probing his raw lip. It was wet and shiny in the dark, juicy pink from blood or friction, I wasn't sure.

"Sorry," I said.

There was no blame in his eyes. This time, though, just when I thought I should excuse myself and disappear into the supply closet until everyone left, he leaned towards me again, and we were kissing. Spearmint and black coffee succumbed to blood and saliva in my mouth. I worked that little scrap of his skin between my teeth, enjoying the gummy resistance of flesh against enamel.

Anne rolled over my shoulders, light at first, then staccato, vibrating.

Our kissing was only interrupted again by a blinding flash,

like lightning splitting the screen.

A few heads turned back to the projector window behind us as Stu and Billy's whining and wailing flooded back to life. Then the picture crept back: pale blue, beige, and red slashes on the white screen, bleeding out from the center. Another graceless splice, Randall would say, but he didn't see what I did.

The faint outline of a face and torso emerged on the left edge of the screen, thickening like smoke against the burgundy wall. A fringe of eyelashes darkened, cheeks surfaced in a gentle swirl, lips bloomed into a small smile. Anne pattered down my spine, then wrapped around my stomach, a gentle squeeze of excitement, recognition.

Grinning, Jamie turned back to the screen. I ran my tongue along the back of my teeth, pushing the torn bit of skin from his lip between an incisor and canine. For later. For tonight in bed, when I could luxuriously provide my sister all the fleshy details.

We were right, Caroline. That's me up there. Every time you touch him ... I can feel things. I can feel my arms.

Feel? So that body on the screen—her body—wasn't just an image?

As if to demonstrate, Anne lifted off my shoulders. I could barely feel her—just a brush against my neck—as her image on the screen vibrated, manifesting an arm, filling out the woman in profile. The emergent arm lifted, its hand pushing against the screen, denting the vinyl as if trying to break through. Trying to step out of the film ...

"Holy shit," I gasped.

Jamie turned to me. I leaned towards him and sucked the fresh bead of blood from his lip.

✳✳✳

The next week, Jamie came into the theater for every one of my shifts. It was a welcome distraction; I could picture us together, Anne and me adding him to our little family, taking care of each other, weeknight dishes and Sunday breakfasts in bed. With a body, Anne could work, too. Three incomes meant no more waiting for the bus with a garbage bag full of leftover popcorn, jeered at by frat boys as they lobbed lewd jokes at me. No more perverts shaking my ladder, running their hands up my pant leg as I changed the marquee. No more begging Randall for another twenty-five cents an hour at my next review. No more lonely midnight shifts.

For Anne, it would be a world of firsts—things we would still be sharing—but this time, the experiences would be fully hers, as well: the contentment of rubbing lotion on our legs, the relief of a full bank account, the satisfaction of tearing the tenderest meat from bone. The pleasure of Jamie on both our tongues.

While Anne chirped about all the things she would do, my eyes wandered to the screen during every kiss. A simple swap of saliva wasn't enough; my sister didn't appear in the film when Jamie and I touched, when our teeth snagged each other's lips, when our hands wandered up each other's shirts or into each other's jeans. Like with the milk when we were kids, it was a valiant but wasted effort.

By the next Saturday, I was ready for more than this over-the-bra build-up. As usual, Jamie came in for the midnight screening, but this time he didn't even make it into the theater. While Abby and Jonah were counting out the drawers, I was fucking Jamie in the supply closet.

Like the kiss, it was clumsy and rough at first, easing into a pleasant rhythm as we got comfortable atop boxes of fifty-four-ounce soda cups. The metal shelving unit thwacked against the wall with our movements, and Jamie paused, a look of chagrin on his face, but I leaned into him, my ass against his stomach, one hand behind me and squeezing his thigh in encouragement. I wanted Abby and Jonah to hear.

Holy shit, Caroline! Is this what it feels like all the time? I can feel him.

So now my sister had other parts with nerve endings and blood flow and pleasure centers that reacted in time with my own? I pressed my lips together, suppressing the "what the fuck" threatening to bolt from my tongue. Anne's body was forming on a screen in the next room, her reach expanding outside of me.

I need to taste him. This is not the time to hesitate.

Swept up in the moment, throbbing against the back of my neck, she was more present than any other moment in my life I could remember. I knew what my sister saw, what she couldn't stop thinking about: Jamie's right hand braced against the wall next to my face, fingers spread, his thumb inches from my lips. And nestled against the nail of that thumb, a little flag of stiff, bleached cuticle, pointing right at me.

I pulled his thumb into my mouth. He moaned as I sucked, his hand twisting as the rest of his fingers brushed against my cheek. He was salty with sweat, wet, hot enough to make my gums ache. I ran my bottom teeth against his nail bed and he moaned again. That little point of skin—his hangnail—scraped my tongue, caught my lip as I eased his thumb out of my mouth. Anne was silent, but I could feel her like a held breath. Before Jamie could brace his hand against the wall again, I caught the hangnail between my teeth and bit.

He yelped and jerked his hand in my grip, but that only helped me. His hangnail tore off in a strip of skin, unpeeling down past the knuckle, only stopping at the side of his palm. Our bond broke when he was finally able to yank his hand away from me, severing the strip of flesh pinched between my teeth.

"What the fuck?"

Holding up his injured hand, Jamie backed away from me. We both stared at it, a glossy pink cleft snaking down the side of his thumb, blood pulsing behind a thin veil of raw flesh, a body not even aware of its power, how it was making cells form and features materialize, building a girl kiss by kiss, nip by nip.

I sucked the ribbon of skin into my mouth and tucked it under my tongue.

"Shit, I got carried away," I said.

Jamie's expression was inscrutable, but all I could think was that I'd gone too far. That I'd never see him again. And now Anne would be trapped half-formed in that movie screen for all eternity, hating me, too. And I'd be trapped working in this theater, forever apologizing to a phantom.

The apologies came tumbling out of my mouth, blurred by the strip of Jamie's skin nudging the underside of my tongue.

"I'm sorry. I didn't mean to … I'm sorry."

He didn't respond. Instead, he slid his injured thumb into his mouth and sucked.

Hard, spattering slurps. Lips curling under teeth, puffy and white-pink as his thumb succumbed to wet engulfment. Jamie kept his eyes on me as his cheeks hollowed into a vacuum seal. Was he angry, or was he unable to resist? I imagined the minerally salt coating the tip of his tongue, the same taste that haunted my own mouth.

Abby and Jonah exchanged a wide-eyed look as I burst from the supply closet into the lobby. I didn't look back to see if Jamie was still in there, pants down and thumb in his mouth. Still buttoning my own pants, I darted into the theater, took a seat in the back and waited for Anne to press down on me, scold me for my lack of finesse, but instead I sensed that warm washcloth lifting from my shoulders again, same as the night I scratched the back of Jamie's neck.

On the screen, dead-center, a woman appeared. Not a hazy profile this time, not a whisper of lips and cheeks and eyelashes. She was solid pink and enamel white and shiny auburn hair, sharper and brighter than the drab, humidity-faded figures of *Kids* lazing and dirt-bagging behind her. She had arms and legs, and she was using them to push against the screen, smiling right at me.

***

The silence, the lightness that came after my tryst with Jamie—that left me hollow. Rudderless.

I spent that night wandering my apartment, my pace increasing with my panic, as I waited for Anne to tell me all about her new limbs, her body forming on that movie screen. She had to be bursting, finally able to *feel* something, finally having something all her own. I was excited for her; I wanted to know if her body felt the same as mine, if her limbs had the same weight, the same flex, the same urges. Did she smell like me, the stink of sludgy, orange popcorn oil I could never fully wash off my hands, the sour gape of my bellybutton? Was her growth as reckless and cumbersome as my puberty?

When she didn't respond, I sat in the dark, in the silence, willing her comfortable weight to return, to fill the chasm it had carved in my body since before we were born. I felt insubstantial without her. Alone. The air in the room no longer had heft. My bones felt thin, hollow, my brain in a chaotic race to fill the gaps Anne had left.

With every nip and nibble of Jamie, she was fading from my body and manifesting four-and-a-half miles away at the movie theater. Wasn't this what we always wanted, though? The freedom of being apart—as an option, even if we never explored it—tethered by the invisible, elastic pull of always coming back together, because we couldn't exist without the other?

I rolled the ribbon of skin from Jamie's thumb on my tongue, sucking sweat and the promise of plasma from it, tucking it back into my nightstand drawer when it got too soft, too thin—a delicate comfort for later.

He would understand about Anne. I could feel it in the way he savored the pain that tinged his pleasure, the way he'd tithed his flesh between my teeth and his blood in my mouth.

But I had gone too far in that supply closet. Now he would never return to the theater, and Anne would stay trapped on that screen, her eyes pleading for another taste, another jolt of life from the boy I'd chased away with my impatience.

Anne was silent because I had failed her. Instead of being trapped in my body, my sister would be trapped on a movie screen, helpless and silent while the shitty theater fell to ruin around us both.

***

He's here, Caroline. I need you. We need you.

The sound of my sister's voice—the first time she'd spoken to me in almost sixteen hours—was as alarming as it was comforting. I didn't even clock in or return Jonah's greeting before dashing into the theater.

I found Jamie immediately, the only person there for the 3:45 screening of *Velvet Goldmine*. As I slid into the seat beside him, it was obvious that he wasn't watching a holographic-sequin-coated Jonathan Rhys Meyers strutting around.

Instead, Jamie's gaze was fixed on the left edge of the screen where my sister stood, twenty feet tall and even more solid and saturated than the last time I'd seen her, so much more than a projection on a white screen.

When we were little, we used to imagine what she would look like, if we would be identical or fraternal twins. If our hair color was the same, she would wear it short while I kept my long waves. If our mouths were indistinguishable, I would wear dark lipstick because I liked those colors better. It was a fantasy that kept us entertained in study halls and church pews. I never thought I'd see Anne come to life on a movie screen. I never expected to see her even more tangible and radiant than we'd imagined.

I can feel my body, Caroline. All of it. I have a body! Look at me! We're so close.

"What do you want me to do?"

Jamie turned to me as if to answer. I looked down at his fingers spread atop his thigh, his cleft thumb winking at me under the film's sparkling lights, a sticky pink coated in saliva. There were new wounds, too: three knuckles split and raw, exposed and sticky like his thumb. They looked chewed, as if he'd bitten each one and peeled his flesh in strips down the back of his hand, like chicken from the bone.

"Your sister," he said.

On the screen, a feather-trimmed Jonathan Rhys Meyers was

singing in close-up. The fat, pink slopes of his lips bobbed up and down, as wet as Jamie's wounds. My sister grinned her approval.

See, he wants this as much as we do, Caroline.

I reached over to brush aside an errant lock of Jamie's hair, but he caught my wrist, pushing me away. He had to be upset that I'd left him pants-down in the supply closet last night. When I reached for him again, a small smile parted his lips and he said, "We don't need you."

On the screen, Anne vibrated, leaning towards us, her reach a push against my back, towards Jamie.

This time, Jamie didn't resist when I slid my hand around the back of his head. He let me guide him towards me, his mouth turning wet and hungry so that I knew I was right, Anne was right. His sigh was hot against my cheek as I trailed kisses across his jaw to his ear. More weight lifted from the back of my neck, my own or Anne's, I wasn't sure.

I suckled Jamie's earlobe, the supple bounce of flesh yielding to my lips, my tongue lapping at peach fuzz, a gentle tug as I gnawed another piece of Jamie between my teeth. Heat bloomed thick from his face to his hands now roaming my breast, my thigh, and I caught the scent of pork fat beneath the spice of his deodorant.

Gently, gently, I tested the pressure of my teeth against his earlobe, and his hands pressed harder into my flesh. My mind wandered to the ribbon of skin in my nightstand drawer, a piece of Jamie dried to detritus now that it had served its purpose.

Did I ever feel anything for him, or was it the promise of what he could do, that his body gave Anne corporeal form? Was my initial attraction to him nothing more than my sister's instinct deep in my DNA?

From the movie screen, Anne whispered ecstasy in time with Jamie, and I abided.

A pinch, a release—once, twice—a test that wet the whorl and hollow of his ear. His lobe so delicately suspended between my front teeth, an elastic bounce that teased. It was Anne this time, coming down on the back of my neck, the muscle memory of my body carving space for what should've been hers. She lifted when

I bit down.

Jamie yelped, but he didn't pull away. His fingers tightened on my breast, a nudge that would've been my sister's doing if he had been any other man.

I sunk my teeth all the way into his earlobe.

Blood rushed into my mouth, filling the well beneath my tongue where I had stowed less significant pieces of Jamie. Hot, rancid-sweet, viscous as cum slinking down the back of my throat—all of it was a surprise, perhaps more than I'd been prepared for.

The severed earlobe sat oyster-slick atop my tongue as I savored his blood on my lips. Anne responded with staccato beats of humidity against my shoulders and the sides of my neck.

Jamie's grin stretched into the smear of blood that painted his cheek. Hand clamped to the new wound, he tipped his head towards the screen.

There was no flash of light this time, no dramatic cleaving that could masquerade as a broken projector or poorly spliced reel. The film was simply gone, bare torsos and psychedelia replaced by twenty feet of Anne, center screen, pushing against the plastic. Her body solid, fighting its way out from two dimensions. She was a deity behind pearlescent vinyl, a never-ghost with one last obstacle to vanquish.

We're so close. I can't wait to be with you.

"I can't wait either," Jamie said.

He raised the underside of his wrist to his mouth and bit down.

Blood streamed down the right side of his head, down his forearm—the odor of stale popcorn overcome by a metallic tang as thick as swamp air. Jamie tore at his arm, ripping skin and meat and loosing veins from wrist to elbow. Every piece of him fed my sister, breathed blood and bone into a hollow image, lifted her from the phantom I carried to a real person now, visible and audible not only to me. Existing in the world beyond me.

Separate from me.

I grabbed at Jamie's right arm, but he slipped out of my grip before I could bring it to my mouth. I chased him through the theater, up the stairs to the stage so that we were both standing in front of the screen. Anne loomed over us, grinning open-mouthed, saliva like bright, white starbursts gathering at the corners of her lips, eyes narrowed in soft repose. Hands lifted, she pushed the limits of the screen as Jamie raised his bleeding arm to her.

As his blood drained, the screen fell away from Anne, disintegrating into the humid, metallic air, sparkling particles that draped her now-solid body in an ethereal mist of theater lights and blood. Arm still raised, Jamie fell to his knees. He kept his eyes on my sister, glossy with reverence, and she beamed in appreciation.

It was supposed to be me, not Jamie.

I was supposed to be the one who brought my sister to life.

The one who made her real.

I pulled Jamie's arm to my mouth. Weak and drained, he didn't fight me this time. As my teeth penetrated skin and muscle, I looked up at Anne, willing her to turn her gaze from Jamie to me. Without me—without that first kiss, that first nip, tearing the hangnail from his thumb, ravaging his ear—none of this would have happened. The offering had to be presented by my teeth, passed from my lips, to free her.

Anne was born from my efforts, not Jamie's.

Still, she wouldn't look at me. She was stooping now, focused on Jamie, one hand caressing his jaw as his eyes grew heavy and he deflated before us. His pulse didn't quicken as I ripped free a mouthful of his flesh—supple, springy, fatty on my tongue, slipping like a thick, slick fish between my teeth—instead slowing, fading with him. I rolled the pulpy skin around in my mouth, his blood running rivers between my teeth, the mealiness of overripe fruit blooming in the back of my throat and in my nostrils.

I closed my eyes. I waited for my sister's voice to ring bright and clear through the cavern of the theater.

"We did it, Anne," I murmured. "You're free."

When I opened my eyes, the theater was empty. I was on my back, slick and sticky, limbs slipping against more blood than could've fit in a single human body. My tongue probed my gums, swollen and itchy, the crevices of my molars, the pockets of my cheeks. I tasted nothing more than the paper-bag mustiness of a dry mouth. Jamie was no longer on my tongue, between my teeth, on my fingers.

He was gone.

Anne was gone.

I scanned the theater. The projector was running again, limning endless rows of empty seats in white gloss. The movie's credits were playing now, but the words were meaningless shapes I couldn't discern. Up the aisle, the double doors opened, blasting the bright lights of the lobby through the darkness.

"Any garbage?" Jonah called down to me, clutching a black plastic bag in one hand.

I stood, finding my footing easier than I anticipated. I was so light now. Nothing on my shoulders, nothing on my back, nothing against my neck. My bones knit around the void she left behind, testing this new shape of absence, not even the reassurance of a phantom limb to ease the transition. My skin was cool and weightless and I thought for sure I would float away.

The Clover Cafe
Amanda Cecelia Lang

CONSCIOUSNESS RETURNS SEVERAL SECONDS before Sam opens her eyes. In this brief and cottony haze, she can still pretend.

She's home in bed, buried in blankets, stretching luxurious bones while the house stirs around her. Footsteps on the stairs, kitchen cabinets banging open. Any minute now Claire is gonna smack her with a pillow or spray a whipped cream flower on the tip of her nose. *Wake up, nerd, it's waffle-thirty.* She can practically smell the hot butter and cinnamon. They'll pig out on the couch and watch their parents' ancient stash of VHS movies all throughout the morning, quoting the cheese-ball dialogue and snickering into each other's shoulders. Sam in her ratty UCLA sweats, and Claire with no makeup and those goofy, blue bunny slippers—and, *gasp*, what would the cool kids say? Luckily, Claire's brat pack friends won't be around to judge. Sunday mornings are just for sisters. Best hours of the week. Laid-back, cozy, and it sounds like rain today. Even better.

With a lazy smile, Sam opens her eyes.

Claire stares back.

Half-lidded, vacant. Face bloodless and doughy, one cheek scrunched against grimy floorboards.

Claire?

Overhead, rain patters against an unfamiliar roof, the relentless tapping of ten thousand fingers trying to get inside Sam's head. Lightning branches outside a broken stained-glass window, flash-illuminating the splintery innards of the church and the pickaxe lodged in the back of her big sister's neck.

Claire!

Sam's mind throbs. She tries to sit up, but the last three days pile back in, crushing her with the weight of corpses. Literally. On top of her. The entire brat pack pins her down, sagging limbs and torsos: Shawnee, Brie, Jake. And Claire.

A surge of nausea rises from Sam's guts and exits in a scream.

She lashes an arm free. If she can reach Claire maybe one of them will wake up, a jump-scare in her bed, like the old movies they watch every October. But Claire is real, and so is the tender, cavernous gash in Sam's temple. Her hand comes away red. *He thinks he killed me.* She remembers now, her one semblance of a plan. Stay under the bodies where he left her, play dead, pray for help to come. Not that any prayers were answered this weekend.

Over the rain another noise rises, scraping, urgent, the grave-work of a shovel.

He's out there.

Oh, God. She whimpers, shrinks smaller. She wants to lie here, stay buried, *be buried.* What's the point without Claire? Claire was the fighter, the one who stood a chance. The one who helped her survive this lonely life. What else is there now but to sink into the floorboards and wait for oblivion?

Claire stares at her. Observes her spinelessness with dead marble eyes. Practically imploring her.

That fucker can't get away with this!

Everything hurts; her head feels gooey and soul-drained. But Sam shoves out, dislodging herself, sending corpses lolling to one side. *Oh, God, oh, God, I'm so sorry.* She wanted them out of Claire's life, but not like this. She was going to steal her away to college, they were going to be roommates and — and now —

Sam limps past their bodies, past the altar to the broken window. The bones in her right ankle crunch hideously, so she stands on her left tiptoes and peers out.

Gravestones haunt the driving rain. Vengeful angels, winged demons, and, at the center of it all, the animated hulk of the priest wields his shovel.

Digging five graves.

Sam turns away. The church is a dilapidated husk full of weapons. Razor shards of stained glass, iron shackles bolted to the pews, toppled candlesticks and crucifixes.

But something in here is much deadlier.

"I'm sorry," she whispers, yanking the pickaxe from the back of Claire's neck. The body lurches, then slumps to the floorboards.

Don't think about it! Just go! Now! For Claire!

The front door releases a splintery shriek, but the rain is too loud, the rhythm of his shovel too satisfying. He doesn't see her staggering through the mud, savage determination twisting her once gentle face. The fucker. She'll only get one chance at this. With a silent scream, Sam raises the pickaxe and swings.

***

It's really coming down out there.

Even at full throttle, the windshield wipers can't keep up. Might as well be driving this old rig at the bottom of a lake. With a sigh, Big June flicks the switch for her chicken lights. The eighteen-wheeler's mounted high beams blaze to life and cut through sheets of passing rain. The road beyond remains a spectral gray ribbon. A lesser driver would've pulled over miles ago to wait out the storm. Not Big June. She cranks the gearshift and hammers down on the gas. There's a pick-up scheduled for three a.m. sharp, less than fifteen minutes away.

Big June never misses a pick-up.

Lightning splits the night with a flash of day. The rain turns white, and on both sides of the highway the desert reveals itself. Hard-baked terrain melting into rivers of mud. It's been a while since she's been on a run in these parts—and never in the rain of all things—but she's not surprised. Her line of work lends itself to the middle-of-nowhere. Backwoods roads, sleeping neighborhoods, gone-to-seed summer camps, sometimes all in one night.

No GPS signal way out here, but she checks her mileage. Getting closer.

She pops the CB from the cradle—more dead air. Typical for these runs, but force of habit keeps her honest.

"Come back, Home Base, this is Big June. Getting greasy out

here, but I'm coming up on the pick-up site, ETA three minutes. Will radio again once I'm all loaded up. Please standby."

She re-cradles the CB and looks up as a young woman dashes into the road: stark white in the high beams, bedraggled and waving a pickaxe. *No time to stop!*

A second before the *splat*, the figure lunges sideways out of the lights.

With a yelp and a prayer, Big June pulls the brakes. Air hisses, tires wail. The rig skids into a fifty-foot stop. *Holy good God!* She isn't sure if the poor soul made it until she catches her in the side mirror running the length of the trailer, screaming for a ride.

Three minutes early.

But Big June smiles.

She never misses a pick-up.

****

Sam doesn't remember climbing in. She's chasing the rain-drenched brake lights of an eighteen-wheeler—then she's in the passenger seat. It's that sudden. The interior swims around her, tracers of light from the dashboard, patter on the roof.

She drips all over, rainwater, tears, cries of animal anguish pouring from her mouth. The driver kneels next to her, blurring in and out: a grandmotherly thing, small-boned, long, silver hair and an oversized trucker hat with a four-leaf clover. She drapes a blanket over Sam's shoulders.

"It's okay, sweetheart, Big June's gotcha now. You're not alone. Just breathe, let it all out."

But Sam's mouth is too full, the last three days too unending, everything trying to spill out at once. All she sees are Claire's empty eyes.

"Call an ambulance!"

"Sorry, sweetheart, no signal out here. You know that."

"You don't understand. They're all dead! Please ... *my sister ...*"

"*Shh* ... I know, I know." A hand settles on Sam's arm, achingly warm. "Right now, we have to worry about you. Tell me now, this is important: did you get the bastard?"

"I …" Sam's fingers cramp around the pickaxe, startling her. She didn't even realize she still had it. The steel point rests against the dash, gleaming and bloodless. The rain must've washed away the hair and bone and—*don't think about it, don't!* A sick chill spreads through her, feels like a scream.

"I had to."

"Of course you had to." The woman tucks a sopping strand of hair behind Sam's ear. "By the looks of you, he had it coming in spades."

"He was gonna bury Claire."

"Claire?" The name comes gently. "Your sister?"

Sam starts to nod but ends up hunched over in her seat. She moans and cradles the pickaxe—Claire's final gift to her. She can still feel the sword-in-stone resistance as she wrenched it from her neck. *Oh, God, oh, God, I just left her there!*

"Sweetheart, I know it's awful. But I need you to sit back up. Your cut's still gushing."

Sam shakes her head, but the air shifts as Big June guides her upright. There's a soft tug as the old woman tries to slip the pickaxe free.

"Don't!" Sam recoils, jerking the weapon away.

Big June puts her hands up and sits back calmly on her haunches. "That's okay, sweetheart. Hang on to it if it helps." A first aid kit sits open at her knees. No sudden movements, she produces a roll of gauze and antiseptic. Just a kindly old woman. The priest was kind at first, too.

"Okay if I fix you up a little?"

Sam resists, but only in spirit. She shakes, racked with all-over sobs as Big June dabs the meaty parts of her temple. The antiseptic stings, but the woman's words are brutal. She tells Sam she's brave, she's strong, she's gonna make it through this. *It's not right!* Sam can still see Claire running from the church, the shape of the priest as he filled the candlelit doorway. How will she make it through anything ever again?

"Stay with me, sweetheart," Big June says from the driver's seat.

Sam blinks, her vision unblurs. Outside, the road streaks past, wet and silver in the headlights. *When did we start moving?* She touches her temple, surprised at the bandage.

"Where're we going?" She sits up straighter. "I can't leave her!"

"Somewhere they can help," Big June promises. "Just down the road."

"No." Sam's fingers tighten around the pickaxe. "There's nothing out here. We hiked this road for a day before he found us."

"It'll be there, trust me."

Trust you? But bone-heavy exhaustion pins Sam to her seat. The miles pass, fast and slow all at once. At some point the rain starts to thin and a hazy green glow appears in the distance.

A mounted radio crackles with a distant broken voice. *"Big June, this is … come back … that pick-up?"*

Big June snaps up the handset. "Home Base, this is Big June. That's affirmative. Just crossing out of this darn storm. Got you on my horizon. ETA two minutes. Standby."

The radio voice responds drenched in static, some code impossible to decipher.

"Tell them to call someone," Sam says. "Tell them we need the police!"

"They already know, sweetheart. I promise. Help is coming."

Sam keeps one hand on the axe, one on the door handle.

With the final mile, the storm lets up. It's almost as if they drive right out of it. Rain gives way to dry asphalt and a nightscape blanketed in moving fog. That green glow at the end of the road pulls closer and takes form: a cheery little building with a jukebox sheen and a flickering neon sign.

The Clover Café.

Big June turns into the empty parking lot. Despite the middle-of-night hour, the place is open. Sam sees people inside occupying several booths and a long counter.

Before she knows it, she's limping across the parking lot with Big June as her crutch, cocooned in a blanket, clutching the pickaxe to her chest. They pass under the buzzing green neon. The café door opens with a jingle and the sweet aroma of a thousand Sundays engulfs her. Warm butter and cinnamon.

"Come in, Sam," the voice from the radio says. "We've been expecting you."

***

"Wake up, nerd. First day of October, you know what that means."

An M&M bounces off Sam's forehead. Eyes squeezed shut, she feels along her pillow, then pops the chocolate into her mouth. Three more plink off her head.

"All right, I'm up, I'm up." She smiles and cracks one eye.

Claire stares back.

Face screwed up, tongue twisted out, completely juvenile, irredeemably goofy.

Sunday mornings are the best.

Comfy-clad, they shuffle down to the rec room, carrying plates of Claire's world-famous cinnamon butter fried waffles and bags of Halloween candy to honor the month.

Claire plops down in front of their parents' sacred wall of VHS and selects three classics. She holds up the cover art for Sam's inspection.

"Which one first?"

A wooded summer camp framed inside the silhouette of a knife-wielding killer.

A young woman terrorized in her bed by a bladed skeletal hand.

A skin-masked maniac waving his chainsaw overhead.

They all make her shudder, but Sam points.

"That one. It's got the best ending."

***

"Welcome to the Clover Café, Sam. We're so glad you made it. Do you prefer a booth or the counter?"

"I ...?"

Sam squints against an assault of polished tile, immaculate

countertops, shiny vinyl seats. The voice from the radio manifests before her as a trim middle-aged waitress in a pale green uniform. Neat red lipstick, vintage platinum curls. She lingers inside the heaven-scented entranceway with a menu and a sly smile.

"They call me Goldie." She steps closer. "It's an honor to meet you. You're an incredibly brave girl."

Sam shakes her head. *An honor?*

"It's okay, sweetheart." Big June nudges her forward. "You're in good company. Miss Goldie runs this old joint. She'll have what you need."

"What I need?" Like that ambulance she asked for? That cop car? Transportation back to a life that's been forever gutted? What's the point without Claire? Surviving makes even less sense in the light.

"First things first." Goldie loops an arm around Sam, helping Big June keep her upright. "Let's get this wildcat off her ankle. I'd say a booth is in order."

Sam sobs. "You don't understand …" *Claire* would've wanted a booth; she'd stretch her legs out the length of the seat and flirt with the waitstaff, order fancy desserts she knew they didn't have. All Sam wants is a dark corner, somewhere she can crouch into a ball and scream. This place was here the whole time?

Customers dot the seats, amorphous bodies on the too-bright edges of her awareness. They talk in late-night voices, and somewhere, somebody goes on laughing. It's not fair. They've never watched someone they love slump to her knees. They've never been dragged away, reaching and screaming as the soul faded from her eyes! They shift in their seats and side-eye Sam's soggy bandage and the pickaxe-shaped lump inside her blanket.

Chin down, Sam asks Goldie for the bathroom in a voice about to break.

"Of course, how thoughtless of me. You'll want to wash off the night."

Goldie and Big June help her down a hallway ending in two doors, both marked with the same symbol: ♀.

"Here we are, ladies' choice," Goldie says, "And …" She produces a neatly folded sweat suit and a washcloth. "Something clean and dry from the gift shop."

Sam stares at the offering. With every kindness, it's harder to breathe, harder to trust.

"Go on, sweetheart," Big June says. "All for you."

Sam accepts the clothing, slowly, letting her blanket slip from one shoulder, exposing the smiling curve of her pickaxe. Like Big June, Goldie doesn't even blink.

"Hope you hurt him good."

Sam shakes her head. "He said he was a priest. Do you know him?"

"Not him. But we know the breed." Goldie and June exchange dark glances. "Sooner or later, they come for us all."

"We were driving to California," Sam says, "to tour UCLA … but now Claire … she'll never … we'll never …"

"Oh, sweetheart, we hear you, we truly do." Big June squeezes her shoulder. "It feels like these monsters take everything from us."

"But they don't, Sam," Goldie says. "They *don't*." She pushes open a bathroom door, exposing a room of clean white tile. "How about a little privacy?"

Sam nods, already unhooking herself from Big June.

"Go easy on that ankle, sweetheart." Big June lets her go. "That bastard's done enough damage."

Except that's where the old woman is wrong.

The priest didn't crack Sam's ankle.

Claire did.

"Anything at all," Goldie says, filling the doorway. "Just holler."

Sam turns to thank them to get them to leave, but a novelty sticker on Goldie's collar gives her pause: a happy face and the line BE KIND REWIND. Above that a faded purple scar snakes across the waitress's throat.

"Help will be here soon, Sam," she promises, closing the door.

Sam twists the lock, then hobbles to the sink and sets the pickaxe on the counter where it's fast to grab. There's a mirror, but all it reveals are bloodstains and bruises. There's nothing vital underneath, nothing left of her. The congealed remains of her t-shirt and shorts fall away like scabs as she peels herself raw and naked.

She fills the sink, but her hands hesitate and her gaze gets lost in the shimmering white-blue water. The priest gave them water. Their throats were dry and swollen; their skin sunburned from the endless walk for a gas station. He offered them freshly pumped well-water in shallow silver bowls, one for each of them.

Even then, Claire's brat pack had snickered.

What a primitive. Dude doesn't even have working faucets.

They should have been more concerned about the ghost-town vibe, the mounds of fresh earth they passed in the churchyard, the muddy-red stains on the vestments he wore. But they were so thirsty and he promised his new congregation would arrive soon.

Sam doesn't remember who drank first, only that Brie was the first to collapse.

Hell came fast after that. Faces doubling and blurring, bodies slumping to the floorboards. Something in their water.

Nothing holy.

Sam woke to Shawnee and Brie screaming. She tried to stand, but dizzy, sleepy tendrils pulled her back down—that and the shackle securing her ankle to the pew. Claire sat chained to the next row, terror elongating her face, fire rippling in her eyes.

The church flickered, aflame with candles. The first corpse of the weekend sat slumped against the altar. Eyeballs red and bulging, face a purple bruise, a golden cincture knotted brutally around his neck. Jake. The only male member of Claire's brat pack, maybe the only one the priest saw as a threat.

That's when Sam started screaming, too.

Pleased, the priest stepped forward, dressed in ceremonial vestments and a ravenous smile. He appraised his remaining captives, their long, tan legs and pretty faces, and pulled the vestments over his head. No need to disguise himself behind kind gods any longer. There was nothing ordained about this maniac.

But he was their kingdom now.

The sound of her own weeping snaps Sam back to the present, and the bright white bathroom reclaims her pulsing vision. She reaches for the washcloth—except, it's already in her hand. The water in the sink ripples, dark pink. She blinks at the mirror. She's clean, scrubbed raw and breaking out in gooseflesh. As if time sloshed forward while she was haunting the past. She drops the soggy washcloth into the water and presses a palm against her temple.

Hastily, she dresses in the sweats Goldie gave her. They're a size too big and easy to hide in. Hugging the pickaxe to her chest, she limps out into the hallway. Nobody stands waiting for her, but the air is cruel with warm butter and cinnamon. She holds her breath as she creeps into the dining area.

"There you are, sweetheart."

Big June rises from the nearest booth.

Goldie appears at the kitchen door with a plate of waffles.

Sam limps toward Big June, but as she does the people turn in their seats to watch her, and the café finally pulls into focus.

And Sam sees them. *Really* sees them.

Goldie's other customers.

Young women with blankets and bloody bandages. Smeared mascara, swollen lips. Girls with bruises and stains, slashes and gashes.

An entire slaughterhouse worth of injuries inside one little café.

They gape silently at Sam, exhausted and broken. Sam gapes back.

"Who are you people?"

✳✳✳

"Oh, man, now that's an ending!" Claire reaches for the remote and hits Rewind. "I always forget what a beast that girl is with a machete. Final girls are so badass."

"The killer sure didn't see her coming," Sam says, crawling off the couch, feeling a little green. October is awesome but intense. Inside the VCR, gears and wheels hum, spinning the tape back to the start. "What's next?"

Claire considers the array of video boxes on the coffee table and sighs.

"I'm really gonna miss this."

Sam's hand freezes over the Eject button. "Don't say that."

"It's okay to face it, nerd. Our Sundays are numbered."

"Maybe they'll be a little different," Sam hedges, and those world-

famous waffles turn to rocks in her stomach. "I mean, there's no way Mom and Dad are gonna let us take their video collection to L.A. But we'll have wi-fi in our dorm, we can stream, and we'll bring a waffle iron or—"

"Stop it." Claire nudges her with a bunny slipper, hard. "You know that's not what I mean."

Sam knows. But.

"It's not too late for you to apply," she says. "I can help you. We can take a road trip, tour the campus. Once we see it for real, you won't wanna leave, I know it."

"Snap out of it, Sam." Claire's smile goes flat. "Seriously, stop fooling yourself with this fantasy dorm bullshit. College is never gonna be my jam."

"Then what is? Barhopping with your stupid friends? A different hook-up every night? You wanna be a waitress forever?"

"Wow. Tell me how you really feel."

"I didn't mean it that way."

"Sure you did. And it's fine. Let's face reality."

"You're my big sister, I'm not supposed to leave you behind. If you come with me, we can help each other. Study, party. Like a team."

"And when did that ever work for us?"

Every Sunday morning.

"I can't move to California alone, Claire."

"Sure you can. You got accepted without me, didn't you? I mean, look at you." She chucks an M&M at the UCLA logo stamped across Sam's sweatshirt. "You've been wearing that ugly thing since junior high. It's your dream."

"You were supposed to be there, too."

"You're strong enough without me."

"You're wrong."

"Shut up, nerd, you're gonna be fine. Just remember the number one rule for survival." She slides the next movie across the carpet. "When shit gets real, the boring, smart chicks rise up and leave the foxy, fun ones in the dust."

****

The women in the Clover Café regard Sam and her pickaxe with tired empathy, then turn slowly back to their tables.

There are so many of them, ravaged and damaged, hair and darkness in their eyes. One girl sits slumped over an entire pot of coffee, her high-necked nightgown hanging in ribbons. In the next booth, a blonde in a blood-matted wool sweater stares anxiously out the window at the neon parking lot and the rolling fog. Someone in the far corner cackles endlessly and tragically, while, at the counter, another tormented soul clutches a blanket to her chest with an arm that ends in a bandaged stump.

"We're all survivors, Sam," Goldie says. "Like you."

"Try not to stare, sweetheart," Big June says.

But Sam can't help herself. There's something achingly familiar about these girls, like phantoms from a past life.

"Did the priest do this?"

"They have their own monsters, Sam. You know that." Goldie sets the waffles on Big June's table and steps back. "Sit, please, you need your strength."

"Strength for what?" Her head throbs, her ankle burns. The scenery keeps titling.

"To make it through this." Big June stands, and together she and Goldie guide Sam into the booth, forever unfazed by her pickaxe. Their kindness weakens her. Her axe-arm slumps to the table. She loosens her fingers but doesn't let go completely.

They sit across from her with gentle eyes.

"What's next for me?" Sam whispers, reluctant. The question spills past the night, past tomorrow, it bleeds into a thousand Sundays.

"It's different for everyone," Goldie says. "Tonight, for you, help is coming. But only you can decide what you do with it."

"I don't understand."

"That's why we start small."

Big June nudges the waffles across the table. "I hear these are world-famous. Cinnamon fried."

Sam's stomach crawls. Hunger is for people who still have sisters.

"These were her favorite."

"Tell us, sweetheart. Tell us about her. Tell us anything you need."

"She was … she …" But there are no words. How do you sum up someone who was *everything*? Sam swallows a sob and shakes her head.

"That's okay. Maybe it'll help if *we* start." Big June sets her trucker hat on the table and pulls back her long silver hair. Her left ear is missing. "There're lots of stories here tonight."

"We're the lucky ones." Goldie lifts her chin, exposing that ropy scar. "I know that doesn't feel true. But there's one thing every woman here can hold on to, one thing that makes us very rare, but very important."

Big June leans in. "We got the bastards that did this to us."

The two women replay their victories for Sam in low voices. Stories of courage, of resilience, of overcoming the darkness against all odds. They tell her about the other survivors, too, filling Sam's head with masked killers and relentless maniacs—and all the impossible, beautiful ways these everyday girls took the bastards' heads or burned them alive or simply kicked their asses back to Hell. With every tale, Sam's mind spins faster, whirring round and round, until she's certain she's heard this all before. Dread closes around her, icy fingers of déjà vu.

Out in the parking lot, the fog thickens and the first falling lines of raindrops glow green in the light from the neon sign. The storm is catching up with her. Sam's fingers twitch around the pickaxe; the clean steel head catches the light and winks. Her heart starts pounding.

She takes a deep breath.

"He kept us in the pews for three days."

"Oh, sweetheart." Big June squeezes her hand.

"The first days were hot, Jake's body started to rot and stink. But on the third day, the rain came …"

Sam can still see him, enormous in the candlelight. He paced in front of Jake's bloating remains, raving about the stench, blaming the girls and their sticky bodies. So vulgar, so weak, so deserving of punishment. At first, the fury of the storm punctuated his words, but eventually the thunderheads outperformed him. The monster stepped down from his altar.

But only to baptize his trembling sunken-eyed congregation.

He removed their shackles, one savaged girl at a time, and took them into the rain. While he was outside with Brie, Claire sprung to life.

I saw tools in the graveyard before. I'm gonna try and grab one. This is our chance, Sam, do you hear me? You gotta be ready to fight!

When it was Claire's turn for the rain, she locked eyes with Sam.

Be ready.

But nothing could've prepared Sam for the last five minutes of her sister's life.

Even over the storm, the roar the priest let out shook the bones of the church. Seconds later, Claire burst inside dripping rainwater and hoisting a pickaxe over one shoulder. She rushed to Sam's side, powerful and radiant. Shawnee and Brie cried for her help—but it was Sunday and on Sundays sisters come first.

Show me your ankle, nerd.

With shaking hands, Claire slid the point of the pickaxe into the shackle, between the cuff and Sam's ankle.

Do you know what you're doing?

Saw it in a movie once.

I love you.

I love you, too. But after I do this, you have to run, okay, nerd? Run like hell and don't look back. I'll be right behind you.

"But she wasn't," Sam sobs. "She stayed to help her friends and he came back and ripped the pickaxe away and he … that fucker, he …"

"It's okay, sweetheart," Big June says, drawing Sam back into the present. "You don't have to say it. Not this part."

"But, please, Sam." Goldie leans forward, a gleam of urgency in her eyes. "Tell us how you ended him."

"He killed the others, and he chased me through the rain, didn't take him long with my ankle. He dragged me back inside."

"What happened next?"

"He slammed my head against the altar. That was it. He thought he killed me. He piled me with their bodies and I slept for the longest time. I wanted to die. I wanted it to be *over*. Claire was dead. I wanted to be dead, too. If I was stronger, if I was Claire, maybe I could get up and fight. But then what? Claire messed up my ankle when she broke my chain and I was still lost in the middle of nowhere. Even if I killed him, I was gonna die out there. But then. But then I got up."

"You got up?"

Goldie and Big June lean in. The rain beats against the window.

"I took the pickaxe and I—" Sam's mind flashes bright white. The swing of the pickaxe and then—then she was chasing the brake lights on Big June's eighteen-wheeler.

Someone screams.

"Out there!" The blonde in the wool sweater backs away from the window.

The café erupts. High-tension girls flock to the windows to get a better look. The blonde raises a machete; another holds a crucifix to the glass.

What's happening?

At first, Sam misses it.

Nothing out there but fog and rain and random cracks of lightning.

Then a hulking shape materializes inside the misty ether, stepping forward, moving with slow and sinister intent toward the café.

"That's the thing about these bastards." Big June slides her hat into place and stands to face the night. "Sometimes they come back."

***

The survivors line the windows and watch the spectacle of the shape lurking in the rain.

"What's he doing?" someone cries.

"Who is he? Can you see his weapon?"

"This can't be happening! I won't survive a second fight."

Several girls shout in agreement. Others want to rush out and brawl. Every voice rises up at once. Sam would cover her ears, but a dark certainty freezes her in place. The shape faces the café, waiting, watching, as if scanning a smorgasbord.

"It'll be okay, ladies," Goldie says, but a crack in her voice tells Sam otherwise.

"Does anyone recognize him?" Big June sounds equally tortured, as if she's selecting a maiden for sacrifice. Nobody answers, but Sam's heart thunders.

The shape in the rain produces a shovel. The girls cry out, but he doesn't come forward.

He starts digging.

His shovel should strike sparks on the asphalt. Instead, the rhythmic gritty sound of metal biting through grave soil fills the café as if blasted from overhead speakers.

"He's mine," Sam hears herself say.

She slides from the booth and starts to swing the pickaxe over her shoulder. But her hand hangs empty. Her weapon is gone. Vanished!

"My pickaxe! Who took it?"

"Did you ever really have it?" Goldie and Big June step backward, and their expressions conceal something terrible.

"Help is coming," they say, but Sam's beginning to think they're just blowing air.

The shape of the priest and his shovel dissolve into the thickening downpour. Sam only knows he's still out there because his shovel is relentless.

Digging and digging and digging.

The edges of the windows fog over and shards of moving color spread across the panes like a plague of stained glass. Everything coming together and unraveling at once. Axe-hand as empty as her future, head spinning, Sam starts to shout.

"He can't be alive!"

Digging and digging.

"He can't! I killed him, I—"

But the untruth in her voice is as sharp as the sudden jingle of the front door swinging open. The others cry out, and an unexpected visitor steps inside, dripping rain across the floor.

A foxy redhead with blue bunny slippers and a stack of old

movies.

"Hey, nerd," Claire says. "Ready to go?"

***

"How do you think they get home?"

"How does who get home?" Claire grabs the video from the VCR, makes sure the tape matches the box, then shelves it.

"The boring, smart chicks," Sam says. "After they decapitate the monster or whatever, ninety percent of the time they're still stranded in the middle of nowhere. All by themselves."

"I don't know, they hitchhike. Some old lady trucker'll find 'em."

"And then what? Go to some clueless police station, some cold hospital to be poked and prodded? What happens when the authorities don't believe their stories? Their best friends are gone. Their lives will never be the same. Doesn't get more isolating than that. So, what then? How do they figure out their futures all alone?"

"You're overthinking it, nerd."

"Am I?"

"We still talking about movies here?"

"I don't know. Yes." Sam crosses her arms over her UCLA sweatshirt.

Her big sister appraises her, seems to be deciding how serious she wants to spin this.

The spirit of Sunday mornings wins out.

"If it was up to me, they'd all end up at the same shiny, little roadside diner, a meeting place for the sisterhood, every last boring, smart chick to ever kick ass and live to tell about it. And the waitress who runs the joint will serve waffles—they won't be as good as mine, of course—but she'll listen to their horror stories forever and ever and—"

Sam snickers. "That sounds amazingly awful."

"Right?" Claire flashes a goofball grin. "Lucky for you, nerd, it's all pretend."

***

Claire stands in the doorway.

Every survivor in the Clover Café holds her breath. Every heart misses a beat.

Then Sam runs to her big sister.

She throws her arms around her and squeezes tight, so, so tight. It's impossible, Claire shouldn't be here, but it doesn't matter. In this moment every Sunday in history collides. They're a team, everything will be just as Sam always imagined.

Except, Claire isn't hugging her back.

The videotapes waterfall from her hand and her rain-soaked body presses against Sam, cold and stiff. Lightning cracks the sky, flash-illuminating the pickaxe protruding from her neck.

Oh, God, Claire …

"Good luck, sweetheart," Big June says. "We truly hope you make it."

"Yes," Goldie says. "Come back soon."

Sam lets go of her sister and steps back, breathing through the scream. For a heartbeat, Claire remains upright. For a heartbeat, their eyes seem to lock.

You gotta be ready to fight!

Digging and digging and digging.

The neon sign in the parking lot goes dark. All the beautiful, badass survivors nod at Sam then sink back into their seats as the interior of the Clover Café flickers and dims. Vinyl seats and polished countertops decay and dissolve into the ethereal darkness at the back of Sam's mind. Warm butter and cinnamon become a putrefied reek. This wistful other reality exhales a death rattle and in a blur Claire and Sam are all that remain. Them, and the scrape of his shovel.

Digging and digging.

Claire topples forward, knocking Sam down with her. They land inches apart. The stiff weight of several corpses presses the air from Sam's chest while Claire goes on staring. Face bloodless and doughy, one cheek scrunched against grimy floorboards. Her marble eyes implore Sam. Then she too fades into the dark.

Out in the rain, the shovel stops. He's coming.

No pretending this time.
You gotta fight!
Sam opens her eyes.

Open All Night
L.S. Johnson

THE PLANE BOUNCED AND LURCHED THROUGH THE AIR, making everyone huddle deeper in their seats, as if that would somehow make a difference. The little window was smeared with rain; through the gray-black clouds Erin could glimpse lights far below, their distance speaking of long, straight roads through acres of wheat or corn. What else grew in fields that large? She didn't know, and felt foolish for not knowing.

The plane gave a sickening, sideways jerk and she clutched her knapsack tighter. Everything important to her was inside. She had two weeks before rent was due again; she had one more paycheck coming but it wouldn't be enough to cover it. She had already started giving away possessions in case she was evicted, though she could not quite fathom it. How had it come to this? She could not say, could not put her finger on exactly when her security had started eroding, or when that erosion had become an avalanche. There was no one she felt comfortable asking for help, not four-figure help, not *can I sleep on your couch indefinitely* help. Everyone was so scattered now, their communication intermittent if at all, and now this family death: her last uncle, and with his passing a last, morbid glimmer of hope, for he had left her something in his will.

It said something, that this plane ticket was cheaper than her rent, even if she had paid for it with miles from her now-maxed credit card. It said something, that she was flying back on her cousin's blithe announcement, so casual over the phone. *Looks like he kept his promise to leave everything to us kids.* It said something that Erin desperately needed to be a *kid*, just once more.

The plane rocked and jittered and suddenly, terrifyingly, fell. A straight drop, long enough for her to think *oh, God, oh, God, I'm not ready*. There were screams, cries; a cart sailed halfway down the aisle, spewing dirty food trays and wadded-up napkins. Her heart pounding, bile in her mouth, cold sweat drenching her—

And just as suddenly the plane settled again, as if nothing had happened. The woman next to her began weeping, holding a shaking hand over her face.

"Sorry about that, folks," the pilot said, as genially as if they'd run out of pillows. "We're being instructed to land and wait this storm out. We'll be touching down at the nearest airport."

Another chorus, this time of groans and curses. Still the woman wept, taking shuddering breaths to try and calm herself.

Erin turned back to the window, her heartbeat thudding in her ears. Lightning flashed in the clouds, the mark of some dread god at work. And if they had kept falling, had gone down into that sparse grid of lights nose-first like a cartoon? An explosion, a spray of debris. The rescue crews picking over it in the morning, holding up the sorry remains of her sorry life. Dying wherever this was, neither where she was supposed to be nor anyplace she could even name. A good a way as any to just *stop*.

✳✳✳

Wherever they were, it was the smallest airport Erin had ever been to. It was so small there were no jetways; they had to wait while stairs were brought, because there were only two sets and other planes had landed before theirs to wait out the storm. They finally disembarked in a swirl of soft, white snow that was gathering on the runway. The lights of the terminal showed the flurries in sharp relief; beyond the single building sat the dark, hulking form of a second plane, snow already blanketing it. If there were other planes, she couldn't see them.

They hurried into the warmth of the building where a long, winding line led to the only open desk. Others pushed past her, eager to get ahead; she started to join the line but something about their faces, grim and bathed in bluish fluorescents, made her turn towards the phone booths. The stores were shuttered; half the overhead lights were dark. She should at least tell her cousin what had happened, where she was.

The receiver was crackling, but it managed to connect, the ringing hollow and tinny. And ringing and ringing, no answering machine, no one home. The enormity of it hit her then: how far she still must be, too far for a taxi or a bus or perhaps even a train. How little money she had on her. And if she didn't make it? Her family liked performances, they liked theatrical hugs when greeting and thank-you cards for the smallest gestures and somber, all-black grief at funerals. If she wasn't there, if she wasn't *making the effort*, if she couldn't even *show up when it mattered*, what would become of her inheritance?

Shaken, she joined the back of the line again. The man in front of her was fumbling through his briefcase, pulling out one paper after another; he gave her a disapproving look.

"You should have gotten on line when you first got here. Now you might not get a room."

Erin shrugged. She couldn't afford one anyway. She just wanted to know when they'd be taking off again, or if they'd be moved to another flight. Her indifference seemed to further annoy the man; he turned his back to her and kept pawing through his briefcase. The papers inside were densely handwritten, some stapled together in thick booklets.

"If you don't get a room," he said to the papers, "don't say I didn't warn you."

"What room?" a woman asked derisively from further up the line. She was craning her head back, watching them intently from behind cat's-eye glasses. "We're the fourth plane routed here. You think they got rooms for a thousand people in a place like this?"

"Where are we, anyway?" another man asked. Younger than Erin, but his jacket was leather and the suitcase in his hand was monogrammed. No one answered his question. He was eating a sandwich, still half-wrapped with wax paper; people were watching him surreptitiously, their lips miming biting, chewing. A little girl reached for it and her mother pulled her back hard.

Still the line didn't move. People began to look ahead impatiently, straining to see what was happening. Erin leaned forward, stretching her sore back. Had someone gone to the airport to meet her? Would they know, would they understand what had happened? She checked her watch, thinking to call again, but it had stopped.

"Do you have the time?" she asked the man before her.

He was turning a paper one way and another, reading the lines of tight script that ran to the edges and then up and down the sides. When she asked him again he glared at her.

"Why should I tell you that?" he demanded, his voice loud enough that others turned and looked at them.

She flushed and looked away. Why should he tell her that? Why should anyone do anything for her? There was no reason. *Just an old man*, she told herself, but it did not stop the tears from stinging her eyes, her throat from closing. Abruptly, she walked towards the darkened hall and the signs that said Taxi and Baggage Claim. Like a little girl. Ridiculous to be so upset. But as soon as she rounded the corner she leaned against a wall and cried, her tears hot and wrenching, and then just as swiftly the storm vanished. She wiped her face, trying to think.

"You can't stay here," a woman's voice said.

Erin looked up to see an older woman in a plain blue smock. *Hel*, her badge said.

"You can't sleep here, if that's what you're thinking," she continued. "They shut this place completely for a few hours each night. Bathrooms are already locked." She nodded over Erin's shoulder, back at the fluorescent glow. "They'll find you a place to stay. City's only an hour ride from here, the hotels've been sending shuttles."

"Oh." Erin tried to think, where could she go? Past Hel she could see wide glass doors. Snow swirled in the pools of yellow light, gathering in drifts. "Do the shuttles go downtown?"

At her question Hel frowned, then came close. "There's nothing open downtown, hon," she said more gently. "We got laws about that. No place you can ride this out, not without paying for a room. Everyone has to pay here."

"Oh," Erin said again. She suddenly felt very small, and afraid. She looked down at her thin canvas sneakers; she imagined the snow seeping in, that icy wetness. Swallowing, she began to turn. "I, ah, I guess I'll get in line then—"

"How much money do you have?" Hel asked. Her lined face earnest. There was a haze of gray where her roots were showing beneath the reddish-brown dye. Chunky plastic butterflies dangled from her ears.

"A hundred and thirteen dollars and twenty-seven cents," Erin blurted out. Enough for a taxi from the airport if no one was waiting, and black stockings, and to pay her way at meals. Enough to look like she wasn't desperate. One more paycheck coming, but it wasn't enough for the rent. How had she let things go so far?

"Better than I thought," Hel said, and she smiled then, revealing a line of pearly capped teeth. She dug in the smock's pocket and came up with a business card. "Go out to the taxi stand and ask for Steve. Tell him your ride's on Hel. Rooms here are about thirty bucks."

Erin took the little white rectangle. *Candlelight Inn*, the front read, above a drawing of a candle with a moth circling it. On the back it said simply *Open All Night*.

"Thank you," she said.

"No need to thank me. I was once just like you. Someone helped me get where I needed to go, and now I do the same." She laid a warm, comforting hand on Erin's shoulder. "I hope you get to where you need to be."

Erin thanked her again. She felt Hel's gaze on her back as she followed the Taxi signs, but she didn't turn around, felt she shouldn't turn around. Only when she was nearly at the doors did she realize she didn't know when to come back to the airport, or how she would get here.

I can call from my room, she thought, and kept moving. Getting where she needed to be.

***

Erin had forgotten snow. Not the cold of it, or the wet seeping into her sneakers as she found Steve's taxi and clambered in, but the way the cold damp painted her sinuses. It brought back a flood of memories: of being small, of school, of being another person. Her apartment now was in a western city, bone-dry air and only brief, terrible rains. This snow felt like taking up a long-forgotten burden.

She huddled on the back seat, her face parched by the heater, listening to the squeak-slap of the wipers.

"Hel's good people," Steve was saying. He was balding; plastic stays poked through the frayed collar of his blood-red shirt. Erin remembered her father, a sharp, painful memory that she pushed away. "We go way back, Hel and I. Been lost ourselves. Maybe she told you."

I'm not lost, she started to say, but wasn't she, in a way? Unable to find her way home, and where even was *home* anymore?

"Hel's very kind," she said instead.

"Not much of that left in the world. Good music and kindness: both started disappearing after '69." He leaned over and turned up the radio. "Hear that? Now that's real music. That there is the Creedence Clearwater Revival."

But Erin knew that already. Everything was prodding at her, reminding her of moments she had long pushed away. *Let me remember things I love.* For a moment it wasn't Steve in the front of the car but her parents, singing; where had they been going? To some relative's house. Perhaps the uncle who had died. All so long ago.

She saw Steve's eyes on her in the rearview mirror, realized he was waiting for a response.

"My parents liked Creedence," she said.

"Then your parents had taste. They still around?"

"No." No one was around anymore. She was falling through the snowy darkness and there was no one to catch her. Betting her future on the will of a man she hadn't seen in years. What a fool she was.

"My condolences. But you're proving my theory: that's a little less taste and kindness in the world, with them gone."

Had her parents been kind? Erin couldn't remember. She remembered hugs, singing. Franks and beans for dinner. Watching her father's hands, how she knew when his knuckles shifted from pink to white that she needed to apologize, that she had something to be sorry for.

The music changed, thankfully losing that awful specificity, still familiar but in the way supermarket music was familiar. Snow whipped past the window, obscuring her view. There was only darkness, punctuated by the occasional streetlamp; sometimes she saw a pinprick of light, but whether real or imagined she could not say. She could be anywhere. Perhaps the plane had truly fallen; perhaps she was dead. Snow and the oily heat of the car and rock 'n' roll: there were worse afterlifes, or so she had been told by her fervent grandmother, pulling Erin close in the kitchen and drawing heaven and hell on a memo pad. The one filled with smiley faces, the other with frowns and pitchforks.

Good girls go here.

How long since she had thought of any of this? Was there something wrong with her?

You're a strange stray cat, the radio sang, as if in explanation.

"So, hey, miss. I don't know if Hel told you about the Candlelight?" Steve's voice jerked Erin back into herself; she forced a smile as she caught his gaze in the mirror again. "The place is fine, great people there. They'll take good care of you." He hesitated. "Only—if you need something to eat, the only food is the diner at the crossroads, and it's pretty rough. All-night truck stops are no place for a woman alone. If you're hungry, ask Todd to order something for you. Don't go there yourself. Okay?"

"Okay," Erin said.

He seemed about to say more, but a glow filled the windscreen, soft at first and then brightening. They rounded a bend and the crossroads came into view. A gas station, the diner, a large parking lot filled with trucks, and, atop a little rise, the Candlelight Inn. Each planted at one corner of the crossroads. At the center of the intersection, atop a traffic island, a sign on an impossibly high pole read OPEN ALL NIGHT, sun-bright. In the distance she could just glimpse paired lights moving back and forth: a highway of some kind.

She kept looking at the diner as the taxi wound its way up to the inn's office. The big, glass windows were brightly lit, showing a classic diner interior, all chrome and vivid colors. It didn't look so terrifying. A lot of men sitting alone, and a woman, too, seated at a central booth. She wore something sleeveless and black, and her dark brown hair hung loose down her back; before her was a tantalizingly large plate heaped with red. There was a waitress in a pink uniform, walking the aisle with a pot of coffee. Safe enough for them. Steve probably thought Erin was younger than she really was; many men did.

You're a strange stray cat

He pulled in front of the office door and turned around, laying an arm along the seat back. "Here you go, Erin. Take care now. You need another lift, you tell Todd to ring me."

"Thank you," she said earnestly. "I really appreciate it."

"I know you do," he said.

She gathered up her knapsack, smiled and nodded. The cold shocking after the car's heat. Hurriedly, she got out, sinking into ankle-deep snow, and shoved the door of the taxi closed. Steve watched her as she stepped onto the concrete walkway, stamping the snow off her feet, and went to the glass door of the office, a blue-white rectangle in the darkness.

At the door she gave an awkward little wave. Still he lingered, his somber gaze on her. Only when the door shut behind her did he roll away, the snow churning around the car like a ship cutting through surf.

Inside, the office was painfully bright from the massive, buzzing fluorescent light overhead. Walls, ceiling, and floor were all flat white, though the floor was marred by years of scuff marks like strange writing. There was a vending machine with toiletries, and a dusty plastic ficus in a corner. At the furthest point from the door was a window set into the wall, a rectangle of thick plastic with wire embedded in it and a round grille, like a bank teller's window. There was even a little hollow in the sill beneath.

Melting snow trickled down Erin's legs and formed dark spatters on her too-thin coat. As she tried to wipe it off a man came to the window, emerging from what seemed like a showroom's worth of office furniture crammed into the room behind him. Sprays of pimples dotted his forehead and chin, yet lines crinkled around his eyes. On one of the desks was a bowl of nachos, bright yellow cheese and orange chips; though she knew they would taste revolting her eyes kept coming back to them.

"You Hel's girl?" the man asked as he slid a piece of paper and pen under the window.

Erin hesitated, then nodded. Maybe she was getting a discount of some kind. She filled in the form, then pushed it back through.

"That'll be thirty-two ninety-nine, cash only," the man said. "And I need to see your license."

She put the money and her license through the little slot and waited while he withdrew into the forest of office furniture. As soon as she got to her room she would call. Stranded. Not her fault. Perhaps, too, she could risk a little lie, something about a rebooking fee, about a too-expensive room and taxi, if perhaps she could just borrow some money once she got there, she'd pay them back as soon as she returned home —

Or got her inheritance?

Oh, please, oh, please, let there be an inheritance …

The door flew open, letting in a gust of icy air, and a woman came in. Older than Erin, wearing only a tank top and drastically ripped jeans despite the weather, though her feet were clad in thick furred boots. She barely glanced at Erin, instead going straight to the vending machine where she began feeding in coins.

From the midst of the desks, the man looked up, frowning; his frown deepened when he saw the woman, but he went back to his paperwork.

At last, the woman yanked on a knob: a shaving kit, tiny razor and tiny can of foam. The metal coil holding the kits duly rotated, but when it stopped the foremost one was balanced on the edge, one corner still stuck in the coil.

"Goddamn it!" The woman jerked the handle back and forth,

but the kit didn't budge. She tried to shake the machine, then raised one booted foot and gave the machine a hard kick. The sound loud enough that Erin flinched instinctively.

"Hey!" The man came to the window. "Don't you fucking do that! Don't you fucking do that, you hear me?"

"You said you were getting it fixed, *Todd*," the woman retorted. She kicked it again.

"Do that again and I'm calling the boss. Understand?" He raised his thumb and pinky to his face, miming a receiver. "And for the last fucking time, stop calling me Todd." With a grimace he pushed Erin's change and license under the window. "Just gotta get your key," he added, his face flushed.

"Who's gonna evict me in this weather?" the woman asked, clearly not expecting an answer. But she didn't kick the machine again; instead, she sidled up beside Erin. She smelled of cigarettes and a too-sweet shampoo. "Come on, Todd," she said, her voice coaxing. "I'm going out tonight. Don't you have extras back there?"

"Call me Todd again, Marion, and I'll make that phone call," he retorted, unlocking a cabinet on the wall.

"Who's Marion, Todd?" But she turned to Erin, holding up her arms. "Would you go on a date with pits like this?"

There was indeed dark stubble; Erin made what she hoped was a sympathetic noise.

"Here you go." Not-Todd pushed a key with a large plastic diamond attached to it, showing a number 6. "Checkout's at noon. Oh, and don't go down to the diner. If you want something to eat you can tell me. I'll take care of it."

Erin took the key. Her eyes flitted to the nachos again, and her stomach growled.

"A sandwich would be nice," she blurted out. What would be cheapest? "Just—just cheese, or tuna salad? Something light," she added hopefully. Light was usually less money.

"Why shouldn't she go to the goddamn diner?" Marion put in. "No one warned me about the goddamn diner when I first came here. Why does she get a warning and I didn't?"

"I wouldn't know," he snapped, "as I'm not fucking Todd." He turned back to Erin. "I'll call your sandwich in. Go to the far end of the rooms, turn left at the laundry. You'll see number nine."

A 9, not a 6. Of course: she was looking at it upside down. She turned to go, only to see Marion staring at the key; she felt oddly ashamed and shoved it in her coat pocket.

"Thank you," she said to not-Todd, and then to Marion, "I hope your date goes okay."

Marion blinked, then smiled at her. "Aw, you're sweet. Sweet enough to eat, my mom would say. Don't let him spook you about the diner. Delivery will take forever in this weather, and a woman can't live her life afraid."

Her father's white knuckles. Of course you could live in fear. People did it every day.

"It's fine, really. I can wait. Goodness knows I'm not dressed for snow."

"God helps those who help themselves."

"Leave her alone, Marion," not-Todd said.

"I appreciate it, but I'd rather wait all the same." Erin gathered up her knapsack.

"Too sweet for your own good," Marion said. "Reminds me of another woman who stayed here once, what was her name?"

"What does it matter what her name was?" not-Todd said. "Everyone's someone else here."

And there was something in his voice, a sharpness, that quieted Marion at last. With an awkward smile and nod, Erin took the opening and hurried to the door. Again, the staring, the two of them watching her open the door, watching her step outside. She pulled the door closed behind herself and still they watched her. Snow seeping into her already-soaked shoes, she began picking her way through the rising drifts to the low strips of rooms.

****

There was a parking lot between the office and the rooms, not that large, but it seemed to take ages to cross. The drifts were rising, and

176

when Erin twisted her ankle on some hidden hazard—a pothole?—
she took to raising her foot high and stepping cautiously before
moving her full weight forward. The last thing she needed now was
to injure herself—or was it? She thought of a hospital bed, a quiet,
dim room, the steady beeps of monitors. She thought of everything
being put on *hold*, and was startled when her eyes welled.

Amidst the gusting wind came a cry, halfway between a shout
and a scream, and she froze in place, looking around in the
darkness. Again, that cry. She looked towards the crossroads and
saw a man standing outside the diner, his arms splayed wide, his
head thrown back to the night. Behind the glass windows the men
and the lone woman kept eating. A third cry, and he seemed to
deflate then, his whole body rolling forward into a hunched
stance. Slowly he turned and shuffled back into the diner.

And Erin was going to catch her death if she didn't get inside.
She continued her plodding journey towards the rows, groaning
a little as she saw the first room number: 36, then 35, then 34 …
the low numbers would be furthest in the back. Past each row of
rooms, twelve rooms to a row, each with a parking space in front,
lights showing through the drawn curtains. Many more lights
than cars out front. At last she reached the back row, longer than
the others because of the laundry room, and a sign with an arrow
pointing left: 1–12, and, underneath, No Outsiders Permitted.

Past the laundry room, where she glimpsed a middle-aged
woman folding clothing while a little girl in pajamas ran in circles
around her, making a cawing noise not unlike the diner man's
howl. Erin shuddered and curved widely to the left to avoid being
seen. 12, 11, 10, and at last 9. The key was smooth in the lock and
she felt something unknot in her shoulders as she opened the
door. Inside the room was dark. Her wet shoes squelched against
a linoleum floor; she shut the door and then felt on the wall for
the light switch. When she finally found it, a pendant light in front
of the window turned on, just enough to see by. A table and chair,
a dresser with a television precariously atop it, a queen bed—

And a suitcase, sitting on the bed.

It was a plain blue suitcase, one of thousands such. She had owned one just like it once. A spray of worn, dirty butterfly stickers covered its surface. Even in the dim light it seemed unnaturally vivid against the dark brown blanket.

She stared at the case for a long moment, thinking perhaps that cold and hunger were making her hallucinate. But the case remained, and when she finally stepped close and touched it, the hard blue plastic was solid beneath her fingers. No name, no tag, nothing to show whose it was.

And she was suddenly, unbearably tired. Another complication. Her feet were numb; she was wet through. She put her knapsack on the table and went to the bathroom; here another fluorescent buzzed merrily when she turned it on, painting her face in bluish highlights that made her look like a corpse. There was nothing in the bathroom save a wrapped bar of soap and a few folded towels. She peed, washed her hands and face with hot water, gratefully pressed the thin but wonderfully dry towel to herself.

Even when her back was turned she could feel the suitcase on the bed, filling the room with its presence. She considered bringing it to the office, but the thought of that long, cold walk made her shudder. Instead she picked up the phone.

"Yes," not-Todd answered without preamble.

"This is room nine—"

"I know. What's wrong?"

She took a breath. "There's a suitcase in my room."

"Okay."

"Well, what should I do with it?"

"Just put it aside," he said. "Someone will take care of it in the morning."

Her toes were stinging. She flexed her hand, marveling at how chapped her knuckles had become in such a short time.

"What if the owner comes back for it?"

"Room's been empty for three days," he said. "No one's coming back."

"Oh." Still she felt uneasy. She didn't even want to touch it; it felt wrong to touch it. "Couldn't you come and get it?"

"I'm locked in, sorry."

"Oh," she said again.

"Was there anything else?"

"No—wait," she said hurriedly. "If you're locked in, how will I get my sandwich?"

"The diner's taking care of it." He sounded annoyed now. "There're vending machines in the laundry room in the meantime. Sodas, chips, that sort of thing."

"Oh." She heard herself and felt foolish. "Well, thanks?"

"Sure," he replied. "Was there anything else?"

"Should I say something when I check out? About the suitcase?"

"*I'll* tell Todd when he comes in." His voice was sharp, the same tone that had silenced Marion. "It's my job after all."

"Of course." Then, before she could help herself: "Only—when does Todd come in?"

"Whenever the storm's over," he said, and hung up the phone.

****

Before she began to peel off her wet things, Erin ventured forth once more, to the laundry room at the end of the row. *Vending machines*, he had promised her. *Sodas, chips*. It was something, and her mother had always said something was better than nothing.

Why was she thinking so much about them, why were they in her head at all?

The lights from the laundry room glowed like a beacon. Past 10, dark and silent; past 11, blue-bright from television; past 12, with only that front lamp on. There were pictures taped to the window of 12, coloring book pages of butterflies like the ones on the suitcase. How long had these people been here, that they were decorating the window? She thought back to Marion, calling the clerk by the wrong name: like a routine.

But her musings were blasted away by the dry heat of the laundry room. She felt scalded, painfully aware of every spot of moisture pressing against her skin. Every dryer was spinning, their combined movement like the engine of some great ship. The

179

middle-aged woman was still there, folding a vast amount of laundry with steady, precise movements. Three tall, plastic bins surrounded her, each heaped with clothing; on the chairs were smaller bins labeled with numbers. When Erin shut the door the woman gave her a brief smile.

"If you want your clothes washed, prices are on the wall," she said. "I've got four ahead of you, but I'll get it to you before noon."

"Thanks, but I just wanted the vending machines," Erin replied, surveying their contents. As not-Todd had said: sodas and chips, but there was also a bag of mixed fruit and nuts, and a row of cans labeled Juice Drink.

She fumbled in her pocket for her loose change when a small voice behind her said, "Are you staying here?" Looking down, she saw the little girl, now snug in a hooded sweatshirt, eating from one of the potato chip packs.

"Uh, yes." She smiled briefly at her, and the little girl smiled back.

"We're in room twelve, aren't we, mama?"

"That's right, sweetie," the woman at the table said.

"Where are you?" the little girl asked.

"Room nine," Erin said, counting out her quarters.

There was silence behind her. She glanced down at the little girl again and was met with an openmouthed stare. The woman just kept folding, her movements steady, like she hadn't heard Erin at all.

"Don't use your change," the little girl said suddenly. She came around Erin, digging into the pocket of her sweatshirt with a greasy hand.

"Didi," the woman said.

"But you said we ought to help them," Didi replied, a whine in her voice. When her mother stayed silent, she drew out a dollar bill with a long strip of plastic attached to it—packing tape, Erin realized, folded over to make a kind of tail.

"What would you like?" she asked.

Erin pointed at the fruit and nut pack. Didi made a face but handed Erin her half-full packet of potato chips, then moved close to the machine. Whispering nonsense syllables, she carefully inserted the dollar bill. Just as it seemed to vanish she yanked it back by the tape, then pressed the buttons for the fruit and nut pack. The coil spun, the pack dropped, and she held it out to Erin with a flourish.

Erin exchanged the fruit and nut pack for the potato chip bag. "Thank you," she said.

Didi clapped her hands, beaming. "Now, what would you like to drink—"

"That's enough now," her mother put in. "You know how Todd feels about your trick. Everything has to be paid for in the end, remember?"

"I can pay—" Erin began.

"No, no, it's done now." The woman sighed. "But you're better off without any of those sodas, they're far too sweet. Drink one now and you won't sleep tonight, and you need to sleep through this storm."

"Is it going to get worse?" Erin asked.

"Everything gets worse before it gets better," she replied.

"I'm supposed to fly out tomorrow."

"Oh, I wouldn't bet on that." The woman glanced at her, her gaze hard. "I wouldn't bet on anything right now." Before Erin could reply, she went to a dryer, opened it, and began pulling out what looked like army fatigues.

"Well." Erin felt scolded and uneasy, why did she feel uneasy? "Thank you for the snacks. This should tide me over until I get my sandwich."

At that, the woman spun around.

"You're going down to the diner?"

Didi gasped, her eyes huge again.

"No! No, I mean, the man in the office ordered a sandwich to be sent to my room." She smiled reassuringly.

The woman nodded, but her expression was still uneasy. "Well. Todd's not the worst, all things considered. Just be careful where and how you go. With a storm like this anything could happen."

"I will." She looked down at Didi. "Thank you again."

"Welcome," the little girl replied, then stuffed a fistful of potato chips in her mouth.

Outside the snow was falling more heavily, or was it just in her mind, responding to the woman's suggestion? *Worse before it gets better. Anything could happen.* All distinction between walkways and parking lot seemed to have vanished, smoothed into one blue-gray expanse dappled with lights. A small, bare strip remained in front of the doors to the rooms, where the overhanging roof kept the snow at bay. Everything else was being erased.

Which was a ridiculous thing to think. Erin felt faint; she was hungrier than she had realized. Would anyone be able to get food to her? She went to the far end of the laundry room, stepping tentatively lest she twist her ankle again, and peered down at the crossroads. In the swirl of white, the buildings were barely visible, but she glimpsed men outside the diner. Shirtless men. They stood in the glare of the windows, forming a kind of circle, while two grappled in the center; they shook their fists in the air and slapped each other on the shoulder. Inside the diner, the woman was watching, kneeling on the bench seat to get a better view, her shadowed face pressed against the glass—

Erin blinked to get the snow out of her eyes, and when she looked again all she could see was white.

Unnerved, she went back to her room. As she passed the laundry room once more she saw Didi feeding the soda machine her dollar bill, her lips moving as she did so. The woman was staring at the window, at Erin, her arms overflowing with satin underthings.

Erin quickened her pace, wanting nothing more than to shut the door on all of it.

***

Back in her room, she locked the door, then prized her wet shoes from her feet and put them under the heater, laying her drenched socks over the vents. Out of her pants, wet to the knee, and into the sweatpants she had brought to sleep in, to chat with whichever of her relatives would put her up, the better to pretend she was there out of the kindness of her heart.

Out of the kindness of her heart, she finally picked up the phone and called. This time, however, there wasn't even ringing, only a staticky buzzing in her ear. She hit the receiver and tried to dial the front desk: the same noise. The storm must have pulled the lines down. She ate a handful of fruit and nuts and turned on the television. Her stomach nearly cramping over the food as she flipped through screen after screen of snow, the lines of static laced with images of cars backed up, snow in drifts, flames in an open space with toy-sized fire trucks before it—a crash? There was no way to adjust the picture; when she turned up the volume there was only the gentle *wooosh* of static. The clock radio the same: faint, incomprehensible voices between walls of noise.

She ate more of the fruit and nuts, went into the bathroom and poured herself a little glass of water. The face in the mirror was more lined than she knew it to be, her eyes sitting in purpled sockets. Like looking at herself five, ten years hence. Like looking at herself made undead.

From the window, Erin watched the whiteness pour down from the sky, saw with alarm how the snow was piling almost to the windowsill. She might be snowed in tomorrow; she might not be able to get back to the airport. How many days could she afford to stay here? How would she eat? No delivery would make it tonight, that was for certain. Panic made her mouth taste sour; she wanted nothing more than to sleep it all away.

But that meant dealing with the suitcase.

She had been circling it all this time. Contorting herself to avoid touching it or sitting next to it. It occupied the bed as a drunk had occupied her bed once, long ago when she shared a house: half-awake, belligerent, grunting every time she tried to move him. She had slept in a corner of her room that night, hating herself for not being more assertive. The story of her life: making herself smaller and smaller when imposed upon, until she had nothing, was nothing.

The drunk had been gone when she awoke that morning, but

the suitcase—she was stuck with the suitcase, at least until she could carry it down to the office. She knew, instinctively, that neither Todd nor not-Todd was going to bother removing it. The Candlelight Inn was not a place that helped you with your baggage.

And she was being ridiculous again. It was just a suitcase. She could put it in the closet and forget about it. Tomorrow it would be someone else's problem.

She downed the last of the fruit and nuts, took a sip of water, and grabbed the handle. As she lifted it up the suitcase opened and an astonishing quantity of clothing tumbled onto the bed. Where there had been one neat suitcase, there was now a riot of fabrics, from wool to satin, with a pair of shiny black pumps sticking out from the folds.

Groaning, she laid the open suitcase on the bed once more. How had it all fit inside in the first place? It looked like three suitcases' worth. But there was nothing for it now. She would have to handle everything, and hope she was long gone before the owner returned.

She began folding the clothes, packing them in as tightly as she could. Slinky cocktail dresses, dainty camisoles: the kinds of things she never wore herself. Always she had felt too exposed, every roll and bulge laid bare to the world. Still, whoever their owner was, she and Erin were the same size, and they had similar taste. Erin found herself before the mirror with a particularly lovely silk dress, holding it up to herself and imagining herself on a warm summer's day. A different Erin, confident enough to wear a dress so thin, just a slip underneath. Confident and secure, with money in the bank, with no fear of the future.

Another Erin, in another universe.

She put away the dress, tucked the pumps in the suitcase, though she checked inside them as she did: again, just her size. She usually wore flats out of fear of twisting her ankle, but these were low, the heel thicker than usual and the leather buttery. Perhaps one day, perhaps if the inheritance was good.

When our ship comes in, as her mother would say.

She reached again into the pile of clothing and felt something rectangular and leathery. Her heart skipped a beat as she pulled out a long, slim wallet.

For a moment Erin just stared at it, and then, her hands trembling, she opened it. Credit cards, a driver's license. Money. Not a vast amount, not a criminal amount, but over a hundred at first glance.

Credit cards. Money.

She took the wallet over to the light, her heart racing now. The license even looked like her. *Reminds me of another woman who stayed here once.* Not a perfect likeness, no horror movie doppelgänger; but it looked more than a little like her. The dark brown hair was smooth, blunt cut, not Erin's overgrown layers; but the eyes were brown like hers, the straight nose, the hint of olive in the skin. Close enough that no one would look too closely, if they had no reason to.

Brenda Scapelli. Almost like a lyric, a rhyme. She could remember it easily enough. The signature on the cards was clear and rounded. With practice—

How long had the suitcase been there? Not-Todd had said three days, and the storm would make it difficult to return. What if she took the wallet and hid the rest in a drift? Why had she called the office and told them it was here?

It could be *something*, the something Erin found herself silently begging for, the outstretched hand, the erasing of her woes. If nothing else, it could guarantee that she would get to the funeral, no matter the weather …

She lay down on the bed, pressing her hand to her eyes. Her head was spinning from hunger and exhaustion both. Could be, couldn't be. What did the money, the credit cards matter right now? Nowhere to go, nothing to buy. She would have been better served to find food in the suitcase, say granola bars, or a bag of candy. She would commit violence for a steak and potatoes, for the sickly-sweet feeling of being gorged to fullness.

It was with visions of red meat that she fell asleep.

Open All Night

****

Erin awoke in the night to a muffled popping like fireworks. The room cold, so cold; the heater had stopped and the lights were out. Stiffly she went to the window. The snow had tapered off a little, but all of the inn was dark. The only light was the OPEN ALL NIGHT sign, as vivid as a full moon, and beneath it the glow rising up from the crossroads.

Another pop, and another; a faint sound like a scream. Erin jerked back from the window, frightened and shivering. Drew the curtains, checked the lock on the door. The clock radio was frozen at 11:59, the phone still a staticky buzz. Why hadn't she wound her watch earlier? It seemed important to place herself in time.

She heaped all the clothing atop the bedcovers and slid beneath the pile of fabric. Shivering, she could not stop shivering. But she had slept colder in her life.

And when she finally fell asleep she wasn't in the Candlelight Inn, broke and frightened and alone. She was a child again, at her grandmother's house, all her family reunited for a weekend. Sitting on the stool in the kitchen and everywhere women, her mother and grandmother and aunts and cousins all crowding together. She was watching as her mother scooped up ladleful after ladleful of macaroni and cheese and poured it into three aluminum trays, filling them nearly to the brim before sprinkling all with buttered breadcrumbs. Voices everywhere, music in the backyard. *Someday*, an aunt said, *you'll have a house just like this, with all your children.* Her child-self watching the knuckles of the men as they passed through, feeling at once separate and part-of, wanting to hide from them all even as she wanted to scream *look at me, see me —*

And then she was grown, in her first year in her new city, far from everything she knew, eating catered macaroni and cheese at a work party. Only this time it was made with a blend of artisan cheeses and dotted with ham and broccoli and topped with sourdough breadcrumbs, and it had tasted like shit, it had tasted

186

like the most bittersweet of victories, and every victory has a price.

***

The door to the room opened, letting in a gust of icy wind that tasted of damp. Erin rising to meet her—to meet *herself*—for her contours were as familiar as Erin's own, her shadowed face a shrouded mirror. Herself, her mother, her grandmother, friends she had lost over the years, they were all there, this *ur-woman* her dreaming brain managed, calling forth a phrase from college. All these women and now Brenda Scapelli, incongruous in a sleeveless black dress despite the snow falling around her.

Her face was expressionless as she surveyed the mound of her clothing, but when Erin began to explain she simply opened her bare arms wide and embraced Erin. Her body warm, her dress smelling of barbeque and her grandmother's roses, thick and sweet. Erin began weeping, weeping as she had not done since she was a child, and the woman steered her to the bed and sat them both down, pulling Erin onto her lap and rocking her as her mother would do.

I'm sorry, Erin whispered, or was it the woman? *I made so many wrong choices. I'm so sorry for everything. I—I just need someone to make it okay again. Please. Please just make things okay again. Please.*

As Erin's crying quieted, the woman began crooning, a tuneless singing that whited out all other sounds, even Erin's own heartbeat. She drew back then, trying to study the face smiling at her, but she could not focus on it. The features seemed to slide and reform in the darkness, the only constant that curving mouth, lips slightly parted. The arms were still loose about her; now they fell away, leaving her bereft. From the pile of clothing the woman drew forth a silk slip, gauzy as film, stroking the fabric with that same wondering smile. Erin found herself smiling too: it was as if this other-she had discovered silk for the first time. She drew the silk over her arms and face, then did the same to Erin. The fabric like a butterfly's kiss. The woman slid it again, and again, and then draped it completely over Erin's head. The world darkened further, shapes becoming gray-black fuzz. Erin smelled something in the fabric, a human smell, tang and pepper, and she began weeping again. It had been so long.

Cool hands smoothed the silk against her features, fingers stroking and pressing as if molding a mask. Erin inhaled and silk jerked against her nostrils; she inhaled again, the sharp gasp of a drowning woman, only to feel lips press through silk against her own, alien and intimate all at once. Still she struggled to breathe, the air clogging in the fabric. She parted her lips and tasted another breath, sour and without heat; she reached out to push back the crushing mouth but all she felt was cold air, as if the very storm was embracing her. Her nostrils flaring, silk flicking in and out like tiny bellows, and then a silk-covered tongue pushed into her mouth and she gulped air and silk, the silk was sticking to the back of her throat, she flailed at the cold air—

She looked wildly around and saw, framed by the half-drawn curtains, Didi's terrified moonlit face pressed to the glass—

Erin wrenched her arm from the cold and waved at the window: *run, get away!* The effort made lights dance in the corners of her eyes. Reflexively she inhaled, lungs pulling with all their might, and the silk filled her throat and the cold filled her bones.

***

Erin was lying on a pile of clothing, pants atop blouses atop dresses atop the flat mattress. Her lungs were still, her heart was still, but she was *aware*, she was suspended in her motionless body and she knew, somehow, that to try to speak, to try and so much as blink, would make her deathly stillness real and she would be snuffed out like a candle.

She was still Erin, and she was nothing. Her arms were folded against her chest, her knees were bent and swung up until she was curled in a ball. The hands busily began folding the fabric over and around her, swaddling her, the layers thickening like a cocoon.

More fabric was tucked gently over her face, smothering her completely. The total darkness.

And then she was bodily swung upwards and down again. Pressure crushed the thick layers above her, pushing her further down, down. The latches of the suitcase snapped like gunshots. The sound filled her with a bright panic that set her straining against her folded body, and then she wasn't there at all.

***

The fluorescent bulb hummed into life and Erin spilled the make-up into the bathroom sink, rummaging through brushes and compacts and tubes until she found the lipstick, worn to a bright red knob, all the edges gone.

She ran it with a practiced hand over her lips and in the mirror she was her grandmother, doing the same before going shopping; she was her mother in the early morning before work, already tired and her day not yet begun. Three strokes: the two halves of the bow of her upper lip, down to the corners, and then that thick glide along the plumpness of her bottom lip. As red as blood, as life.

You're a strange stray cat her lips mouthed.

She blotted her lips on a square of toilet paper, leaving the red O floating in the bowl.

***

In room nine, the men from the diner crowded in shoulder to shoulder, filling the space. They knelt in the center of the bed and sat on the edges, they sat on the table and the chair, they hunched in the closet and pressed into the corners of the room and blotted out the window. All of them bulky and warm and smelling of food, of hamburgers and meatloaf, of chili and chicken fried steaks and pot roasts. Dark and light, unshaven and layered with fat, some bespectacled and others wearing hats, in flannel shirts and sweatshirts with sports logos and graying t-shirts with quilted shirts over them. All of them in jeans worn to their bodies' contours.

Erin began to move through them, the silk dress making her slither past their fleshy bodies, aware of them silently watching her. Ahead, the door stood open, showing the clear dawn sky. She twisted and turned with each step, her shiny black pumps finding just enough space around their sneakers and construction boots. One draped his quilted shirt over her shoulders and she shot him a grateful smile; another held out her suitcase and she took it from him, returning his serious nod. Everything important to her inside.

She pushed and slid and twisted, holding the suitcase before her like a prow cutting surf, until she finally reached the door. The line of men ran all the way to the diner, just enough space between them for her to walk, the snow tamped down by their feet into a melting path. In the distance she saw the steam rising from the diner's kitchen. All the food she would eat.

Hands helped her down from the concrete walkway and across the parking lot, steering her around the potholes and steadying her over the lingering patches of ice. The morning was still and crisp-cold; the room windows were all the neutral beige of their drawn curtains. Behind Erin the men crowded in, following her, matching her pace like an army following their general. Grease on the wind, fresh and hot. Their outstretched hands touching her. Their expressionless faces watching her every move. Her stomach cramping in anticipation as the diner doors opened and the pink-uniformed waitress waved her inside.

Closing Time
Shanna Germain

DAL CAN ALREADY TELL IT'S GOING TO BE A BUSY NIGHT, but she doesn't mind. The more deals she makes, the sooner she completes her own deal, the sooner she finds out what's next. Or, rather, finds out if there is a next. She doubles the recipe for the pie crusts she's making, and watches the parking lot fill as she kneads the dough.

Not even dusk, and the lot is near-to-full, the easy spots long-gone, and then the gravel and grit ones going, and now, lastly and with some trepidation on the driver's part, the ones with the tall grasses and dirt divots, too. Another dozen people without vehicles, trying to look as if they belong here, in this diner parking lot, in their long-way-traveling clothes and their faces full of need and hope. One leans on the dumpster trying to pretend like they've got nowhere else in the world to be, like they haven't just found themselves in this weird and smelly place where they're second-guessing their life choices.

Dal's got a few daytime customers left, scraping their last bits of cherry and strawberry and lemon-curl pie off their plates, taking their last lukewarm sips of decaf. She doesn't hurry or worry them. She doesn't need to. Come the gloaming, something in them will tell them to go, and they will gather their things carefully, somehow also knowing that it won't do to forget a wallet or coat or loved one, and then they will walk out beneath the neon Crossroads Cafe sign and murmur to each other about how wonderful their pie was and how sweet their waitress was (they can never remember Dal's name, even though it's in big blue letters right on her nametag) and never come back.

Dal digs fistfuls of small ivory spheres out of the bowl on the counter, filling each pie crust with their heft. Then she slides the unbaked crusts into the pie case, where they will disappear and be replaced by whole, fresh pies in time for the night. Dal makes the day pies—simple apple and cherry and banana cream, and, when she's feeling ambitious, a cinnamon chocolate mousse topped with brown sugar whipped cream—and the night crusts, but she doesn't know where the night pies come from, and she doesn't have anyone to ask. They appear, and she best-guesses at their flavors based on smell and color and crust (she has never even tasted a single one; they are not for her, not since she arrived here). There are always six flavors, including one that is the baker's choice, with its intricate latticework crust and special gold tin. No one has ever ordered that one, in all the time she's been here.

"Hutch fry," Hutch says, from her precarious perch on the top of a napkin holder. The raven's too big for the space she fits herself into, too black and billed for how invisible she is, too large of wing and big of voice for all the times no one notices her.

"No fry, Hutch," Dal says. "Only pie and coffee, remember?" They haven't served fries or any other real food in at least twenty years, not since the fryer crapped out one afternoon, sending burning oil everywhere and nearly causing the diner to burn down. There are some days Dal wishes she hadn't worked so hard to save it, had just stood back and let it burn. But not mostly. Mostly she is glad to be here, doing this work, paying her dues.

"No fry?" Hutch cocks her head at Dal, confusion on her black-bead eyes. Hutch forgets sometimes. She's ancient, way older than Dal, and Dal feels pretty damn old some days. "Hutch crust?"

"Yes, Hutch crust." Dal tosses her a leftover piece of pie crust, a practiced move that would land it right in Hutch's maw even if Hutch wasn't so fast to snatch it up. She wonders how many times she's tossed a piece of crust to Hutch over the years, how many times the raven has caught it, how many times they've done the thing they're doing here now. The crust is long-gone already, and Hatch is dippering her head into the goldfish bowl on the counter for a drink.

"Hutch fish soon," the raven says, her bill dripping.

"Hutch fish never," Dal says. "Don't eat the fish, Hutch."

"No eat," Hutch says, as if Dal has not understood her true desire. But how well Dal knows the raven after all these years, knows that she will bend the rules if she can, forget what she cannot have, take advantage of every little opportunity. She imagines what kind of creature Hutch would be if she were human instead of raven. A thief in the night perhaps, digging trinkets from pockets. Or a witch of the woods, gathering herbs and shinies from passersby.

The last of the day customers slides out of their booth, gathering their things, putting their cash down on top of the blank slip of paper Dal has given them (they're a cash-only joint; they've always been a cash-only joint and no one ever stiffs her on the tip).

By the time twilight fully falls, the sky going blue-gray and the trees on the other side of the road throwing up their long black shadows, the diner is empty but for Dal and Hutch.

Hutch has flown to the perch on the back of the corner booth, the one that curves around like a lazy U. She scans the parking lot, head cocked.

"Busy," she muses. "Small fry."

"No fry," Dal says automatically. Hutch clicks her tongue and shifts her position, but knows better than to ask Dal for more food when they're about to open for the night. When Dal turns back to the pie case, tonight's pies are here. So fresh they're still steaming.

"Dark-dark," Hutch says. "Deal time."

"Deal time," Dal agrees. She curves her hand gently around the top of the bird's head, and Hutch leans hard into her touch with a quiet sigh.

"Love you, bird," she says, and then goes to open the front door.

***

The line's orderly and careful and long, loose-weave along the front of the diner and around, no one too close to anyone else nor too far. No one fights or pushes, no one cuts. If you can find the diner in the dusk, then you already know its rules. First-come, first-serve. Order the pie. Pay what you owe.

The parking lot and the rest of the world is pitch outside of the diner's lights. Dark-dark has come and with it, the enveloping shadows that seem to hide and highlight the diner both. Most can't see the diner this time of day, drive on by it along this gravel-spun ghost road and never even notice its neon red and orange that flashes OPEN beneath the cursive *Crossroads Cafe.* Dal suspects they would not see it even if they were looking for a restroom or a respite, for a piece of homemade peach pie. You have to need it like you need to breathe or eat or dream.

"Come in," she says to the first person in line, a middle-aged man who has his hat in his hands in a way that feels old-timey, how his fingers curl tight around the brim, the way it brings his shoulders in. He slides into the corner booth with the movements of a body and mind that hasn't yet gone to rot but is starting its slow decay, and orders an Arkansas half-and-half and a cup of coffee. Unlike the day diners, night diners can see Hutch, and he gives her a reverent nod as he sets his hat on the seat next to him.

Dal figures out the pie—it's the one that literally looks like it's two different pies on top—and cuts a slice that gives him a little of both.

Back in the booth, she wraps her hands around a mug of warm water and watches him eat. Everyone does this different, and she learns a lot from this. Is there precision? Appreciation? Is it something to get through? Do they use their fingers or fork or knife or spoon?

He eats carefully and slowly, small bites so as to not spill or hurry what's coming. And yet, he was first in line. Regret? A change of heart? Fear? No, Dal doesn't think so. Something else then. The pace, she thinks, of someone who wants so badly and is so afraid that nothing, none of this, not the wait or the pie or the diner or the raven or even Dal herself, will be able to give him what he wants.

When he puts his fork down across his plate and takes his napkin from his lap, she asks, "What is the deal you wish to make?" She's said this, must be, a million times since the time it was said to her, and some nights she wishes she could give a warning with it, and some nights she wishes she could give a gift. This is the true complexity of what she does; she loves it and hates it both in equal measure. She wishes she were done, her soul-cost paid, but wonders what she would possibly do with herself then? Where she would possibly go. She does not wish for the world nor for death, but knowing what she does not wish for is a far cry from knowing what she does.

"My wife, Agnes," he says, bringing her back, and she knows from his tone what he will say before he says it. "She's dying."

"We are all dying," Dal says, but it is not flippant. She is never flippant. She is true.

"Not all," he says, and he's looking at Hutch. He's not wrong, although Dal suspects Hutch is not immortal, just very long-lived. Birds of a feather and all of that.

"Hutch crust?" Hutch asks, eying the crumbed plate, always knowing when to take advantage of an opportunity.

"No crust," Dal says. Hutch harrumphs over her shoulder, ruffles her feathers. "Why have you come to the Crossroads?"

"I would like her to live."

"For how long?" Dal asks. "A week? A year? You're trading your soul for this. You would do well to be specific and sure."

He starts, as though he hasn't thought about this, which is why Dal is asking. Grief bargains are hard bargains, perhaps because they are rarely thought through. He wraps his fingers around his napkin and the gesture clatters his fork against the plate.

"I don't know. Longer than me."

"So that she may watch you die and mourn you, the way you are mourning her already? Truly, you would ask that of her? Or perhaps she doesn't care enough to mourn you?" It aches Dal to say these hard words, prickle-pointed and well-aimed. But she was too easy in the beginning, too soft, and she made too many deals that still haunt her.

His eyes, already red around the edges and leaning a little heavy into their cataracts, blink closed, and his pain radiates like an oven.

"Maybe we could … go together?"

"Not without her here, to give her say-so. You know that, surely."

"What then?" he says, and there it is. The push, the break, the knife point to the crust. She sees the man he was once—fists and fury, a hard man to love and be loved by—but he is that man no more and she knows he knows it is because of Agnes. Beneath the grief, guilt. And fear. The fear of being unmade, returning to what he once was after his Agnes goes.

"Would you not just ask to be a better version of yourself? To become the man alone that you are with her? That's what you really wish for, is it not?"

He takes his time with this question, a good sign, and at the end, he nods, more to himself than to either of them. "Yes, it is," he says. "But not as much as I wish a longer life for her. I will give what I must. Happily. Happily."

Dal thinks he is telling the truth, but is it enough? Will this bargain break him or take him somewhere else? She can't tell.

"Hutch hat," Hutch says.

Dal lifts a brow, surprised at Hutch's quick agreement. Now she too must choose.

Dal scans the man's near-empty pie plate, looking for answers in the crumbles and swirls. She takes in his wedding ring, a simple gold band worn thin along the edges, the indent all the way around his finger, how she doesn't think it would come off over his knuckle anymore. He knows not what he asks, but none of them ever do. She can only do her best to give the worthy and the non- exactly what they truly need and deserve.

The easiest ones to say yes to are the mean ones, the hard ones, the ones who want something selfish and stupid like to win the lottery or become the boss or burn some small corner of the world. She will happily make that deal, few questions asked. They already believe they are soulless and so it's nothing to them, to lose this tiny bit of themselves. But Dal knows better. Giving up a soul is no small thing, and if they had more than one, she would gather them all.

The harder ones are the ones who want to make something beautiful. Music, art, poetry. The world needs those things so, so badly. But, oh, the cost. She gives them extra pie on the way out the door, sometimes an entire one, even though she's not sure she's supposed to. But pie eases the hurt for a little while, and she can do that at least.

The hardest are the ones who are already so broken they don't understand that the thing they seek will break them. Who don't understand that they will not be around to see what they've traded for. She never makes those. Never. Not even if Hutch says yes, which she rarely does.

This man is not that. He's just a person who is broken and grieving and growing. He is somewhere between Easiest and Harder. He will not make the world worse, but he will not make it better either. Which is the truth of most deals with the devil, she has come to believe.

"The Crossroads accepts your bargain," she says.

The man nods and lifts the hat across the table to Hutch, who takes the brim in her beak and looks exceedingly pleased with herself. Dal resists the urge to roll her eyes as she digs in her apron pocket for her pad. She rips a piece of paper off and sets it down on the table, her palm resting on it for a moment. It is blank. They are always blank. And yet everyone knows the price.

"What will happen to my—to me?" he asks.

She doesn't answer, because she can't. She has tried, sometimes, when she thought it might change a mind, but no words will come. It is, she thinks, part of the deal. You must make your bargain not knowing, you must be willing to step into that vast unknown for what you desire.

"The bill," she says, "must be paid before you leave. Take your time."

***

So the night goes on. So every night goes on. Dal doesn't hurry anyone. She doesn't have to. The night will stretch as long as it needs to find room for every person who has come to make a deal.

Dal sometimes gets exhausted, but she never gets tired.

As morning nears, showing itself through the dark in tentative streaks of potential light, Hutch has accumulated quite a pile of things, shiny and not, one from each agreed-upon deal, and she has placed them all on the counter in a long neat row so she can see them from her perch on the booth.

Dal has accumulated things, too. She makes the deals that she wishes, and hopes she's doing the right thing, and at the end of each, she lifts the small ivory orb from the blank slip of paper and puts it into the bowl with the others. Unlike Hutch, who keeps all her shinies, the souls are not Dal's to keep. She understands she is just the dealer, the midpoint between here and something else. What that something else is, she still does not know. She's not sure she wants to know, and yet. She would ask, if given the chance. She would know what else there is.

She remembers making her own deal, although not all of it, the edges blurred like a day-old dream. She was Dalia then, just a girl, coming to this crossroads in the gloaming—no diner then, before neon, before the road—just a small house in the woods. Drawn by something outside herself, as all are. She'd knocked on the door and been served pie—what flavor? she doesn't remember, doesn't remember eating it, just remembers what came next—when she'd asked for something, anything, that was different than what she had, which was nothing and no one. A home, a friend, a purpose. And she remembers too, the woman, black-robed and black-eyed, who said, "Choose one," and Dalia had refused, greedy needy thing, and said, "All. All. All."

And here she is, all these ages later. A diner for a home, a raven for a friend, a devil's deal as her purpose. She does not think she has regrets, but she also no longer has hopes. This is her trade-off, her bargain, her eternity. No one knows what their deal will truly cost them.

"Last call," Hutch says.

The night is coming to an end, but Dal's still surprised when she opens the door and there is only one person left standing in the neon glow. A young girl, dirty and worn, a pink barrette that's been left in her dark hair so long it looks like a permanent fixture.

"Small fry!" Hutch croaks from her booth, opening her wings wide-wide-wide, and now Dal understands. *Small fry*. Not small *French fry*. Hutch has a soft spot for the kids, perhaps because they get them so rarely. Dal can remember three, and none as young as this, and all three with an adult, for better or worse.

Dal's heart slow-sinks to see this girl here, to take in her holes-in-the-toes sneakers, the skinned shins, and what looks like dirt or a bruise or perhaps both blooming big and dark along the side of her collarbone. But she cannot, as her heart wishes, turn this child away at the door. She has to hear her out, has to give her pie, has to let Hutch make her decision, and then has to make her own. It's the way of things. It's always been the way of things.

"Come in," she says.

The girl hesitates so long Dal hopes that day will make a mistake and arrive before she gets inside. But the girl enters and makes her way to the corner booth, sneakers squeaking across the tile floor, her fingers fisted, her eyes everywhere. More wild animal than human, Dal thinks, and these are the moments when Dal's careful choices feel like they're not enough, never enough. Yes, she's keeping the wolves from the door, but what is she letting in instead?

A hint of a smile flutters on the girl's mouth when she sees Hutch, who has puffed herself up into all shiny and soft feathers, begging for a pet. Sometimes an expression shows more than it means to, and in that slight, nervous twist of lips, Dal sees the girl who might have been. A girl with someone to keep her from showing up here, to keep on driving and not notice this diner in the middle of nowhere in the middle of the night. A girl with shoes that fit, with barrettes done fresh, a girl who knows where her laugh is and keeps it in a pocket for easy access.

"Pie?" Dal asks.

"No, thank you," the girl says, and her voice is an echo from behind locked doors, from crawlspaces and back seats, from hidden corners and don't-see-mes. Her hands are clasped under the table and she no longer has even a ghost of a smile for Hutch, who is sidling across the back of the booth, one ridiculously slow step at a time, as if she's trying to sneak up on the girl. Dal gives the raven an eyebrow, and Hutch practically shrugs her little bird shoulders at her like, *what?*

Dal presses gently, hugely aware of her own power to rip and tear. "You have to choose."

At this, the girl looks up, brown eyes like big spills of coffee. "I don't think I like pie."

Dal, weirdly, doesn't like pie either. She's much more of a cake person herself, ideally with too many sprinkles and a layer of lemon between the layers. But cake is not an option here and she cannot remember the taste or feel of cake in her mouth.

"I don't think it matters if you like it."

"Can you choose for me?"

No one has ever asked her that before. Everyone who walks through that door has known which pie to order. It's rolled off their tongue like saying *hello* and *goodbye* and *I want to make a deal with the devil.* Dal doesn't even know if it's in her power to choose. She looks to Hutch, but Hutch has no eyes for her, just for the *small fry,* still playing her wiggle-and-step game to get closer and closer to the girl.

"Hutch," Dal warns, and Hutch practically rolls her black-black eyes at her, but she stops and stays, one foot cocked half-up in a step.

"Gold," Hutch says.

Dal squints at her. They haven't even heard the deal yet, and the girl certainly doesn't have any gold on her.

"What?"

"Choosechoosechoose." The words run together, like they do when Hutch gets overly excited and it takes a Dal a moment to figure out what she's saying and then to understand its meaning.

"Oh," she says, and something inside her rocks her back so that she clutches the edge of the booth, fingers curled around it like talons. "Oh."

Choose. Baker's *choice.* The first time it's ever happened and she doesn't know why this makes her feel so off-kilter, why this whole thing feels like she is about to topple from a great height.

"Yes," Dal says, when she can get her voice back, when she knows it will be soft and free of thorns. "I can choose for you."

She takes the gold-tinned pie from the case, surprised at its weight, its heft. When she slices a piece, it is everything somehow, all the pies she's ever served and will ever serve, layered into one, but in a way that makes it seem delicious instead of awful. Meringue and strawberry and mousse and cherry and—Dal can't even count all the layers, each is so thin, but she can smell them all and it reminds her of her deal from long ago, something she didn't forget, but which she buried down deep, another place, another night, the whoosh of feathers and a blank check.

Dal shakes it away and sets the plate in front of the girl, slides into the booth. Hutch is at the girl's shoulder now. Sometimes Dal swears the bird is laughing and this is one of those times. She can't shake the feeling that the raven and the girl are sharing some secret joke that she hasn't been let in on.

That feeling deepens when Hutch says, "Hutch crust," and the girl picks a piece of the edge off her pie with her fingers and hands it over her shoulder to the raven as though she's already done this a dozen, a hundred times. Dal's stomach cramps up with some weird combination of fear and jealousy, that ongoing sense that she's very high and the ground is very, very far below.

"Who *are* you?" Dal asks.

In answer, the girl slides the pie to the middle of the table, then further, until it nearly reaches Dal.

And everything is wrong. Everything is topsy-turvy. Is this what happens when she screws up (if that's even a thing?) and whatever is on the other end of this diner, of all these crossed places in the world, that being or beings that she collects souls for, whoever and whatever they are, is this what happens when she screws up and they come for her? In the guise of a little, broken girl? She runs fast through all the deals she's made this long, busy night. Which one was her undoing? And she thought she wanted to know, but now she absolutely does not.

But, no, Hutch is acting like everything's normal, everything's hunky-dory, except for taking a bit of crust from the girl's fingers before the deal's been decided. Dal can chalk that up to Hutch being Hutch, a greedy little glitter-thief woods-witch-wannabe before all else. And the girl has already said she doesn't like pie, so of course she wants to give it away, piece by piece.

Dal watches the girl, who watches her, tries to recalibrate.

"What is the deal you wish to make?" she asks.

"I want a job," the girl says. And Dal almost laughs, but catches herself. This girl isn't a power, a reckoning. She's just a lost girl, seeking something better than what she's got, and why not? Why not, indeed. After all, Dal was once in her shoes—less holey but just as ill-fitting—and didn't know what she wanted. Only what she did not want.

Everything rights itself, and Dal is herself again.

"Look," she says softly, turning the pie plate around and around in her fingers, much like you would a hat, a planet, a soul. She could use the help, she thinks. Someone to fill the sugar and make the coffee, someone else to entertain Hutch and to feed the fish. "You don't have to make a deal for that. Jobs are easy to come by. In fact, if you come back in the morning, I can see about—"

"No," the girl says. "*Your* job."

There's a place and time, perhaps in another universe, in another Dal, where she understands what is happening right now. But this is not it. Now she does laugh, the sound soft and, to her ears, a little scared, despite the absurdity of the proposed deal.

"You can't have my job," Dal says.

"Barrette," Hutch says, and Dal wants, suddenly and for the first time she can remember, to cry. How can Hutch say yes? Betray her after all this? She wants to put her head down on the booth and weep and sleep and when did she get so damn tired?

"No," Dal says. "Hutch, no."

"Hutch yes," Hutch says, and there's something in her deep black gaze that Dal can't quite sort out.

The girl fumbles with her barrette, trying to get it out of the tangles of her hair, and, despite everything, Dal has the urge to reach out and offer help, to be the fingers that undo whatever's been done to make this mess. Finally, the girl gets it, pink and toothed, still holding onto a hair or two, and holds it out to the raven, who takes it in one claw.

"Dal pie," Hutch says.

And Dal understands so much now. She understands why no one's ever made her choose. Why the baker's choice pie is all the flavors she's ever served. Why she didn't think she actually likes pie. The pie is for her. She can't remember the flavor of pie she ate when she came here, because she did not eat it. She looked at the woman across the table from her and said "you choose" because something inside her told her that was the way to get what she wanted. Didn't she wonder what would become of her after? And now that moment might be here, and she is afraid-afraid-afraid, her heart a wild beat of wings inside her chest.

Dal is tempted to spell out all the reasons the girl doesn't want this job, all the reasons it's not worth losing her soul over. But she knows they wouldn't be true. This job, after all, is what saved her. And isn't her job, after all, to offer a kind of salvation? Maybe for them, maybe for her, maybe for the world. She doesn't know. She isn't sure of anything right now. It's the first time she's felt that in so long that she doesn't have a name for it, this unknowing.

She looks at the raven, who is looking at her, holding the girl's barrette, waiting for her to decide.

"The Crossroads will accept your bargain." Dal pulls her notepad out of her apron pocket, with its pages that never run out and can never be written on, and slides it across the table to the girl.

"Thank you," the girl says, and in her face, there is, for the first time in Dal can't imagine how long, a flicker of hope. A ghost of a smile that forgot it was alive. The girl reaches out and cups Hutch's head, and the touch is so soft, so loving, that it brings tears to Dal's eyes. How long since she has been touched like that? Ever?

"What will become of me?" she muses, not meaning to say it out loud, her voice thick.

She is surprised, for once, to hear an answer.

"Dal Hutch. Hutch fish," the raven says. And, once again, Dal is taken aback that she could be alive so long, watch so many humans come and go before her, and still not see the obvious. This is what's next in the bargain she made. Girl Dal. Dal Hutch. Hutch fish. And after that? After that is another vast unknown. Perhaps she will become a soul or a being with a soul again. Or perhaps she will become a pie, a berry, a crust, a pink barrette dangling from a bird's claw, a bright strip of neon in a sign that only some can see. Or the sun rising in the sky. Who is to say? Who is to know?

Dal pulls the plate toward her. It's a perfect piece, cut with love and care, and she can smell the sun-ripened blackberries, the sweet honey, the butter in the crust. She takes a single bite, lets it melt on her tongue. It takes her no time at all to finish, save for one piece of crust, which she tosses to Hutch. One last time.

Dal throws, and, in the same motion, she catches.

Outside, the neon light flickers off as the sun stretches and yawns, spilling its light into the diner. An ebony fish splashes around and around a small bowl on the counter. In a corner booth, a girl gently cups her soft hand around the head of a small brown robin. "Love you, bird," she says, and the bird, who has not yet taught herself to speak with this new mouth and these new feelings, leans into the touch and spreads her wings as far as she can, which, she is delighted to learn, is very far indeed.

About the Authors

Russ Bickerstaff is a critic and author living in Milwaukee, Wisconsin.

Lydia Bugg lives in Nashville, Tennessee, with her husband, dogs, cat, and all the little forest creatures who dress her in the morning and do her chores. Her comedy writing has been featured on *1900Hotdog.com, Cracked, BunnyEars, The Reductress,* and *The Trailer Park Boys Get A F#*!ng Comic Book.* She's also written several romance novels and exactly one horror novella. Sometimes, she refers to herself in the third person. It's weird.

Tom Brennan is a working-class, Irish-British writer who lives beside Liverpool's River Mersey with four cats (all related, it's a long story) and he enjoys watching the ships glide past, particularly at night when they're illuminated and look like cities on the move; he also enjoys reading and creating a wide variety of fiction and his stories have appeared in the US, Australia, Canada and the UK.

Nathan Crowder is a writer of weird stuff currently haunting the Pacific Northwest. Mostly known for his superhero fiction set in Cobalt City, Nate also crafts dark little stories that pop up in other places from time to time. He has a deep and abiding love for jazz music, cross-country road trips, and cornbread.

Laura Garrison lives in Virginia and is slowly transforming into a crazy cat lady. She enjoys weird craft projects, vegetarian cooking, and wandering through moonlit cemeteries in her best nightgown.

If **Shanna Germain** were a god, she'd be the Benevolent God of Rainbow Sprinkles. Sadly, she's only human. She is also an award-winning writer of short stories, novels, games, essays, and poems.

Her work has appeared in places like *Apex Magazine, Best Lesbian Erotica, Best Gay Romance, The Deadlands*, and *Fantasy Magazine*. She lives in a rainforest with a dog named &. Follow her down the rabbit hole at ShannaGermain.com.

Elena Greer (she/they) is a disabled, Indigenous, lesbian writer from the northeast of Ohio, who writes fantasy and horror stories for Indigenous queer people such as herself. Their writing most often explores the complicated variety of human nature, as well as the intersections between disability, queerness, and her reconnection with her Indigenous identity. She can be found at their website, ElenaGreerWrites.carrd.co, and on Twitter at @GreerTragedy.

Eirik Gumeny is the editor of Atomic Carnival Books and author of *Beggars Would Ride, The Greatest Gatsby: an American Werewolf in West Egg,* and the *Exponential Apocalypse* series. His short fiction has appeared in, among others, *Impossible Worlds, Kaleidotrope, Soul Jar* (Forest Avenue Press), and *Escalators to Hell* (From Beyond Press). His nonfiction has been published by *Cracked, Wired*, and *The New York Times*. In 2014, he received a double lung transplant and technically died a little. He got better. Find him at EGumeny.com or on Bluesky.

Rik Hoskin is a multi-award winning writer of novels, graphic novels, video games and animation. He's written comics for *Star Wars, Superman, Doctor Who* and various other properties, and won the Dragon Award for Best Graphic Novel 2018 for *White Sand* (with Brandon Sanderson), which also made *The New York Times* bestseller list. He writes SF novels under his own name and as "James Axler." He also writes video games, where he has served as head writer, and has written animation for BBC television in the UK.

L.S. Johnson lives in California with a spouse, six and a half cats, and a rapidly-depleting goldfish population. She is the author of the *Chase and Daniels* quartet of queer gothic novellas and over forty short stories. Her first collection, *Vacui Magia*, won the North Street Book Prize and was a finalist for the World Fantasy Award. Her second collection, *Rare Birds*, was an IPPY medalist and longlisted for the Stoker Award. Her Enlightenment-era serial, *Prima Materia*, about vampires and alchemists and a returning serpent god, is happening now. Find her online at TraversingZ.com.

Megan Kiekel Anderson (she/her) is a nerdy queer neurodivergent dark fiction writer. Her work can be found or is upcoming in such places as *Flame Tree Press*, *The Arcanist*, *Dark Recesses Press*, and *Nightmare Magazine*. She lives in Kansas City with her chaotic family including too many cats, chickens, and foster kittens. You can find her on Twitter and Instagram under the handle @megan_nerdnest or at her website at MeganKiekelAnderson.com.

Amanda Cecelia Lang is a horror author and aspiring recluse from Denver, Colorado. As a die-hard scary movie nerd, her favorite things are meta-horror, '80s nostalgia, and the rise of a fierce final girl. Her stories haunt the dark corners of many popular podcasts, magazines, and anthologies, including *NoSleep*, *Cast of Wonders*, *Dark Matter*, *Uncharted*, *The Dread Machine*, and Flame Tree's *Darkness Beckons*. Her short story collection *The Library of Broken Girls* will debut in the Spring of 2025. You can stalk her work at AmandaCeceliaLang.com—just don't be surprised if she leaps out at you from the shadows.

Steve Loiaconi is a journalist and a graduate of George Mason University's MFA program. His fiction previously appeared in *Griffel*, *MysteryTribune*, *Samfiftyfour*, *Tales of the Fantastic*, and *The Saturday Evening Post*, as well as the anthologies *Dracula's Guests*, *P is for Poltergeist*, and *Dragon Gems (Summer 2023)*. He lives in Washington, DC with his wife and son.

J.A.W. McCarthy is the Bram Stoker Award- and Shirley Jackson Award-nominated author of *Sometimes We're Cruel and Other Stories* (Cemetery Gates Media, 2021) and *Sleep Alone* (Off Limits Press, 2023). Her short fiction has appeared in numerous publications, including *Split Scream Vol. 3*, *Vastarien*, *PseudoPod*, *Apparition Lit*, *Tales to Terrify*, and *The Best Horror of the Year Vol 13* (ed. Ellen Datlow). She is Thai American and lives with her husband and assistant cats in the Pacific Northwest. You can call her Jen on Twitter @JAWMcCarthy, and find out more at www.JAWMcCarthy.com.

Danger Slater has been a pet sitter, a delivery boy, a courier, a stock person, a shoe salesman, a security guard, a liquor store clerk, a paid taste tester, and an author.

Bailee Smith-Garcia lives in Arizona, where she enjoys writing spooky stories. "Whispers in the Dark" is Bailee's first in-print short story. Her essay "The Queerness of *Scream*" appears on the Divination Hollow Reviews website. Her short story "The Apple" appears in Outrageous Fortune's online magazine. When she's not writing, you'll find her rewatching the *Scream* franchise. You can find her on Instagram or X (Twitter) @BaileeSG or her website, BaileeSmithGarcia.home.blog.

Patrick Tumblety is an author of horror, science fiction, and poetry. He has been featured in numerous anthologies, including *Tales of Jack the Ripper* from Word Horde Press, *The Dead Inside* from Dark Dispatch, *Gothic Fantasy: Science Fiction* from Flame Tree Publishing, and *Dark Moon Digest* from Perpetual Motion Machine Publishing. He has also been published by and is an active member of the Horror Writers Association. His work has been described as being able to deliver both "genuine fear and genuine hope" by Amy H. Sturgis, award-winning author and professor of Narrative Studies.

Special Thanks
to Our Kickstarter Backers

Akis Linardos
Al Rodriguez
Ally Malinenko
Amber Bennett-Groves
Anne M. Gibson
Brandi Martinez
Buzz
Catherine W!
Chris Sandoval
Colleen Feeney
Dominick Cancilla
Eileen Gettle
Erik M Johnson
Eron Wyngarde
Janet B
Jay Gironimi
Jenny Ortiz
John Fanelli
Jonathan Gensler
Joseph Jerome Connell III
Kath
Kerry Goode
Laura Garrison
LS Johnson
Matt Brandenburg
Quin Boyce
Used Gravitrons
Vi and Sar
Victoria Nations
Yesenia Pelaez

www.ingramcontent.com/pod-product-compliance
Lightning Source LLC
Chambersburg PA
CBHW020034310726

48970CB00007B/2260